Guardians of Glede:
Next Generation Book 3:
The Coven

By JennaKay Francis

Writers Exchange E-Publishing

http://www.writers-exchange.com

Guardians of Glede: Next Generation Book 3: The Coven
Copyright 2007, 2015 JennaKay Francis
Writers Exchange E-Publishing
PO Box 372
ATHERTON QLD 4883

Cover Art by: Laura Shinn and Jatin

Published by Writers Exchange E-Publishing
http://www.writers-exchange.com

Second Edition

Other Books In The Series:

Beginnings Book 1: The Triskelion

Beginnings Book 2: Dark Prince

Beginnings Book 3: Sorcerer's Pool

Beginnings Book 4: Dragons of Mere Odain

Beginnings Book 5: DragonMaster

Beginnings Book 6: For the Love of Dragons

Beginnings Series Collection: Books 1 - 6 in one volume

Next Generation Book 1: Caves of Challenge

Next Generation Book 2: Blood Sacrifice

Next Generation Book 3: The Coven

Next Generation Book 4: Fire Stone

Next Generation Book 5: The Fane Queen

Next Generation Book 6: Battle for Argathia

Reckonings Book 1: Dukker's Revenge

FAMILY TREE

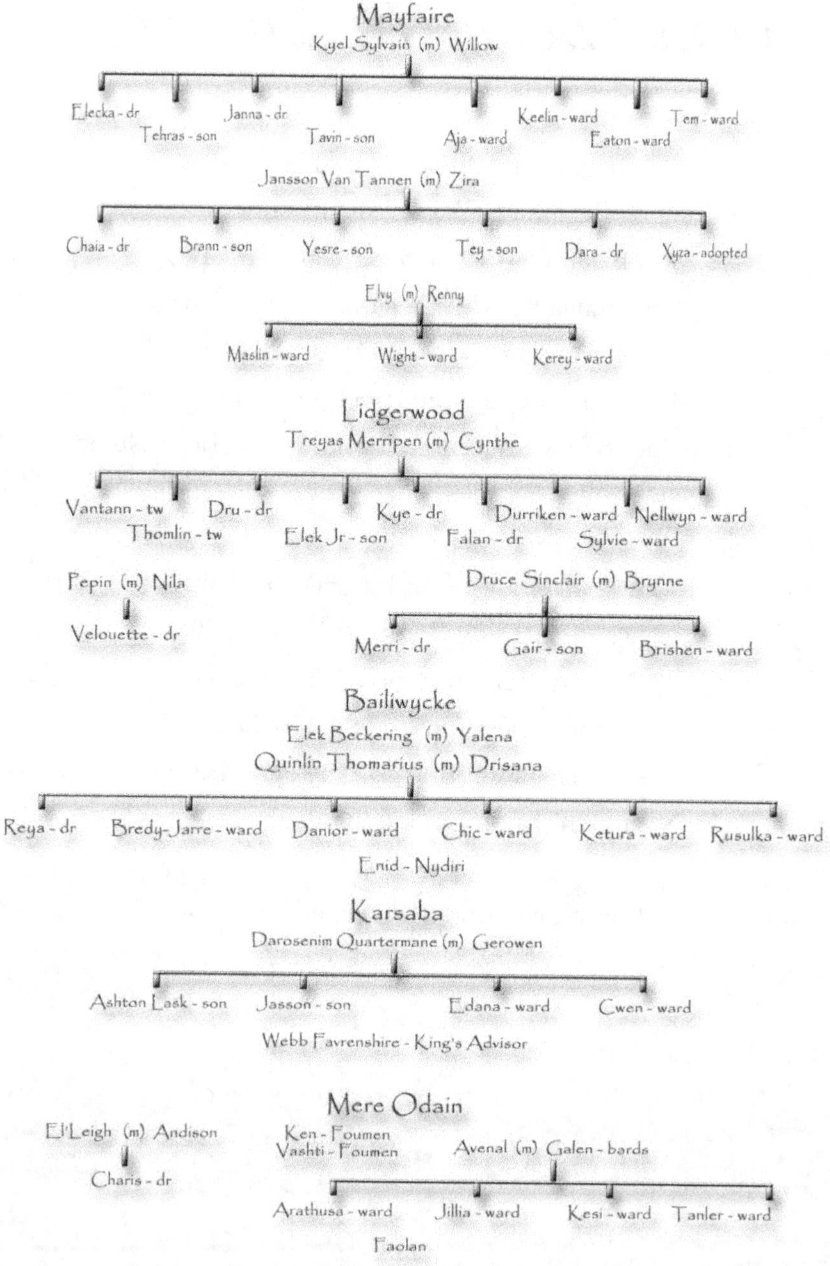

Mayfaire
Kyel Sylvain (m) Willow
Elecka - dr
Tehras - son
Janna - dr
Tavin - son
Aja - ward
Keelin - ward
Eaton - ward
Tem - ward
Jansson Van Tannen (m) Zira
Chaia - dr
Brann - son
Yesre - son
Tey - son
Dara - dr
Xyza - adopted
Elvy (m) Renny
Maslin - ward
Wight - ward
Kerey - ward

Lidgerwood
Treyas Merripen (m) Cynthe
Vantann - tw
Thomlin - tw
Dru - dr
Elek Jr - son
Kye - dr
Falan - dr
Durriken - ward
Sylvie - ward
Nellwyn - ward
Pepin (m) Nila
Velouette - dr
Druce Sinclair (m) Brynne
Merri - dr
Gair - son
Brishen - ward

Bailiwycke
Elek Beckering (m) Yalena
Quinlin Thomarius (m) Drisana
Reya - dr
Bredy-Jarre - ward
Danior - ward
Chic - ward
Ketura - ward
Rusulka - ward
Enid - Nydiri

Karsaba
Darosenim Quartermane (m) Gerowen
Ashton Lask - son
Jasson - son
Edana - ward
Cwen - ward
Webb Favrenshire - King's Advisor

Mere Odain
El'Leigh (m) Andison
Charis - dr
Ken - Foumen
Vashti - Foumen
Avenal (m) Galen - bards
Arathusa - ward
Jillia - ward
Kesi - ward
Tanler - ward
Faolan

Chapter One

"Father?"

Crown Prince Treyas Merripen looked up from his paperwork with a smile. He beckoned the young elf into the room as he rose from behind his desk.

"I'm not interrupting anything am I?" the brown-skinned young man asked.

"Pepin, you are never an interruption," Treyas replied and embraced him warmly. "In fact, I'm glad you're here. I was finalizing our travel plans to Dalziel and I realized I never got your supply request. If you want to,"

"Papay," Pepin interrupted softly, "I'm not going."

Treyas looked at him in surprise and puzzlement. "What do you mean? Is something wrong? Is someone ill?"

"No, no. Everyone is fine," Pepin assured him.

"Then..." Treyas shrugged.

"It's not my place to go, Papay," Pepin said.

"Of course it is. You're in line to the throne."

"That's just the point," Pepin said with a sigh of exasperation. "I'm not. Not really."

Treyas' face grew firm. "Pepin, you're my son."

"Yes, by choice not by chance." Pepin took hold of his arm, his dark eyes searching Treyas' face. "You've been my father since I was seven years old. There's not a day that goes by that I don't thank you with all of my heart for adopting me. But *you* adopted me, Papay, not the elfin empire. I should not be in line to the throne. That right belongs to Vantann. He is your first-born son, not me."

Treyas stared at him in shock, then annoyance settled in his mis-matched blue and green eyes. "Who's been talking to you?"

"No one." Pepin released Treyas' arm and walked over to look out the tall, mullioned window. He could feel Treyas' gaze burning into his back.

"Then where did you come up with this idea?" Treyas asked. "Aelfdene and the elves accepted you as my son fifteen years ago, Pepin. They expect you to follow me. I expect you to follow me. What's happened that's changed that?"

Pepin hesitated, toying idly with the drapery pull. "Father, I have a legacy," he finally said. "A role to fill. But it's not in Aelfdene. You know that."

"I know that you're an honorary Prince of Mere Odain," Treyas said tightly, "and that you still oversee the DragonRiders there, but I was under the assumption that Faolan had filled the role you speak of."

Pepin closed his eyes, the chill in his father's voice eating at his heart. He took a deep breath, opened his eyes and turned to face Treyas. "I've taken the position back, Father," he said quietly. "I am now officially the DragonMaster of Mere Odain."

Treyas stared at him, stunned. "When?"

"Six months ago," Pepin replied. "On my twenty-third birthday."

"Six...why didn't you tell me?" Treyas exploded. "Was it supposed to be some sort of secret? Was I supposed to find out the day you left home? Gods, Pepin! I'm your father! Does being twenty-three relieve you of common courtesy? I should have been told, Pepin! No! Dammit! I should have been asked!" He jerked toward the door as a soft knock sounded. "What is it?" he snapped.

Druce Sinclair, Treyas' squire and SoulMate, stepped into the room, his dark eyes darting from Treyas to Pepin and back. "You wanted to know when Elek had arrived," he said. "He's downstairs with the children."

"Where, Druce?" Treyas demanded hotly. "Downstairs is a bit vague."

"In the kitchen," Druce answered slowly, then added, "He's sitting in the chair closest to the fireplace and has had three cookies and a half a glass of milk."

Treyas glared at him. "Don't patronize me," he seethed, then glanced at Pepin. "We're not through with this discussion, Pepin. Until we are, I forbid you to return to Mere Odain!" He strode from the room, angrily pushing past Druce.

Druce watched him storm down the circular stairway, then turned to Pepin. "What was that all about?"

Pepin shook his head and flung himself into a chair. "Nothing!"

"That was nothing? Come on, Pepin, what's going on? You and Treyas never fight."

Pepin rubbed wearily at his face, then looked up at Druce. "I've officially assumed my title as DragonMaster."

Druce's eyes went wide. "I see. When did this happen?"

"Six months ago. I know I should have told him then. I just couldn't. Half the house was sick with poujo, and Mamay and Papay,"

"You haven't told your mother?" Druce interrupted, aghast.

"Not yet," Pepin mumbled, picking at the green brocade on the chair arm.

"Coals, Pepin, and you think Treyas took it hard."

Pepin slouched further into the overstuffed chair. "I know, I know, but at least Mamay will understand." He surged to his feet to pace. "Gods, Druce! What is it with Papay and Mere Odain? Why does he go wild every time I mention it? You'd think he'd understand. I'm half Merian, my father was the DragonMaster. I'm his only son. It's my legacy, it's part of who I am. I can no more ignore that, than he can ignore his naiad half. Why does he make this so painful for me?"

Druce winced. "Because it's so painful for him." He touched Pepin's arm lightly, stopping his pacing. "He's been fighting against Mere Odain's pull on you for over fifteen years, Pepin. That's a long time. A long time to be waging a personal war only to find out he lost it six months ago."

Pepin regarded him with a frown. "I really messed this up, didn't I?" He sagged back into the chair.

"Well, waiting to spring it on him the night before you're supposed to leave on a diplomatic visit probably wasn't the wisest course of action," Druce admitted, sitting in the chair next to him. "Why didn't you just wait until you got back?"

"I couldn't," Pepin replied. "I'm not going."

Druce sighed in amazement. "This just gets better and better. Why aren't you going?"

"Because, like I told Papay, it should be Vantann going, not me. Vantann is related by blood. The lineage runs through him and Thomlin, not me. And besides," Pepin took a deep breath, "Queen El'leigh has ordered Dragon placement in Akuri Kelta. They leave in two days. I'm the overseer."

Druce sat back with a groan. "Oh, gods, Pepin." He was quiet for a long moment.

Pepin spoke up. "You being a Merian, I thought you'd understand."

"Being a Merian, I do understand. The Akuri can't be given any slack. We've all seen what they're capable of. But, being your father's SoulMate, I know how he's going to take this."

"Uncle Druce," Pepin said, sitting forward, his voice low, "he doesn't have to know. At least, not until he gets back from Dalziel. I would prefer it that way."

"Pepin, I can't keep this from him," Druce replied in astonishment.

Pepin hesitated. "I could order you to," he said slowly.

Druce stiffened. "I suppose you could. I would hope that you wouldn't."

Pepin eyed him steadily. "Will you keep quiet?"

Druce returned the gaze defiantly. "No."

Pepin clenched his jaw and rose. "Then consider it an order, Druce. Papay is to know nothing about this until I tell him."

Druce also rose, his voice cold. "Consider it done, Prince Pepin. I only hope you know what you're doing."

Pepin watched him leave, then exhaled sharply. This had not gone the way he'd intended. Not only was Treyas furious with him, Druce was as well. And since Treyas had forbidden him to go to Mere Odain, he would have to go against his father's wishes to follow Queen El'leigh's command. That is, if he wanted to truly be the DragonMaster of Mere Odain in more than just title.

He left the study and began the walk back to his living quarters. The Elfin Council Chambers had been his home for sixteen years, ever since Treyas had plucked him out of Sarben's clan to assist in finding King Jansson van Tannen. Pepin had had more than one opportunity to claim his position as DragonMaster and always he had turned it down. He was comfortable with his elfin half, though even that was not pure. He was a brownling. His mother had been a black elf, his father a white Merian. Sarben's clan had been the only place he was accepted until Treyas had brought him to Aelfdene Valley. For a while, even that was hard.

Treyas, being the true heir to the Crown, had appointed Kyel Sylvain, King of the Black Elves, to rule over black and white elf alike. Since Kyel's wife, Willow, was a white elf, it didn't take long for other brownlings to appear. Then, Treyas had relocated Sarben's entire clan of brownlings to Aelfdene Valley, ensuring that Pepin would never be considered an outcast again.

So, what am I doing, Pepin thought. *Why am I going against the one man who has made my life complete?* He sighed and opened the door to his and Nila's solar. That was the problem. His life wasn't complete. True, he was an honorary Prince of Mere Odain and as such, could still be involved with his beloved dragons. But it wasn't enough. His legacy called to him, begged him, seduced him. He was meant to be the DragonMaster. It had ceased to be a choice. It was a command, given to him by a power he didn't understand and couldn't ignore, though he had valiantly tried for many long years.

He collapsed on the settee, lay back and stared at the ceiling. And what of his elfin allegiance? What of the fact that he had pledged his loyalty to King Sylvain and the elfin crown? How did one go about changing that allegiance? Did he really want to? Or had he already done so when he had accepted his Merian title? Gods! Why did everything have to be so complicated?

"Papay!" A sweet, little voice reached him and he sat up with a smile. His five-year-old daughter, Velouette, took the last stair, wriggled free of her mother's hand and raced to the settee. Pepin swept her up in a hug and showered her with kisses, until she was giggling happily.

"How did it go?" Nila asked, approaching him.

Pepin looked up at the black elfin beauty. "Not well. Papay was furious. He forbade me to go to Mere Odain."

Nila sat down beside him and handed Velouette a silver plated brush. The little girl squealed with delight and immediately stood behind Pepin to brush at his dark shoulder length curls.

"Did you tell him about El'leigh's orders?" Nila asked.

"No." Pepin winced as Velouette caught a snarl and yanked it free. "The way he went off, I didn't dare. I'll just have to wait until he gets back from Dalziel. Hopefully, I'll be back before then anyway."

Nila took his hand and kissed it. "I wish you weren't going at all," she murmured.

Pepin gave a small smile, looking into her blue eyes. "So do I, Nila, but if I'm going to be the DragonMaster, I need to be with my dragons."

"I know," Nila replied quietly.

Pepin kissed her gently. "I wish Papay understood as well as you do."

Nila smiled wryly. "I don't know that I do understand, Pepin. I only know what makes you happy. Being with your dragons makes you happy. Doing what was born into you makes you happy. Being DragonMaster of Mere Odain makes you happy. I know it, but I don't really understand it."

Pepin chuckled and drew her into his arms. He laid one hand on her belly. "Just as I know there's a child here, though I don't understand the miracle of its growth. Some things just are, Nila. Maybe they can't be explained. Maybe if we explain them, we take away their mysterious beauty."

Nila smiled. "You should have been a bard, Pepin."

He chuckled grimly. "My life surely would have been less complicated if I had. Ouch!" He cringed, then reached back and snagged Velouette, hauling her onto his lap. "Leave some hair there, you," he teased. "What are you still doing awake anyway, miss?" He tickled her gently.

She giggled and flopped backward onto Nila's lap, then turned her head and kissed Nila's protruding stomach. "Sister," she said.

Nila laughed. "Now there's a mystery for you. She takes turns referring to the baby as sister or brother."

"So? She's guessing."

"No, no. I mean, she never makes a mistake. It's always sister, then brother, then sister and so forth. I've been writing it down out of curiosity. She hasn't made a mistake since I started keeping track. How does she do that?"

Pepin shrugged. "Maybe it's twins. After all, my mother was a twin."

"Don't remind me," Nila said with a shudder. "Your mother's twin could have easily substantiated Winze's belief in the demon twin. Come on, Velouette, it's time for bed. Are you coming up, Pepin?"

"In a bit."

"Don't be long," Nila said, scooping Velouette into her arms. "I'm sure to have nightmares now." She kissed him lightly and went up the stairs to the bedroom.

Pepin sighed. He needed to talk to Treyas.

"How could he do this?" Treyas raged, pacing furiously. "How could Pepin do this to me?"

"I don't think he intended to do anything to you," Cynthe answered softly.

Treyas turned to look at his wife, who was perched on the side of the bed, one hand gripping a bed poster. Though her words were calm, her rigidity belied her emotions. "How can you take this so lightly?" Treyas cried. "Pepin has taken on the role of DragonMaster! Do you know what that means? It means he's transferred his allegiance from Kyel to El'leigh. It means his loyalties now lie with Mere Odain and not Aelfdene. It means..." he paused, taking a deep breath, "it means, I've lost him to his past."

Cynthe rose, walked to him and took him into her arms. "Myshay, you haven't lost Pepin. You could never lose Pepin. He's your son."

Treyas looked at her sadly, then pushed away to go stand before the window. He stared out at the quiet gardens, the stables, the dark woods beyond. This was his home, had been for over fifteen years, since he was seventeen years old. His gaze lifted to the western skies. The sun had already set in Bailiwycke, filling the coastal skies with hues of red, gold, orange, touching the silvery water of the cove outside of Ravenscroft. Treyas missed seeing that, missed Ravenscroft and the carefree days of his first fourteen years. The days before he had discovered who he was, who his father was, what his future entailed. Crown Prince to the Elfin Empire. It was a long way from fisherman's apprentice.

He snorted softly. As if he had ever really been Quinlin Thomarius' apprentice. Quinlin was a member of the Elfin Royal Guard, had been assigned to protect the little five-year-old prince, the prince hidden away from the eyes of the elfin royalty. That Quinlin had grown up in Ravenscroft and knew about fishing was a bonus. But while he was a fisherman by choice and trade, Treyas was no more his apprentice than...than...he sighed heavily...then Pepin was an elfin prince. Just putting someone in a particular place and wishing a life for him, didn't always work out. Treyas was proof of that.

His father, Crown Prince Tehras Merripen, had tried. He had sequestered Treyas in Bailiwycke with his dear friend, Elek Beckering. Elek had been sworn to secrecy regarding Treyas' true identity, his heritage. As had Quinlin. Tehras had wanted Treyas to grow up free, away from the pressures and constraints of royal life. For fourteen years he had. Fourteen, long, wonderful years.

Until the Triskelion had resurfaced, plunging Treyas into a nightmare years in the making. His peaceful existence had been shattered violently and permanently. He had witnessed horrors he had never dreamed possible. He had been involved in desperate life or death decisions. He had seen friends die, and he had killed. He shuddered now, then started when Cynthe laid her hand on his shoulder. "I wanted to protect him, Cynthe," he murmured. "I wanted to protect Pepin just as my father wanted to protect me. But we can't change who we are, can we? Our past finds us and claims us. It claimed me and now it claims my Pepin. Gods, Cynthe, will the pain of my life never end?"

She leaned her chin on his shoulder. "Has it all been pain, myshay? Has no good come of it?"

Treyas gave a small smile, breathing in her sweet scent. He turned and took his wife into his arms. Her waist-length blond hair hung loose and caressed his hands and arms as he held her. "You're right, myshay. As usual. I have you and the children. I have friends who are like brothers. I have people around the world whom I can turn to for help and advice. None of this would be mine if I wasn't who I am." He kissed her gently. "I should be proud of Pepin. My son, the DragonMaster of Mere Odain. Gods! Who would have thought that such a tiny little boy would grow to command a legion of dragons?" He looked into Cynthe's violet eyes, then kissed her again, long and passionately. "I need to go talk to Pepin," he said when they'd parted.

Cynthe smiled and ran her finger down his cheek to his lips. "After that kiss, I hope you won't be long."

Treyas smiled, kissed her finger and promised.

He walked steadily, resolutely toward Pepin's living quarters, taking the long way around to gather his thoughts. *First*, he thought, *I'll apologize. I'll apologize for treating him like a child. He's a man now, a husband, a father himself. I can't forbid him to do anything.*

His footsteps faltered outside a guestroom solar as a hoot of laughter reached him. It was quickly followed by hasty shushings. Treyas glanced at the hall clock. Eleven. Too late for the younger children to be awake. He pushed open the doors to the guest solar, and froze.

Vantann and Thomlin, his fifteen-year-old twins, shot to their feet with a collective gasp. They were dressed only in leggings, their chest and feet bare. Their companions, Rusulka and Ketura, also twins at sixteen, were clothed only in their linen undershirts and hose. A small pile of clothing lay nearby and Treyas' gaze flicked to it briefly before his anger exploded. "What in Tor's hell is going on?" he roared.

"P...papay, we...we..." Vantann stammered, his face going red.

Treyas stormed into the room, snatched up Vantann's tunic and flung it at him. Thomlin hastily grabbed his own and yanked it on. "We were playing Queen's Takeoff," he mumbled, then added quickly, "but we weren't going to take anything else off! Honest!"

"Where," Treyas said, trying to control his anger, "did you learn how to play that game?"

The twins exchanged quick, frightened glances, their blue eyes wide. Vantann swallowed hard. "From Grandpapay Elek."

Treyas stared at him, stunned. He didn't know whether to laugh or rant. His gaze swung to the girls, who had not moved. "Get your things," he said tightly, "and get home. I will discuss this with Quinlin in the morning." They scrambled to obey, fairly flying past him toward the study and the TravelPortal.

"They told Uncle Quinlin they were staying here tonight," Thomlin said, then withered under Treyas' gaze. "But I guess they'd better not."

"Good guess," Treyas replied. He regarded them both for a long moment, then drew a deep breath. "Go to your rooms. You'll be leaving with me tomorrow for Dalziel."

"Dalziel?" Vantann repeated. "I thought Pepin was going."

"There's been a change of plans," Treyas retorted sharply. "Now, go to your rooms!"

They sidled past him and bolted for the door and the relative safety of the hallway. Treyas picked up the deck of playing cards, took a deep, calming breath and went to find Pepin. He met his son just a few steps outside of the young man's solar.

Pepin stopped short, obviously reading Treyas' angry face as being directed at him. "I thought we could talk," he said. "But I see you're still angry."

"No, Pepin," Treyas replied. "I'm not angry with you. Not now. In fact, I was on my way to see you. You're right. We need to talk."

Pepin nodded and led the way back to his solar. Treyas sat down in a soft, overstuffed chair before the hearth and looked absently at the cards in his hand.

"What's that?" Pepin asked, nodded his head at the cards.

"What? Oh." Treyas suddenly chuckled and looked up at Pepin. "I just caught Vans and Thoms playing Queen's Takeoff in the guest solar with Rusulka and Ketura." He shook his head.

Pepin smiled. "I'll bet Grandpapay Elek taught them." He laughed at Treyas' look of astonishment and sat down in the chair opposite Treyas. "He taught me how to play it, too, when I was fifteen. He claims it's a great icebreaker with the girls."

"Gods," Treyas mumbled. "If you only knew how protective, moral and...and boring he was when I was growing up!" He shook his head again and dropped the cards on the table between the two chairs. "Anyway, I'm not here to discuss my guardian's morals or lack thereof. I want to apologize, Pepin. I behaved very badly this evening. I treated you as if you were a child, not a man. You're at the age where you need to make your own decisions. I need to respect those decisions no matter how I feel about them personally. Will you forgive me?"

Pepin sighed and rose. "There's nothing to forgive, Papay. I sort of sprang this on you. I should have told you six months ago. I was wrong not to."

"I can fully understand why you didn't," Treyas told him with a grimace. "I'm sorry, Pepi. I'm sorry that you feared my reaction enough that I couldn't be a witness to your title ceremony." He rose, reached out and drew Pepin into an embrace. "I'm proud of you, Pepin. I really am."

"Thank you, Papay," Pepin said quietly. "That means a lot to me."

Treyas studied him for a moment longer, then turned and re-claimed the playing cards. On impulse he handed them to Pepin. "Let Velouette play with them." He paused, his hand gripping one end of the deck, Pepin's the other. "Pepin, can you postpone your move to Mere Odain until I get back from Dalziel? I just want to be here."

Pepin smiled sadly. "Of course."

Treyas released the cards and went to the door, Pepin trailing. "I've decided to take both Vantann and Thomlin with me to Dalziel," Treyas said. "It's apparent I need to get them away from the girls for awhile."

Pepin chuckled lightly. "Papay, you should know better. If they're truly SoulMates, time and distance won't matter."

"Maybe not," Treyas agreed, "but I'm not letting them marry before they're twenty. I'm just not up to it. Goodnight, Pepin."

"Goodnight, Papay."

Treyas paused outside the door. There had been something else, something he felt that Pepin wanted to share, but hadn't. He wondered if he should press the matter, then sighed, shook his head and shuffled down the hallway.

Treyas set down his empty tea mug with a sigh. "I have to go," he said. "Thanks for listening, Quin. Again."

Quinlin grinned and encouraged his tall, lanky form up from the porch step. "What are big brothers for?" He clapped Treyas on the shoulder and walked him back inside the cottage.

It was early and the rest of Quinlin's family was still asleep, with the exception of his eighteen-year-old daughter, Reya. She sat before the fire, huddled in a heavy, patchwork blanket, her face pale, dark circles ringing her green eyes. Even so, she was beautiful, a copy of her mother with her fair skin and copper hair. Treyas smiled knowingly. "Reya," he said softly, "Cynthe used to get like this too, when she was with child. Gerowen had an herb mixture that really helped. I could have some sent over."

Reya nodded. "Thank you, Uncle Treyas, I'd appreciate that."

Quinlin gently massaged his daughter's shoulders, then looked up as a young, black elf, still dressed in a calf-length nightshirt, stumbled into the room. "Reya? What's wrong? I woke up and you were gone."

"It's nothing, Keelin," Reya replied. "Just nature's way of letting me know I'm to be a mother."

"Oh." Keelin sat down on the floor next to her and rested his head sleepily on her lap. She smiled, draped part of her blanket about him and stroked his dark curls.

Quinlin regarded them with an affectionate smile, then glanced at Treyas. "When you started this mixing of elves, I never thought I'd be part of the experiment."

"I'm afraid it's gone far past the experimental stage," Treyas said with a laugh. "It's become a way of life in Aelfdene."

"And I thank you for that," Keelin mumbled.

"You've come a long way from Reyuann's camp, Keelin," Treyas said. "How do you like being a fisherman?"

Keelin shrugged and Quinlin laughed. "He's a good fisherman. He has a gift for knowing where to put the nets."

Keelin grimaced. "Now if I could only get past spending the first three hours heaving."

"Keelin!" Reya cried and bolted for the bathroom, shedding blanket and husband.

Quinlin laughed, his green eyes twinkling. He gave Keelin a hand up. "Choose your words wisely around a pregnant woman," he advised.

Keelin nodded, scooped up the blankets and went after his wife. Treyas chuckled.

"Eighteen and expecting a child?" He shook his head at Quinlin. "Where did all of that talk of maturity go? You railed on me about having children at an early age."

Quinlin shrugged, then looked over as his wife, Drisana entered the room.

"Treyas! Good morning. You're up early."

The statement held a question, and Treyas headed for the TravelPortal. "I'll let Quin explain that one. I really have to go. The others are probably waiting."

"I'll talk to Rusulka and Ketura about their choice of games," Quinlin said, ignoring Drisana's questioning gaze. "And, Trey, don't lose sleep over Pepin. It'll work out. You'll see. It'll work out."

"I hope you're right, Quin. I'll see you when we get back." He stepped into the Portal, manipulated the TravelStrands and arrived back at his study in the Elfin Council Chambers moments later. As he had predicted, the others were waiting. At least, some of the others.

Kyel and his eldest child, Elecka were there, as were King Jansson van Tannen and Darosenim Quartermane, King of Karsaba. The twins and Druce were not.

"Trey!" Jansson greeted. "Where the hell were you?"

"Jansson," Kyel admonished firmly.

Jansson rolled his brown eyes and corrected his language. "Where were you?"

"In Ravenscroft. I went to see Quin. Where are the others?"

Jansson shrugged, selected another breakfast sweet from the tray and collapsed into a chair. Darosenim shook his head, stroking his full, flaming red beard. "Baerns, Jans, that's about the fifth sweetcake you've had this morning."

"So?"

"So, if you start heaving in the Portal, you'd better be standing away from me," Darosenim teased.

"Men!" Kyel snapped. "And I use the term lightly. We are taking impressionable young minds on this trip. Please remember that."

Jansson glanced at Elecka, then opened his mouthful of half chewed food at Darosenim. Elecka giggled and Jansson suddenly yelped as Kyel gave him a sharp mental magic slap, then turned to glare at Elecka. She shrank back in her chair as the twins and Druce arrived, the former two still adjusting their tunics. Their blond hair was tousled and sleep hung heavy in their eyes as they stumbled into the room. Druce looked frazzled and annoyed.

Treyas addressed the boys. "So? Do we have a reason here?"

"We forgot," Vantann mumbled, heading for the breakfast tray. "I mean, you only told us last night."

"All right," Treyas agreed. "That's fair." He looked at Druce. "Were you able to help them pack? Do we need to wait?"

"No. I've got their packs. I gave them to Elek."

"Good. Did he say when he'd be ready?"

"In about half an hour," Druce replied, his voice weary.

Treyas eyed him, concerned. "Have you been up all night, Druce?"

"No, not all night."

"Just a good portion of it, right?" Treyas gripped his shoulder and propelled him toward the door. "Go spend some time with your family. We'll wait."

"Trey, I,"

"Go!" Treyas gave him a gentle push, almost sending him colliding with Pepin who darted into the study breathlessly.

Druce and Pepin exchanged a long look, then Druce left with a terse nod. Treyas turned to Pepin, puzzled.

"I wanted to say goodbye," Pepin explained. "I was afraid I'd miss you. I thought you were scheduled to leave at nine."

"It's been delayed," Treyas said. "Due to a change of plans. Remember?"

Pepin winced and glanced at Kyel, then dropped his voice to a whisper. "Does he know?"

"Do I know what?" Kyel asked.

"You can't sneak anything past those ears, Pepin," Jansson said. "Trust me. I've tried."

"Perhaps you should share your news," Kyel said.

Pepin flushed. "That's not why I came down here," he mumbled.

"Just the same, you are here. If there is something I should know, then please speak it."

Pepin looked to Treyas for help but Treyas turned away. He wished he could help, wished he could offer encouragement and support but found it just wasn't in him this morning. He waited with a heavy heart to hear Pepin say the words again.

"I...um..." Pepin took a deep breath, then blurted, "I've officially accepted the title of DragonMaster."

Treyas closed his eyes as stunned silence settled over the study. Then Vantann let out a whoop and Treyas' eyes snapped open to see the twins descend on Pepin with smiles and hugs of congratulations. Even Jansson and Darosenim seemed happy for him and Treyas relaxed. Until he looked at Kyel. Gone was Kyel the friend, Kyel the grandfather. In his place stood Kyel the King.

"Prince Merripen," he said, quieting the others instantly. "Am I to understand, sir, that you have transferred your allegiance from me and Aelfdene to Queen El'leigh and Mere Odain?"

Pepin stared at him, obviously flustered. "I...I don't know," he stammered.

"You don't know? Perhaps this is something you should have considered before accepting the title."

"Kyel," Jansson started and was silenced with a look.

The room sparked with tension, and Treyas looked helplessly at Pepin, who stood rigid, his dark cheeks flaming. Treyas' heart went out to his son but there was nothing he could say. Kyel's question was valid. Pepin needed to provide the answer. Only Pepin could.

Pepin's gaze danced over those around him, then settled on Kyel. He drew himself up tightly. "I had hoped, Your Majesty, that a compromise could be worked out. I have no true desire to abandon my allegiance with the elfin empire. I did not choose to be the DragonMaster. It was born into me. It is a calling I have tried to ignore for years. I can ignore it no longer. If there is no possible way for me to retain my allegiance and position within the elfin empire, then I will be forced to give up both."

Treyas sucked in his breath, his heart catching.

"That's not fair!" Jansson cried, startling everyone. Treyas looked at him quickly.

"Jansson," Kyel said firmly, "this does not concern you."

"The hell it doesn't!" Jansson retorted. "You're the elfin king. I'm King of Odora Dava. You're my advisor and my father. Yet, last I looked I hadn't made any pledges to Aelfdene, nor had you to Odora Dava. So, what does that mean, Kyel? If it comes right down to it, you'll go your way and I'll go mine and family ties be damned?"

"King van Tannen!" Kyel snapped. "You are out of line!"

"No!" Jansson advanced on Kyel with a fury driven by his own uncertainty. "No, I'm not! Tell me now, King Sylvain. Just where do I stand with you? Are you my father or do I need to beware my back in a conflict?"

"Jansson!" Treyas cried. He grabbed Jansson's arm and spun him away from Kyel, just as Elek strode into the room. He was a tall, muscular man and his presence seemed to fill the room.

"What's going on in here?" he asked, his gaze moving from one to another. "I could hear you clear down the hallway!"

"It's past," Kyel replied, his voice tight and cold. "Prince Pepin, I will expect you to reflect on my question while I am gone. We will discuss it further upon my return. Treyas, I will wait in the grand hall. Elecka."

She leapt to her feet and followed her father from the room, though her blue eyes flicked briefly to Jansson almost in reassurance.

"Baerns, Jansson," Darosenim mumbled. "Are you desiring a short life or what?"

"It's my fault," Pepin said softly. "I'm sorry. I never should have come down. Papay, I'm sorry."

Treyas went to him. "I wish there was something I could say, Pepin, but you knew it would come down to this." He gave Pepin a gentle hug. "Work on it while we're gone. Present a well-thought out compromise to Kyel and he may just accept it. No matter what his decision, though, remember you are always my son. I'll see you when we get back."

Pepin nodded slowly and turned away, then stopped and looked back at Jansson. "Uncle Jansson, thank you," he said. "I'm sorry that I,"

"Forget it," Jansson interrupted, then gave a wry smile. "Make that a good compromise, Pepin. I may need it."

Pepin sighed, nodded again and left.

Darosenim looked to Jansson. "Come on, Jans, you don't believe that."

"I don't know what I believe, to be honest," Jansson returned. "It's given me something to think about though. I never even questioned a dual allegiance before."

Treyas looked at Elek. "I haven't seen you for days and I need to know about the safety of this trip. I know Kyel has complete faith in Elecka, but the twins are another story."

"What's that supposed to mean?" Vantann demanded.

Treyas shot him an amused glance. "Need you ask, Vans?"

"Treyas, I have been to Dalziel numerous times," Elek said. "I see no reason to think this visit will be anything more than a typical diplomatic session to discuss alliances."

"In another words," Vantann grumbled, "boring."

Treyas turned to him. "But a necessary part of your position, Vantann." He looked at Jansson, who wore a set, grim expression. "Elek, why don't you and the others go on to the grand hall? I want to talk to Jansson for a moment."

Elek nodded and ushered the twins and Darosenim from the room. Jansson frowned. "Are you going to yell at me, too?"

"Of course not, Jans. I'm in no position to yell. I just wondered,"

"About my state of mind?" Jansson interrupted. "About how I dared to speak to Kyel like that? I can't believe he's forcing Pepin to make a choice. He's being a hypocrite. I simply pointed that out to him."

"I wouldn't say you did it simply," Treyas said. "That line about watching your back was a little strong."

Jansson flushed. "I know. It's just that..." He brought his gaze up to meet Treyas'. "It hurt, Trey. The thought that Kyel might turn against me if push came to shove...gods, Treyas! I never really thought about it until now, but it's a real possibility."

"I don't see how, Jans. There's a grand difference between the elfin kingdom's alliance with Odora Dava, and the elfin kingdom's alliance with Mere Odain. Odora Dava and Aelfdene have been allies for decades. Politically we follow the same path. And socially," he draped an arm about Jansson's shoulders, "you're my best friend, Jans. You're like a brother."

Jansson frowned. "Even brother's fight."

"Fighting between brothers and going to war are two different things. You're just going to have to face it, Jans. You were angry and you overstepped your limits. You know it and Kyel knows it. And now, you'll have to apologize."

Jansson grimaced. "Do I have to?" he teased.

Treyas chuckled, guiding him from the room. "You have to."

They walked the short distance to the grand hall to find everyone ready and waiting except Druce. Treyas thought that strange since Druce had a thing about being punctual. He glanced at the large wall clock. Ten. An hour later than the planned departure time. He frowned and turned to the twins. "Thoms, would you go," He broke off as Druce hurried into the room, looking tidier but no less weary.

"I'm sorry," he apologized. "I seem to be having trouble getting going today."

Jansson grinned. "Maybe you need a good dose of that coffee stuff you claim is so good."

Druce gave him a wan smile. "Maybe."

Treyas took Druce by the arm, scrutinizing him. "Are you sure you're feeling all right? Maybe you should stay here and,"

"No," Druce interrupted. "I'm fine, Treyas. I'm just tired. By the way, you didn't tell me if you would be needing the Triskelion. I brought it just in case."

"I wasn't planning to use any magic," Treyas pointed out. "This is, after all, just a business trip."

"True, but why take chances?" Kyel asked, with a slight smile.

Treyas regarded Kyel and Druce him with a small smile. "Cowards."

Druce grinned. "That I admit to."

"Is everyone ready?" Elek interrupted. "I've preset the Spell. We'll arrive in Dalziel's session chambers. Vantann, Thomlin, Elecka, you three hold hands. I don't want to lose you crossing the dimensional border."

"Lose us!" Thomlin cried as they linked hands.

"Have you ever lost anyone?" Vantann asked.

"No." Elek raised his arms. "But there's always a first."

Treyas cast a sharp glance at Elek, puzzled by the ominous tone in the sorcerer's voice, then forced a smile at the look of alarm that swept over the three youth's faces. Elek cast his Spell and sent them all across the dimensional void to Dalziel.

Pepin felt the little surge of Sorcery magic as Elek cast his Spell. Guilt once more flooded through him. Guilt laced with despair. Kyel's question of allegiance still rang in his head. Even though he had known he would have to face it, to hear the words spoken stung. He shivered in the cool air of the stables and nestled further into the loose straw. He had fled here after the confrontation with Kyel. He often used the stables as a place to think. The musty smell of straw, animals, wood and dirt brought a sense of comfort to him, though he wasn't really sure why. He supposed it was because he had spent a great deal of time here after his problems in Mere Odain.

His gaze drifted to the empty stall at the end. It had once housed cages of various sizes and shapes, all built to fit a specific animal. His animals. Pepin had had a lot of them in his youth. He had loved them all with a passion, but knew now that he had simply been trying to fill the void left by Fayemera's death.

His thoughts drifted to the dragon gently, peacefully. It had been thirteen years since she'd died on the ice plains beyond Rune Mountain. Died saving him. He recalled the LifePledge that had drawn him to her at the age of eight, and was once again thankful that Treyas had talked him into breaking that pledge. If he hadn't, Pepin would have died along with Fayemera. Such was the pledge. It increased the power of both dragon and rider but the cost was far too high. For that reason, Pepin had forbidden any of his Foumen DragonRiders to LifePledge with their dragons. To his knowledge, none had with the exception of Faolan, the Lushik Keltin that Pepin called bloodbrother.

Pepin had assigned Faolan the position of DragonKeeper in the long years of Pepin's internal struggle. The action had brought together Merian, Keltin and Foumen for the first time in history. It was a union that was doing spectacularly well and Pepin continually wondered what effect his actions would have. Faolan had seemed happy for him, content to have him in control again. Still, Pepin wondered how deep Faolan's acceptance ran.

He sat up straighter as El'leigh attempted to MindLink him. He had never gotten over his jealousy at her power. MindLinking from such a vast distance was far beyond his capabilities and he once again reflected on the one major difference between him and El'leigh. Their magic. They were both halflings, cousins. Their mothers, Alita and Irida, had been identical twin sisters. Pepin's father, Pe'pinlaidh, had been the DragonMaster, El'leigh's father, Be'an, the king of Mere Odain. Irida had tricked Be'an into bedding her by posing as Alita, and, though Be'an thoroughly despised Irida, he loved their child El'leigh with a passion, and sought to raise her as a Merian princess.

But war had intervened. War that had caused Pepin's father to send him away for his own safety. Pepin trembled now, thinking how his father must have felt when word came, albeit erroneously, that his only son had been killed. Pepin couldn't imagine losing Velouette and still be able to live. It was no wonder that, in his grief, Pe'pinlaidh had taken El'leigh in as his own when Be'an had been killed. Still, it drove daggers into Pepin's heart to know that while he had languished as a loneling in Karsaba, El'leigh had loved and been loved by his father.

Pepin wondered what El'leigh would have been like had she not received seven good years of upbringing from Pe'pinlaidh. Her familial tie to dark magic and necromancy were strong. Still, she had spent little time with her mother, and Pepin often wondered where she had learned to use her magic so well. El'leigh refused to speak of it, and Pepin had given up prying. Thankfully, her penchant for the use of dark magic was tempered both by Pe'pinlaidh's years of guidance and her husband Andison's gentle love. Still, it was dark magic and even now, as she contacted him, he winced at its use.

::I'm here, El'leigh,:: he sent in the usual informal tone he used with her. ::What is it?::

::Pepin, you have to come right away! The Akuri have attacked Graybara!::

::What!:: Pepin came bolt upright in alarm. ::When?::

::This morning, or, last night to you,:: she sent, referring to the time difference between the two countries. ::Jibben only arrived with the news hours ago. Pepin...he says Graybara is gone. He thinks the Akuri had help.::

::From?:: Pepin prodded.

::From some of the Nydiri, Pepin.::

A cold chill swept through him. ::That's impossible! There are no Nydiri left in Kelta. Papay sent them all to a different dimension when he shattered that Dirin barrier years ago. And Dukker wasn't successful in releasing them either.::

::Apparently there are more than that!:: El'leigh snapped, her volatile temper rearing its ugly head. ::Don't argue with me, Pepin. Just get over here. You need to take a DragonFleet down to Kelta and make sure the Akuri go no farther than they already have. Or do I need to have Faolan do it?::

Pepin stiffened in anger. ::I'll be there. I have to get my pack ready and say good-bye to--::

::To Nila,:: El'leigh interrupted, her voice sour. ::I know. Make it quick, Pepin. I'd like you to be in position as soon as possible.::

::I'll be there within the hour,:: Pepin returned, then winced again as she dropped the MindLink. With a heavy heart, he got to his feet, brushed his clothing clean and headed for the house.

He still couldn't understand El'leigh's animosity toward Nila. He hadn't remembered Nila doing anything to warrant it. But then, memories had a way of changing over time to fit what one wanted to believe. Pepin wanted everyone to love Nila as much as he did. He had known Nila since he was eight-years-old. Nila and El'leigh had met six years later, during a conflict in Mere Odain. A conflict in which Nila had nearly died, would have died but for the power of her grandfather and dark magic. If anything, Nila was the one who should harbor ill feelings for El'leigh, not the other way around.

Pepin grimaced, entering the palace through the kitchen tower.

"Master Pepin!" the rotund dwarf cook greeted him happily. "I've come up with a new cookie recipe. Could you taste them and tell me what you think?" She opened the heavy oven doors, releasing a rush of warm, cinnamon scented air.

Pepin drew back, though it was not so much the heat as it was the iron lining of the ovens. He despised iron. All elves did. It was the one thing that could stop elfin magic. It had once stopped him and Nila, leaving them prisoners of the Akuri Keltins. He shook off the unpleasant memories and accepted a hot cookie from the dwarf.

"Zaida! These are wonderful!" he exclaimed. "What's in them besides cinnamon?"

"That's a secret," the cook replied with a grin. She winked, pushed a stray red lock from her forehead and set to work on placing another batch on the cooking tray.

"Too bad the twins aren't here," Pepin said.

"Good thing they aren't," Zaida retorted. "They'd have the cookies gone before anyone else could taste them. I've never seen such appetites! And where does it all go? They're mere wisps of boys, barely there. And you're no better, Master Pepin."

Pepin grinned. "It's the Merian in me, Zaida. You know that."

"And might we be losing you to Mere Odain?" she asked without looking at him.

"Where did you hear that?"

"The walls have ears, young lord, though I can't say as I like what they hear."

Pepin sank down on the bench by the long trestle table. "Am I doing the right thing, Zaida?"

"I couldn't say, Master Pepin. I only know that occasionally a person has to leave their home to answer a calling. I know I did." She placed another tray of cookie dough into the oven and hurriedly closed the door.

"And your calling?" Pepin asked.

"To serve the king, Your Highness," Zaida replied. "I left my home in Wray to come here and care for your father and his family."

"Don't you miss Wray?"

"Of course I do, Your Highness, but your father, bless him, has gone out of his way to make me feel that this is my home as well."

Pepin frowned. "I doubt Queen El'leigh will be so thoughtful." He got to his feet. "Speaking of which, she wants me to go to Mere Odain immediately. Could you make me up a pack with some more of these cookies?"

"I will indeed, Prince Pepin," Zaida said with a grin. "But I'll include some good wholesome food as well. You need a few pounds on you."

Pepin grinned, then on impulse, gave her a light kiss on the forehead. She started, a red flush settling over her plump cheeks. Pepin chuckled and left the kitchen, snagging a cookie for Velouette on the way. His and Nila's tower was on the other side of the palace and, instead of following the hall around, Pepin elected to walk through the interior courtyard.

He liked it here. The air was always cool and fresh, making the scents from the many different flowers seem stronger, clearer. The sound of water gently falling in the many well-placed fountains was soothing and, by the time Pepin had traversed the stone path, he was relaxed, though still not ready to say good-bye to his family. He crossed the hallway and climbed the spiral staircase to his solar. Nila was just coming down from the bedroom. She greeted him with a hug and a smile, which faded as she drew back to look into his dark eyes. "What is it?"

"El'leigh has ordered me to Mere Odain. The Akuri Keltin have attacked Graybara. She wants me to take some dragons down and see what we can do to stop the Keltins."

"When?"

Pepin took her hand. "Now."

Nila was silent for a moment, then she turned back toward the bedroom. "I'll get you packed then. You'd best get to the armory and get your sword and dagger and whatever else you may need."

Pepin drew her back. "I'll get them in Mere Odain at the palace. Right now, I just want to be with you and Velouette." He held up the cookie. "I brought her something."

"She's asleep," Nila told him, but led the way to the bedroom.

Pepin laid the cookie on the dresser and gathered Nila into his arms. He kissed her long and gently, then held her close. "I'm going to miss you," he whispered.

"And I, you," she replied, then moved away. "Well, this isn't getting you packed."

"I know." He helped her gather his things together, but was puzzled when she took his heavy, wool, winter cloak from the wardrobe. "What's that for?"

"It's cold in Mere Odain," she explained. "Especially when you're...when you're..." She clutched the cloak to her chest and began to cry softly.

"Oh, Nila." Pepin took her into his arms.

"I don't like you on those dragons, Pepin. They scare me. Mere Odain scares me. I'm sorry. I tried to understand. I tried to support you but..." Her words trailed off and she pressed against him.

Pepin stroked her short dark curls tenderly. "I know you have, Nila. I know and I do appreciate it and love you for it. This decision wasn't just mine to make. I realize that now, but it's too late to reconsider. At least, for now. I promise you, Nila, when I get back we'll discuss it fully. You, me, Papay and Kyel."

Nila drew back and nodded. "Whatever is decided, Pepin, I'll be there for you. That's my promise."

"Q'egoshay, beloved," Pepin murmured, stroking her cheek gently.

Nila managed a small smile. "Q'egoshay, beloved."

Chapter Three

Vantann yawned widely and flung himself onto one of the beds in his and Thomlin's room. "Gods," he groaned, "this was one of the longest days of my life."

"No," Thomlin corrected, gazing out the wide window, "gutting fish on Uncle Quinlin's boat counts as the longest to me." He stared down at the immaculate gardens glowing in the vibrant light of afterdusk, then motioned to Vantann. "Look. The hedges are cut into a maze."

Vantann joined him at the window. "Gods! That's huge. A person could get lost in there. I wonder what it's for."

"Probably for fun."

Vantann snorted and returned to the bed. "I doubt the Dalzielians have much fun. They seem rather stuffy to me. Although, they do seem to like fancy things." He ran his hand over the purple, velvet bedcover as his gaze flicked over the guest-room.

It was finely appointed with two oak four-poster beds, an oak armoire and an oak table big enough to eat at. There were several richly upholstered chairs with gold threads running amongst the deep purple fabric. A thick rug before the massive hearth had been sewn to match the chairs. Even the heavy draperies matched, and Vantann absently wondered what sort of economics Dalziel had. It had probably been discussed at Session earlier, though he could not remember. Gods! He hoped that neither Treyas nor Kyel would quiz him on the Session meeting. About the only thing he could remember was the wine page's low-cut blouse and Elecka's blue eyes appraising him thoughtfully every time he had ventured to look at that blouse and what lay beyond. He rolled to his side, propped himself on one elbow and regarded his brother. "You like Rusulka a lot don't you?" he asked.

Thomlin looked over at him, obviously surprised by the question. "Yes, I do. Why?"

"Do you think she's your SoulMate?"

Thomlin flushed, returning his gaze to the outside. "I don't know. Maybe."

"Come on, Thoms. You're fifteen. Papay says SoulMates become obvious at fifteen."

"That's not what he said, Vans. He said it was possible to know as early as fifteen. Most elves don't. Because we're half human, it'll probably be closer to twenty-five or so."

"I don't believe that," Vantann said. "Not the way you and Rusulka look at each other."

Thomlin gave him a surly glance. "Well, what about you? You're the same age as me. You seem fairly tight with Ketura these days."

"Ketura?" Vantann snorted, rolling onto his back to stare at the ceiling. "That's how much you know. We're only friends. Ketura has her eye on some fisherman friend of Keelin's."

Thomlin turned to look at his brother. "I'm sorry. I didn't know that."

"It doesn't bother me. Not much anyway." Vantann paused, batting absently at the purple velvet bed curtains. "I was wondering though, about you and Elecka."

"Elecka?" It was Thomlin's turn to be surprised.

"You used to like her quite a bit," Vantann reminded him.

"Tens! That was five years ago, Vans. She never even looked my way."

"Then you wouldn't mind if I took up with her?"

Thomlin's eyebrows rose in amusement. "Why do you think she would want to take up with you?" he teased. "Besides, you're always complaining about how serious and studious she is."

"I don't!"

"You do! All of the time." He turned back to the window, then gasped. "Vans! Come here!"

Vantann leapt off the bed and joined Thomlin at the window. Elecka had just stepped into the gardens and, with a last furtive look over her shoulder, disappeared into the maze.

"Tens! I can't believe Kyel let her out of his sight," Thomlin breathed.

"I'll bet he doesn't know." Vantann grabbed Thomlin's arm. "Come on, let's follow her."

"Do you know how to get to the gardens?"

"I think so. We'll figure it out. Come on." Vantann rushed from the room, Thomlin right behind. They crept past the other guest rooms, then bolted down the stairs. Vantann hurried into the meeting room where the day's Session had been held and pointed to a door against the far wall. "I saw the wine page go in and out that door. It must lead to the kitchen. I'll bet we can get outside from there." He led Thomlin around the long, shiny, wood table to the door, only to find it locked. "Damn!" he muttered, then both boys froze in panic at the sound of voices.

"Here!" Thomlin whispered and ducked behind the heavy drapery covering the large, bay window. He and Vantann climbed onto the window seat and pulled their feet up as the sound of a door opening reached them.

"Everything is proceeding as planned then?" a man's voice asked.

"Yes, M'Lord," another, younger sounding male replied.

The voices were very close and the twins exchanged frightened glances and pressed closer to the window.

"Excellent," the first man said. "A week from now, they'll be so angry with each other, a war will be imminent. The stage will be set for revenge."

"What of the children, M'Lord?"

"What of them?"

"I wonder if there might not be a way to turn them against their father as well?"

The other man laughed, and the hair on Thomlin's neck rose. He knew that laugh! But from where?

"I like the way you think," the man said as the voices moved away. "I like the way you think."

A movement outside caught Thomlin's attention and he poked at Vantann. "Vans!"

Vantann shushed him and took a cautious peek around the drapery. "They're gone," he murmured.

"Vantann!" Thomlin muttered through clenched teeth and jerked on his arm.

"What?" Vantann snapped, then looked where Thomlin pointed.

A tall, thin figure stood outside the window just beyond the planter beds, apparently staring at them. The person was dressed in black and wore a black cloak with the cowl pulled low over the face. In the evening light, it was impossible to tell whether the person was male or female. Whoever it was, stood for a moment longer, in which neither twin dared to do no more than breathe, then turned and strolled away down the gravel pathway.

Vantann uttered a sigh of relief, peered around the curtain once more, then motioned Thomlin forward. The door that was locked before, now opened easily and the boys slipped inside a short, dark hallway that led to the kitchen.

The kitchen, though deserted, was warm and bright and the familiarity of it chased away the chill that had settled over Thomlin. "Do you think that man in the garden saw us?" he asked.

"How do you know it was a man?"

Thomlin shrugged. "The way he walked. Do you think he saw us?"

"I don't know. There were no lights behind us and it was dark outside."

"Who do you think those other men were talking about?"

Vantann shook his head. "I have no idea, but if the Dalzielians are going to war, I'm going home."

"We need to tell papay," Thomlin said.

"What? We can't! We're not even supposed to be down here, let alone eavesdropping on Dalziel officials."

"But, Vans," Thomlin stopped as the outside door suddenly opened and someone dressed in black swept in, along with a cold blast of night air.

"Oh, Your Highnesses!" the person gasped, obviously startled at seeing them. The cowl fell back, revealing a young woman, her brown eyes wide with alarm, her round cheeks flushed with the cold and embarrassment. Her hand fluttered up to smooth unruly brown locks back toward a tight knot of hair at the nape of her neck, before she dropped into a deep curtsy. "Is...is there something I can get for you?" she stammered.

"No," Vantann answered with a smile. "Unless you happen to have any extra dessert."

"I...I'll see what we have left, Your Highness," she replied, still flustered. She sidled past them toward the pantry.

"Were you just out in the garden?" Thomlin asked abruptly, then grunted as Vantann jabbed him with an elbow.

"N...no, Your Highness," she answered and held up a bottle of wine. "I went to the wine cellar. King van Tannen requested..." She stopped, looking from the wine bottle to them to the pantry and back to the bottle.

Vantann chuckled. "He's a king, we're only princes. See to him first. We'll wait."

"Yes, Your Highness." She curtsied again and started from the kitchen.

"Miss?" Vantann stopped her with a gentle word. "Don't you want to remove your cloak?"

She looked down as if she'd forgotten she wore it, then quickly slipped it off, revealing that she was no mere wisp of a girl. She was muscular and strong-boned and Thomlin unexpectedly found himself appraising her with appreciation. She hung her cloak on a peg by the door and with another quick curtsy, hurried away.

Thomlin watched her disappear up a dark flight of stairs, then nudged Vantann. "Come on, let's go find Elecka."

"I thought I'd wait for the girl to come back. She's sort of cute."

Thomlin grimaced. "Vans, must you seduce every girl you meet?"

"Seduce? Oh hardly, Thoms! I'm fifteen, not twenty-five. Gods!"

"Then come on." Thomlin yanked him toward the door and together they stepped outside.

Vantann shivered, wrapping his arms about his chest. "It's cold out here! I'm going back in. Besides, Elecka's probably gone back in, too. She wouldn't stay out in the gardens. Not when it's this cold. Or this dark."

Thomlin hesitated, his gaze scanning the tall hedges before them. They stood like a silent, dark sentry, the opening of the maze gaping like a yawning mouth. He shuddered, then glanced at Vantann. "Did you recognize either of those men by their voice?"

"No. Why? Did you?"

"The first one who spoke. He seemed vaguely familiar. I just can't place him."

"How could he sound familiar, Thoms? The only voices we've heard since we've been here are the Dalziel officials. And they all sound the same. Boring. Now, let's go back inside. I want to see if there's anymore of that berry dessert left."

Thomlin frowned but followed him back into the kitchen. The girl had not yet returned and Vantann sat down at a small worktable, obviously intent on waiting for her. Thomlin shook his head and rolled his eyes. "I'm going back to our room. You come up when you're done with your 'dessert'."

Vantann blushed. "I really do want some more."

Thomlin chuckled, then paused. "I hate to go back through the Session room. There must be another way upstairs."

"The girl went that way," Vantann said, pointing to the dark stairway.

"Then so will I. Good-night, Vans." Thomlin went through the doorway and peered up. The stairs were quite narrow, and curved away into darkness. He started up them tentatively, feeling his way with one hand on the rough stone walls, then stopped as a dim light shone around the corner above. A moment later, the kitchen girl appeared, carrying a candlelamp. She gasped when she saw Thomlin. "Your Highness! You startled me!"

Thomlin smiled. "I seem to have a habit of doing that. I'm sorry. I was only trying to return to my room. Is this the right way?"

"Aye. To the top of the stairs and just down the hall." She peered past him. "And your brother, Your Highness?"

"Oh, his name is Vantann and he's waiting to see if you have any more of that berry dessert. By the way, my name is Thomlin. What's yours?"

"It...it's...um..."

Thomlin laughed. "Um? That's an unusual name."

She stared at him, agape, then abruptly giggled and found her voice. "No, Your Highness. My name's Enid. It's just that I'm not in the habit of visiting with royalty on the back stairs from the kitchen."

"Well, we're informal royalty," Thomlin told her.

"And your brother?"

"Very informal. In fact, if you keep calling him Highness, he may take you to task for it."

Enid looked past him toward the kitchen, her smile gone. "You seem to be honest, Your Highness. Is it truly dessert your brother desires?"

Thomlin felt a flush crawl over his cheeks. "That's all, Enid. Really. He has a ravenous appetite. We're not in the habit of taking advantage of the help. Even if we were old enough to do so."

Enid's gaze shot to his face. "I took you to be my age, sixteen. Are you not then?"

Thomlin paused, then lied, though why he couldn't say. "In a few months, we will be."

She nodded. "I see." She paused, then pressed past him.

The stairs were quite narrow and she came almost nose-to-nose with Thomlin as she moved down a step. And in that brief moment of togetherness, something inside of Thomlin's soul came awake. He stared at her, his heart suddenly pounding, his stomach fluttering like a butterfly gone berserk. Enid returned his gaze, an odd look in her brown eyes, then abruptly she held the candlelamp forward. "You'll need this. The stairs are quite dark."

Thomlin took the lamp, his fingers brushing against hers, sending a tingle shooting through him. Almost reluctantly, he turned away, listening for her footsteps to disappear into the kitchen. Gods! What was happening? *I love Rusulka,* he told himself as he climbed the stairs. *I've loved her for five years! Five years? Tens! I met her when I was ten. What could a ten-year-old know about love? For that matter, what could a fifteen-year-old know? And why did I lie about my age? Almost sixteen? Gods!* He'd just turned fifteen. He shook his head and let out a heavy sigh as he reached the second floor. It didn't matter anyway. They were only going to be in Dalziel for a few days. Hardly enough time to start a relationship, even if he wanted to. *Which he didn't,* he chastised himself. *I'll just stay away from her. I can do that for a few days. After all, she's only the kitchen help. It's not like I'm going to be forced to be with her.* He stopped outside his bedroom and leaned his head against the polished wooden door. *But, oh gods, I want to see her again. Just once. Just to prove to myself that there isn't anything there.*

He looked up at the sound of a soft thud from Jansson's room. He waited but heard nothing else, shook his head and slipped into his own room.

Pepin arrived in Mere Odain via the TravelPortal. Though it had been day when he'd left Glede, it was evening here. He hated the time change. While he was wide awake, everyone else was slumbering, and when morning came, he was expected to be just as alert as everyone else while his body cried out for rest. Usually he gave himself two days to adjust but, if he was hearing El'leigh right, he wouldn't have that luxury on this visit.

He hefted his pack, left the PortalRoom and started down the long, empty hallway toward the guest rooms. As often as he was here working with the dragons, one of the rooms had been permanently assigned to him. As he walked he glanced at the portraits of Merian royalty that lined the hall. In the flickering lamplight, the eyes seemed to move and watch him. He shivered and quickened his pace, rounded a corner and almost collided with Andison, El'leigh's husband, and ArmsMaster of Mere Odain.

"Andison! Danns! You scared the wits out of me!" Pepin cried. "What are you doing still awake and in the guest wing?"

Andison regarded him quietly, his dark eyes flashing, then answered, his voice tight and cold. "Going to my room, Pepin."

"But your room is..." Pepin stopped as understanding took hold. "Oh. Did you and El'leigh have a fight?"

"You could say that." Andison pushed past him to continue down the hall.

Pepin looked after him, empathically sensing his feelings of anger and hurt. "Andison, wait."

Andison froze. "What Pepin?" he snapped, then whirled to face him, fists clenched. "You've taken my job! You've taken my dignity! You've taken my wife! What else do you want?"

Pepin stared at him in astonishment.

Andison exhaled sharply and ran a hand threw his short, dark curls. "Coals, Pepin, I'm sorry. It's not your fault. I know that."

"What are you talking about?" Pepin managed.

Andison hesitated, then motioned him to follow. They went into one of the guest bedrooms a few doors down. Pepin could tell by the disarray and the number of personal items that Andison had been staying here for awhile.

"Would you like a glass of wine?" Andison asked.

"No. You forget, this is morning to me." Pepin dropped his pack and settled into one of the finely upholstered chairs hearthside. A fire had been kindled and Pepin gratefully accepted its warmth. He watched as Andison poured himself a large goblet of red wine, before sitting down in the chair next to Pepin's.

Andison took a long pull of the drink and leaned back. "I think it's over, Pepin," he said softly, staring through his wine glass at the flames. "Between me and El'leigh."

"Over? How can it be over? You love each other. You have a child together."

"Just having a child together doesn't bind a relationship."

Pepin paused, studying him. "Would I be out of line to ask what happened?"

"No, not at all. You see, Pepin, my wife is in love with another man. A man who clearly holds both her heart and a title she deems more worthy than any I could hold." He brought his gaze and his wine glass up. "You."

"Me!" Pepin's mouth dropped open in disbelief and shock.

"Would you like that glass of wine now?" Andison asked, then took another long drink of his.

"Andison, I...I don't know what to say," Pepin stammered. "I don't understand. El'leigh is my cousin, nothing more. I hope you don't think that I,"

Andison waved the rest of the sentence away. "Of course not, Pepin. This is purely El'leigh's doing. Although, in a way, you precipitated it."

"I did? How?"

Andison drained his glass, rose and poured himself another. "By taking on your title. El'leigh assumes that you two belong together now. The DragonMaster and his Queen." He toasted Pepin and swallowed half the wine at once.

"That's ridiculous," Pepin retorted. "I may be DragonMaster but I'm also married. Happily and securely, I might add. For El'leigh to even suggest that she and I...gods! She's my cousin! What on earth was she thinking?"

Andison shrugged and sagged back into his chair. "Who knows?" he mumbled, and took another long drink.

Pepin looked at the almost empty glass and the vacant stare in Andison's dark eyes, realizing that these two glasses of wine weren't his first that evening. "Drowning in wine won't make it better, Andison," he said gently. "And besides, from what I understand, we leave tomorrow for Kelta."

"Not me, Pepin," Andison replied, draining his glass. "I resigned from the DragonRiders."

"What!" Pepin cried. "Why, Andison? You're one of my best riders. No one can come close to your crossbow skills on the ground or in flight. Please,

Andison, I beg you to reconsider." He hesitated. "If you don't want to fly under my command, then how about Faolan's?"

Andison looked up at him and there were tears in his eyes. "I love her, Pepin," he mumbled. "As difficult as she is, I love her. And coals, I love our daughter more than life itself. How can I leave them? How can I simply disappear from their lives?"

Pepin rose and took the empty wine glass from Andison's limp fingers. "You won't have to leave," Pepin replied, setting the glass aside. He pulled Andison from the chair, using his Merian strength to support the man, though Andison was a good foot taller and outweighed Pepin. "Let's get you to bed, Andison. I'll talk to El'leigh. Everything will work out. You'll see." He half-walked, half-dragged Andison across the room and tumbled him into bed.

Andison rolled onto his stomach and clutched his pillow, burying his face in it. He mumbled something to Pepin but it was unintelligible and Pepin snagged a blanket to cover him with. "I'll talk to you in the morning, Andison. Things always look better in the light of day." Pepin retrieved his pack and left quietly, Andison's pain eating at his heart and stirring anger in his gut.

He stormed down the hall to his room, flung open the door and stomped inside. El'leigh uncurled herself from one of the chairs and Pepin stopped with a gasp. She was dressed in a long, white, satin gown, opened loosely at the front. Her dark hair rippled down her back to her waist and she regarded Pepin through dark eyes made hazy by fatigue and drink. "Where have you been?" she asked quietly. "You said you'd be here within the hour. It's been twice that."

Pepin stared at her, aghast. How dare she! How dare she come here dressed like this! How dare she invite herself into his room. Pepin shook off the emotions of love and want emanating from her as his anger exploded.

"What the hell are you doing here?" He snatched a blanket from the bed and flung it at her. "Cover yourself! Then leave!"

El'leigh caught the blanket but draped it over the chair back. She gave a small smile. "Do you really want me to leave, Pepin? Or do you want to know what's going on in Kelta?"

"We can discuss Kelta in the morning," Pepin snapped. "In the study and in proper attire. Now leave."

El'leigh walked toward him slowly, then stopped just before she passed him. They were shoulder to shoulder, facing each other and El'leigh reached up to place her warm hand against Pepin's cheek. She smelled of wine and Pepin's gaze darted to the table. An empty bottle stood near a glass.

"We belong together, Pepin," she murmured. "You love me. You always have. You know it and I know it. Now that you're DragonMaster once again, there's nothing to stop us from being together."

Pepin drew a tight breath, fighting down the emotions she always brought forth in him. "You've had too much to drink, El'leigh," he said, then caught at her as she swayed unsteadily. With a quiet oath, he picked her up and deposited her on the bed.

She smiled, tightened her grip around his neck and drew him close. Her lips brushed against his and Pepin quickly withdrew. He untangled her arms and straightened. "Go to sleep, El'leigh," he said, covering her.

"But what about you, Pepin? This is your room."

"I'm not sleepy. I'll find something to do. Go to sleep."

"Alone, Pepin?"

He eyed her steadily. "Andison's just down the hall. Perhaps if you desire a bed partner, your husband would be the one to turn to."

El'leigh lowered her gaze and turned away. So, Pepin thought, easily reading the confused emotions, she's not so sure of letting Andison go after all. He turned toward the door, but she grabbed his arm, stopping him.

"El'leigh, please," he said quietly. "Please, don't do this."

"You can't deny that you love me, Pepin."

"I do not deny it, El'leigh," Pepin replied, gently pulling his arm away from her. "You're family and I love you as such."

"But not as much as you love Nila?"

"As much, but not in the same way. Think about what you're doing, El'leigh. Perhaps in the past, the DragonMaster and the Queen were expected to be consorts, but it's no longer that way. I love Nila, she's my wife. You love Andison. Think about what you're doing to him, to your daughter."

El'leigh gasped, her eyes going wide. "Charis! Oh, coals! Where is she?"

"I...I don't know," Pepin stammered in alarm. Then anger swept over him. "You don't even know where she is?"

"Yes! I do! She's...she's..." El'leigh looked at him, frowning. "What time is it? Oh, coals, Pepin, I don't feel so good." She suddenly blanched and bolted for the bathroom.

Pepin heard her retching, shook his head and pulled the cord that would summon a servant. He disposed of the empty wine bottle and the glass, then stepped to the bathroom door. "El'leigh? El'leigh, I've called for a servant. Let's get you to bed before they arrive." He waited but there was no answer. He peeked into the lavishly appointed bathing chamber to find El'leigh either asleep or passed out on the floor. Pepin huffed out a breath of annoyance, picked her up, carried her to the bed and tucked her in, just as a knock sounded on the door. He took up his pack, opened the door and addressed the servant. "Queen El'leigh and I were discussing tomorrow's plans when she fell ill. We both thought it prudent for her to stay here and for me to seek lodging in one of the other guest rooms." He stepped past into the hallway, ignoring the look of skepticism on the servant's face. "Oh. She was concerned about Charis."

The servant looked at him, puzzled. "Princess Charis is in the nursery asleep, Your Highness."

"I reassured Queen El'leigh of that," Pepin said, relaxing with his own concerns. "Please contact her personal servant to assist her. If she wakes, tell her I will speak with her further in the morning."

"Yes, Your Highness." The servant bowed and went into the room.

Pepin sighed heavily. First Papay and Kyel's anger, then Nila's upset, now Andison and El'leigh's possible breakup. It was enough to make Pepin wish he'd never taken back his title. With a grimace, he turned his steps toward the outside and the dragon mews. Perhaps he could find some solace there.

Thomlin smoothed his unruly crop of blond hair, then tied it back with a short strip of leather, before turning to his brother, who had stalled sleepily in his efforts at getting dressed. "You'd better hurry," Thomlin urged. "Druce will be here any minute to fetch us."

Vantann finished pulling on his boots. "Gods," he grumbled, "just the way I want to spend my day. With a bunch of boring old diplomats. I would rather be seeing the sights with a pretty lady as my escort."

Thomlin paused a moment, then, hoping his voice sounded disinterested, asked, "So, how was your dessert last night?"

"Oh, tens!" Vantann flopped backward onto the bed. "I think I'm in love, Thoms."

Thomlin gasped, not a reaction he'd intended, then flushed when Vantann looked his way. "You can't be serious, Vans," he mumbled. "You only just met her."

"So? Papay says he knew the minute he met Mamay that she was his SoulMate."

Thomlin's heart fluttered. "You think Enid is your SoulMate?"

Vantann gave him a sly look. "How do you know her name?"

"Sh...she told me," Thomlin stammered. "I met her on the stairs." He looked away at a tap on the door. *Gods,* he thought, *saved.* He hurried to open the door, then frowned. "Druce! You look awful. Are you sick?"

Druce hesitated as if he were going to deny his pallor, the light sheen of sweat that covered his face, or the fact that the doorjamb was about the only thing keeping him afoot. Instead, he nodded. "I am and if one of you could help me back to my room, I'd greatly appreciate it."

Thomlin leapt forward, pulled one of Druce's arms about his shoulders and assisted him next door. Vantann joined them as Thomlin lowered the Merian onto the bed.

"What's wrong, Uncle Druce?" Vantann asked worriedly.

"It's nothing, Vantann," Druce assured him. "Probably just TravelSpell sickness. You two had better get to Session. You'll be late. Vantann, get your hair back. Thomlin, retie your belt. The ends are off." He looked down at their feet. "I see neither of you polished your boots like I told you to. No! Don't rub them on your pants! Coals! They're fine. Just go. Vantann, tell your father I'm a bit under the weather, that's all. I don't want to alarm him. He has enough to think about. Now, go."

Vantann hesitated. "Should we leave you alone, Uncle Druce? I mean, you look really sick."

Druce managed a weak smile. "I'll be fine, Vantann. Go on, before you're late."

Vantann paused a moment longer, then followed Thomlin from the room and downstairs to the meeting hall. Kyel, Elecka, Darosenim, Elek and Treyas were all there. Jansson was not. Kyel appeared slightly annoyed as the Session was called to order. Thomlin had only a few seconds to fill Treyas in on Druce's illness, before the diplomats were deep in discussion. The minutes and hours ticked by and still Jansson did not arrive. Finally, Vantann leaned close to Tryeas.

"Papay," he whispered, "should I go get Uncle Jansson?"

Treyas glanced at Kyel, who pointedly ignored him, then looked back at the twins. He restrained Vantann gently. "Thomlin, you go see what's keeping Jansson."

Vantann frowned and Thomlin rose, drawing looks of question from the Dalziel officials, and a look of reproach from Kyel. He motioned with his hand for the others to continue, and slipped quietly from the room. The Dalziel chambers were crowded with both officials and citizens, and Thomlin walked slowly, remembering his position, tipping his head now and again in response to a silent greeting. It seemed to take forever to reach the second floor and the guest rooms. When he did, he was surprised, and thrilled, to see Enid just leaving a room with a tray of dirty dishes. He called to her softly and she turned with a shy smile. "Good morning, Your Highness," she said, dropping a curtsy and eyeing him in question.

Thomlin chuckled, supposing she was trying to ascertain which of the twins stood before her. "I'm Thomlin."

She laughed softly, her response surprising him. "I know. I was wondering why you weren't at Session."

"I came up to get my uncle, King Jansson. It seems he slept in." Thomlin looked at the tray she held. It was mostly ale steins. "I'll bet whomever this belongs to, slept in as well."

"No." Enid giggled. "He was gone early enough."

"Enid!" An older woman at the end of the hall snapped her name like a wet towel.

Enid gasped. "I have to go, Your Highness. Excuse me." She gave another curtsy and turned away, her cheeks flaming. Thomlin followed.

"Did I get you into trouble?" he whispered.

"Not yet, but keep following me, and you will, Your Highness," she whispered back.

"Can I see you later?"

She shot him a quick glance. "Why?" she gasped, then quickly amended that. "I mean, for what purpose, Your Highness?"

Thomlin grinned at her. "Because I'd like to. Can I?"

"I'll be in the kitchen until late eve, Your Highness."

"Good." Thomlin stopped outside Jansson's door. "Until later then." He watched her walk down the hallway and disappear around a corner, then sighed, suddenly aware of what he'd done. Well, it was too late now. He turned and rapped on Jansson's door. There was no response and he knocked again, louder.

A moment later, the door opened and a very groggy Jansson stood staring at him. He was still dressed in his clothes from the previous day, which were wrinkled and disheveled. His brown hair was tousled and hung limply on his forehead and he brushed it aside with a yawn. "Thoms? Gods, it's the middle of," He broke off as he caught a glimpse through the window across the hallway. His eyes widened and he darted back into the room.

Thomlin followed slowly. His gaze took in the rumpled bed, the three empty wine bottles, the woman's clothing strewn on the floor, and he went red.

"Firesass!" Jansson moaned, then frowned, glancing at the clock in his room. "The clock stopped! Someone was supposed to wake me. Why didn't they? What time is it? Has Session started?" He frantically splashed his face with cold water from the basin, then abruptly ducked his entire head in, drew back with a gasp and shook the water from his hair.

"It's almost lunch," Thomlin said, handing him a towel. "Session's about over."

"Over? Tor's hell," Jansson muttered. He dried his hair, brushed it, then began to strip off his wrinkled clothing.

Thomlin was one step ahead of him and pulled some clean clothes from the wardrobe. He handed them to Jansson, who rapidly donned them, then began a search for his boots. He stopped abruptly, picked up a ladies undercoat and stared at it in puzzlement. His gaze darted to the bed, piled high with blankets. Slowly, he pulled the heavy coverlets aside, then stumbled backward with a gasp.

Thomlin's breath caught in his throat, his eyes widening in shock. A young woman was sprawled in Jansson's bed, completely nude. Her long, dark hair was lying across her face and one shoulder. Jansson quickly recovered her. "What the..." He went red, his gaze darting to Thomlin. "It's not what you...Thoms, I...we..." he stammered.

"Uncle Jansson," Thomlin said quietly. "Session is waiting."

Jansson's gaze swung back to the bed, he nodded numbly and pulled on his boots. Thomlin went to the door, opened it and waited, his gaze once more dancing across Jansson's room. He glanced again at the bed with a frown, then at the wine bottles. He knew Jansson would never forsake his bond with Zira and he also knew Jansson wasn't a drinker. Something didn't seem right, but he couldn't put his finger on it.

"Come on, Thoms," Jansson said, interrupting his thoughts. "Whoever she is, she'll have to get herself up. Gods! Kyel is going to be furious." He paused as he mentioned the black elf's name, his face reflecting both puzzlement and trepidation. He shook his head and motioned Thomlin from the room.

They hurried down to the meeting hall and slipped in quietly. Neslin, the head Dalziel official, looked up with a smile. "Ah, King Jansson, you're just in time."

Jansson froze as all eyes turned his way. Thomlin quickly took his place at the table, daring a glance at Kyel as Jansson mumbled his apologies. Kyel's face was tight, his blue eyes fixed on Jansson like lethal weapons. Thomlin noticed that Jansson didn't so much as glance Kyel's way as he sat down between Elecka and Treyas.

"Gods!" Vantann whispered in Thomlin's ear. "Uncle Jansson is going to catch hell."

Treyas shot him a disapproving look and Vantann slouched back in his chair.

"What is it that I have arrived just in time for?" Jansson asked.

"King Kyel has graciously offered us some land in Odora Dava so that we might establish a post in Glede," Neslin replied happily.

Jansson stiffened, his gaze swinging to Kyel, who stared at him defiantly and pushed the parchment and quill toward him. "It but requires your signature to be finalized, King Jansson," he said calmly.

Thomlin looked from Jansson to Kyel and back. A red flush covered Jansson's face and his dark eyes held anger. Still, he accepted the parchment and began to read it. Thomlin noticed that his grip on the quill tightened as he finished. Apparently Neslin noticed as well. "Is there a problem, King Jansson?" he asked.

Jansson tore his gaze from Kyel and looked at the Head Council. "I'm afraid so, sir. King Kyel has apparently forgotten that this particular piece of land includes the township of Edpahl. I cannot in good conscious sign this over without first consulting Edpahl's citizens. I'm sure you understand that, Head Council."

"I do indeed," Neslin replied. "I had assumed that you and your advisor were on common ground."

"Usually we are," Jansson assured him, "and there may be some point that I have overlooked. Still, since I have regrettably arrived late to this meeting, I would like some time to discuss this agreement before signing it."

"Very well." Neslin rose. "This Session will re-convene after lunch. Perhaps by then, King Jansson, you and King Kyel will once again be on common ground."

Jansson went an even deeper shade of red as the entire group rose and filtered out, Elek leading, leaving only those from Glede in the large room.

"It was nice of you to join us," Kyel said coldly.

"The clock in my room stopped. No one woke me," Jansson replied. "But don't you think giving away a vast chunk of my country was a bit steep as punishment?"

Kyel eyed him stonily. "If you had been here when you were supposed to, you might have contested the suggestion then," he snapped.

Treyas looked at him, startled. "Kyel, that agreement wasn't just drawn up this morning. You know that."

Jansson's eyes went wide with astonishment and he ran his hand over the parchment. None of the ink smeared with the exception of Kyel's signature. He brought his gaze up to meet Kyel's. "What the hell's going on?"

"Might I remind you to watch your language," Kyel retorted. "You are a king. Act like it."

"And you're my advisor," Jansson shot back. "Yet, you seem to be acting as much more. When was this drawn up?"

Kyel stiffened, shooting an incriminating glance at Treyas before answering. "I had dinner last night with Neslin. We drew up a tentative agreement then."

"What!" Jansson stared at him in disbelief and rage. "Don't you think I should have been in on this tentative agreement?"

Kyel gave him a sour look. "I believe you were otherwise occupied."

Both Jansson and Thomlin went red and exchanged startled glances. Darosenim quickly stepped in, taking Jansson's arm in a firm grip. "Why don't we go for a walk before lunch? You both need to cool down."

Jansson started to protest but Kyel abruptly rose. "An excellent idea, Darosenim. Elecka?"

Elecka rose but hung back. "Father, I was wondering if I might have lunch with the twins?"

Kyel glanced at Vantann and Thomlin with a grimace, but nodded. "Very well, but I wouldn't expect them to offer much insight into yesterday's Session. Their minds were quite obviously not on the proceedings but rather on the wine page and her manner of dress."

Treyas' eyes went wide with anger and humiliation, and both twins withered, drawing back a step as Kyel marched past them and left the room. At once, Treyas turned on his sons. "It was obvious to me that neither of you were paying attention yesterday, but the fact that it was obvious to Kyel suggests that the Dalziel officials noticed as well. I will get a copy of the Session minutes and you two can spend the evening memorizing them. I'm going to check on Druce. After lunch, I expect to see you two here and very, very alert. Do I make myself clear?"

"Yes, Papay," they mumbled together, then watched him leave.

Darosenim exhaled slowly. "Baerns! It looks as if everyone needs a cool down walk. Come on, Jans, we'll talk."

"And eat, I hope," Jansson grumbled. "I'm starved."

Darosenim chuckled. "As always," he replied and escorted Jansson from the room.

Thomlin frowned and looked to Vantann and Elecka, but before he could say anything, Elecka grabbed him and Vantann each by one arm. "I need to talk to you," she whispered. "Somewhere private."

Vantann grinned. "I like the sound of that," he said, then yelped when she pinched him on the arm. "What did you do that for?"

"Be serious, Vantann," she hissed. "For once, just be serious. Come on." She headed for the kitchen door.

Vantann glanced at Thomlin, who merely shrugged, and they both followed her. The kitchen was hot and busy as the staff prepared lunch for the council officials and the myriad visitors, Glede royalty included. Enid was at the bread counter, kneading and rolling dough for biscuits. She wore a white apron over her simple blue coarsecloth frock, the sleeves of which were pushed above her elbows. Her hair, which Thomlin now noticed carried hints of auburn, was tied back in a heavy braid. Quite a few curly strands had escaped the tie and hovered about her face like soft little puffs of dandelion. She had flour on her nose and smeared across one cheek. Thomlin saw why when she reached up and brushed her hair aside with the back of her hand. He grinned as she looked up and caught his eye. She blushed, flashed him a quick smile and returned to her work as the twins and Elecka slipped outside.

The sun was shining though the air was cold, and Thomlin wished he'd brought his cloak. Silk dress tunics were attractive but not very warm. Vantann was apparently thinking along the same lines. "Why don't we go to the stables? At least, it's warm there."

Elecka shook her head. "No. I want to be someplace where no one can sneak up on us."

"Oh, for gods sakes, Elecka!" Vantann snapped. "Who's going to,"

"Hush!" Elecka snapped and stomped away.

Vantann rolled his eyes, but he and Thomlin followed. She bypassed the maze gardens and led them into a vast expanse of green lawn that stretched out flat and unbroken for at least one hundred yards. With no shrubbery to block the wind, it blew fast and icy.

"So," Vantann said, wrapping his arms about his chest, "what's so pressing that we had to come out here and freeze our spare parts off?"

Elecka took a deep breath. "That's not my father," she stated. "It looks like my father, but it's not."

The twins stared at her, glanced at each other, then looked back at her. Vantann shook his head with a snort and turned to go back. She grabbed his arm, stopping him and he whirled on her. "Is this some kind of joke?" he demanded.

"Joke!" Elecka cried angrily. "Did that episode back at Session look like a joke? You know as well as I do that my father would never draw up papers of such grave importance behind Uncle Jansson's back."

"He was angry," Vantann retorted. "Besides, he is Uncle Jansson's advisor."

"Well, if you think an advisor has power over the king, I pity Glede when you take the throne."

"Well, that matter has been pretty much settled hasn't it?" Vantann shot back. "You're older than me and Thoms. You'll rule first, after Papay, and I'll get what's left over."

Elecka's blue eyes flashed with rage. "Fine, Vantann, don't listen to me. Ridicule me. But when things fall completely apart at this Session meeting, don't come asking for my insight. That man is not my father. I don't know who he is or what his plan is but,"

"Oh, gods, Elecka!" Vantann interrupted. "If he's not your father, who is he? Just someone who happens to look, sound and act like your father? Someone who knows,"

"Wait a minute, Vans," Thomlin said softly.

"Oh, don't tell me you believe her!"

"I don't know about Grandpapay," Thomlin said, "but something strange is going on. This morning when I went to get Uncle Jansson, he was still asleep. His room was a mess and there were three empty wine bottles."

"So?"

"Uncle Jansson doesn't drink like that, you know that," Thomlin said. "We saw Enid take him one bottle, not three. You were with her all evening, Vans. Did she fetch him any more?"

"No, but that doesn't mean that he didn't already have them, or that somebody else got them for him."

Thomlin frowned and he paused, wondering if he should share the rest. "There's something else. There was a woman with Uncle Jansson, in his bed."

Elecka gasped, covering her mouth with her hand. "He wouldn't,"

"I don't think he did," Thomlin said. "He was still dressed in the clothes he wore to dinner last night. From the looks of them, I'd say he slept in them. Uncle Jansson was pretty groggy, and he seemed to be just as surprised to see that woman as I was."

Vantann and Elecka were silent for a long time before Vantann finally spoke. "I say we go snoop around in Uncle Jansson's room."

"What would we be looking for?" Elecka asked.

"I don't know. Anything suspicious I guess."

"It's a start, I suppose," Elecka agreed.

They turned as one and headed back to the Session Chambers. As they walked, Vantann glanced at Elecka. "Why else do you think that your father isn't your father? I mean, there must be something more than the land episode."

Elecka shrugged. "Nothing firm." She hesitated as if trying to put her thoughts together. "It's like a song. He knows all of the words, but not the tune." She frowned. "I know that sounds strange but it's the only way I can describe it."

They slipped back through the kitchen and Thomlin was disappointed that Enid wasn't in sight. He sighed, reminded himself sharply of Rusulka and followed his brother and Elecka up the back staircase. The hall of the guest wing was empty and the trio crept down it to Jansson's room. After a brief hesitation, Thomlin tapped lightly. There was no answer and he tried the handle. The door opened easily and they slipped inside. The room was cold, the window open wide to allow fresh air to circulate. Thomlin gave a moan of dismay. The room had been straightened and cleaned. "Now what?" he asked softly.

Vantann began to prowl around, looking in the candy dish, under a stack of books, along the cushions of the two chairs. He blew out a puff of air, his gaze narrowed and he dropped to all fours to look under the large, four-poster bed. And saved his life in so doing.

A crossbow quarral hissed through the open window, sailed across the room and embedded itself in the far wall. Elecka let out a little shriek and she and Thomlin dropped to the floor.

"What the hell was that?" Vantann asked, starting to rise.

Thomlin grabbed him. "Stay down!" he ordered and pointed.

Vantann's eyes went wide and he crawled to the open window to peer over the sill. Thomlin joined him, Elecka close behind. The window overlooked another section of the mazes, though there was no one in sight. Vantann fell back against the wall, staring at the arrow. "Gods! This is getting serious. That was an assassination attempt."

"But on whom? You or Uncle Jansson?" Thomlin asked.

"Either way, I don't like it. Come on. I'm going to find Papay."

"And tell him what?" Elecka asked.

Vantann regarded her in astonishment. "How about that someone used me for target practice?"

"And he'll wonder what we're doing in Uncle Jansson's room. Then we'll be forced to tell him about what Thomlin saw."

"But Elecka, he has to know about this!" Vantann protested. "Someone just tried to kill," He broke off with a sudden shudder.

"Gods!" Thomlin breathed and terror swept through him. "Magic! Dirin magic!"

"Look!" Elecka clutched his arm and pointed to the far wall. The arrow was gone.

Down the hall in Druce's room, Treyas once more dipped a cloth in cool water and wrung it dry. He returned to the bed and laid the compress on the Merian's forehead, then frowned as a brief surge of magic touched at him. Magic familiar and yet not. Druce moaned softly, regaining his attention and he sat down in the chair by the bed. What was taking Darosenim so long? Druce was burning with fever, and Treyas felt woefully inadequate to be caring for him. He glanced at the clock. Two hours until Session would start again.

His thoughts drifted back to what he had witnessed earlier between Kyel and Jansson. It seemed so out of character for Kyel to do something as...well, as un-diplomatic. And so mean-spirited. Treyas had seen Kyel and Jansson angry at each other before, even come to sharp words, but he had never seen the black elf do such a brazen act of defiance. One simply did not sign over land that did not belong to one. Treyas shook his head in puzzlement and glanced again at the clock as Druce stirred in discomfort.

"Trey?" Darosenim's soft voice broke in to calm Treyas' increasing panic.

He rose swiftly. "Dar! Gods, I'm glad you're here. He's really sick."

Darosenim frowned and walked to the bed. He laid the back of his hand against Druce's cheek for a moment, then took the compress to rewet it. Treyas watched him, his heart pounding. The look on the mage's face said it all. He knew what was wrong. Treyas waited until Darosenim had replaced the compress on Druce's forehead before speaking. "Dar, what is it? What's wrong with him?"

Darosenim was quiet for a moment in which he pulled magic. Treyas knew from his own research of the Session Chambers that there was every kind of magic available here. The Chambers had been purposefully built on a magic hotspot to allow all visiting dignitaries the opportunity to access their own form of magic.

Druce calmed, his moans ceased and he drifted to sleep, his breathing once again slowed to normal. Still, that did not calm the panic that raged through Treyas, and he clutched Darosenim's arm.

"Trey..." the mage took a deep breath, "Trey, Druce has Yunyo."

Treyas stared at him in disbelief, then staggered backward and fell into the chair by the bed, his face ashen. "No," he breathed.

Darosenim ran a hand over his face, then hunkered down in front of Treyas. "I'm sorry, Trey. Gerowen's been treating him for the last six months, but,"

"No!" Treyas interrupted. "No, you're wrong! He's just sick. He'll get better."

Darosenim nodded. "He'll recover from this setback, but that doesn't change the course of the disease."

Treyas searched the mage's face, his emotions going wild. His gaze flew to Druce, his friend, his partner, his SoulMate, and he surged from his chair, nearly knocking Darosenim over in the process. "You're a mage!" he cried. "Heal him! Do whatever it is you have to do, but heal him!"

Darosenim straightened. "Treyas, magic can't cure everything. You know that."

"I know it can heal! Sword wounds, arrow, knife, poison...for gods sakes, it brought me back from the dead. Why the hell can't it take care of this?"

"Because this was caused by magic, Treyas," Darosenim replied quietly. "The best Gerowen and I can calculate, Druce caught it in Winze three and a half years ago. We think it may have had something to do with Dirin magic."

Treyas shuddered. The Nydiri! Again the Nydiri! They had almost taken the twins lives through a horribly gruesome sacrifice. Now, they were trying to take Druce's life through a horribly painful disease. Enraged, Treyas picked up the first thing he grabbed and hurled it against the hearth. Glass flew in all directions, echoing Treyas' emotions. But the action only served to further enrage him and he reached for another object. Darosenim stopped him, grabbed his arm and plucked the decanter from his hand.

Treyas turned on him, his voice near hysteria. "Dar, you have to do something! He can't die! He can't! Gods! Brynne...does she know?"

Darosenim shook his head. "Druce didn't want his wife or children to know. He didn't want you to know. He's been going crazy trying to Block it from the MindLink. Baerns! He didn't even tell me until six months ago. You know how stubborn Merians are. I guess he thought he could best it on his own."

"I should have seen it," Treyas mumbled. "I should have noticed. He's my SoulMate. We're MindLinked. We're HealBonded. I should have seen it."

"You're what?" Darosenim cried. "Since when have you and Druce been HealBonded?"

"Since that little dagger episode in Winze. Druce insisted. He felt his Merian strength would help me if I ever suffered a near fatal attack again." Treyas looked from Darosenim to Druce, sudden realization taking hold. "And instead, I'm helping him!"

"That explains a lot," Darosenim said. "Gerowen had a hard time believing this was Yunyo since it's usually fatal within the first eighteen months. Druce's affliction is moving at an incredibly slow pace. But, Trey," he took Treyas by both shoulders and forced him to make eye contact, "you can't stay HealBonded to him forever. I know this is a human disease and you can't get it, but if you're HealBonded to him when he dies, you'll die, too."

Treyas felt as if his heart had dropped to the pit of his stomach. "He's not going to die, Dar. I won't let him." He pushed away from Darosenim, his mind racing, frantically trying to think of a way out of this situation. "You said this was caused by Dirin magic, right?"

"We're not positive but we think so. Why?"

"If the Nydiri can cause it with their magic, then maybe they can cure it. Have you contacted Herrick or Anyar yet?"

"No, I,"

"Then we need to do that," Treyas interrupted, beginning to pace. "They may have some knowledge about this that we don't."

"Trey,"

"And the libraries in Mere Odain," Treyas continued, ignoring him. "You said yourself that the library in Wydrell contained more information on magic than anyplace in Glede. We need to do research there."

"Trey, I,"

"We could send Elek to Winze. He can get past their Sorcery Council. And Pepin can get access to Wydrell fairly easily. He's always off in Mere Odain anyway. I'll,"

"Treyas!" Darosenim snapped.

Treyas froze and whirled on him. "What?"

Darosenim drew a deep breath. "Trey, I know what you're going through right now, but,"

"Do you, Dar?" Treyas cried. "Do you really? Have you ever watched your SoulMate suffer like this? Have you ever faced the loss of a SoulMate? Well, it's not going to happen. I will not let Druce die!"

"You can't stop it," Darosenim said firmly.

"The hell I can't!" Treyas raged. "I'll find a way, a cure,"

"Dammit, Treyas!" Darosenim exploded. "There is no cure! There never has been. Wishing there was, isn't going to change that." He took hold of Treyas' shoulders and looked into his eyes. "We all die, Trey. It's just a question of when."

Treyas began to tremble and tears sprang to his eyes. "It's just that..." he choked back a sob, his voice cracking, "it's just...gods, Dar, it just hurts so damn much."

Darosenim sighed and embraced him, offering what comfort he could. "I know, Treyas," he murmured. "I know."

Chapter Five

Pepin woke with a yelp of pain as something large and heavy came down on his foot.

"Laith! Pepin!" Faolan cried. He pushed aside the dragonling he had been leading. The dragonling who had stepped soundly on Pepin's foot. "Did she hurt you? What are you doing out here?"

Pepin sat up, pulling his foot toward him to examine the injury. "Seeking some peace and quiet," he mumbled, trying to remove his boot. He grimaced as pain shot through his foot, then gave the young dragonling a surly glance. "Well, Jevra, you and your big feet. I think you broke my foot."

The dragonling lowered her head, her back scales glowing pale green in the sunlight filtering through the mews' glass windows. She wasn't a large animal, nor exceptionally heavy as far as dragons went. She was only about one-fifth the size of the other dragons in the fleet, standing at twenty hands at the shoulder, with a tail as long. She had a thin, gracefully curved neck that reached up to a somewhat flat head. Her long, pointed snout had two sharp horns flanked by horn fans and she showed her smooth, white rows of teeth as she begged his forgiveness. Pepin grinned despite his pain and reached out to scratch her dark green belly. He had no idea who her parents were or if she and the other five dragonlings were siblings. He realized that he probably should have destroyed them when they'd hatched. They weren't really useful to the fleet, considering their small size and limited wingspan. Plus, with feet as large as their heads, they tended to be rather clumsy and awkward. Still, Pepin had always had a soft spot in his heart for the runts of a litter and had supported the six, sweet-tempered little dragonlings with his own money. Or more precisely, he cringed, his father's money. In that respect, the dragonlings belonged more to Aelfdene than Mere Odain.

Jevra leaned forward and affectionately butted her head against Pepin's shoulder, knocking him backward into the straw.

"Jevra, no!" Faolan scolded and helped Pepin sit up. "Coals, Pepin, I'm sorry. The dragonlings haven't been out to exercise for a few days. I guess they're a little restless. Is your foot really broken?"

Pepin regarded the large, square, twenty-four-year old Keltin before him. He had met Faolan almost ten years ago when the Keltin's father had captured Pepin and Nila in Mere Odain. Faolan had helped them escape and, over the course of their adventure, Faolan and Pepin had become blood brothers. Now, Pepin wondered if that would be enough of a bond to keep Faolan from reacting negatively to the DragonMaster situation. Gently, Pepin probed at the Keltin empathically but got nothing more than concern and mild irritation. The former was no doubt related to Pepin's foot, the latter could be any number of reasons. Pepin sighed and pulled a little spark of magic to stay the pain in his foot, then looked up at Faolan. "Yes, I'm sure it's broken."

"Can you fix it?"

"No. I can't do bone healing on my own. You'll have to help me up to the main house and fetch Seker."

Faolan grimaced but nodded. Pepin well knew of his reluctance to go into any room of the palace save the kitchen. In fact, he had built a very comfortable cottage for himself near the mews and, when he wasn't working with the dragons, he was holed up there, reading or writing. It was always surprising to Pepin that Faolan should have such an artistic, sensitive disposition when he came from a warrior race. He would make a good husband and father whenever he found the right woman. The problem was finding the right woman, or any woman for that matter, in northern Mere Odain. When one was a heavily-muscled, hair-covered, Lashik Keltin, it was virtually impossible. No one seemed to be willing to look past the outward appearances, though by Keltin standards, Faolan was quite handsome with his wide, gray eyes and shaggy blond hair. And while a lot of Keltin women found him highly desirable for his looks, they were put off by his quiet, sensitive nature.

"Let me turn Jevra out to pasture," he said now, "then I'll be back for you. Gods, I am really, really sorry."

"It's not your fault," Pepin assured him. "You could hardly be expected to know I was here."

Faolan grimaced again and prodded at Jevra to get her moving. She hissed at him good-naturedly, gave Pepin a parting shove and ambled on her way. Pepin smiled at the love emanating from Jevra toward him and settled back to wait for Faolan. He was surprised when the Keltin returned just moments later. The walk to the grazing pastures usually took upwards of a half an hour. Faolan caught his puzzled look and grinned. "I forgot to tell you. The dragonlings have learned how to fly."

Annoyance and envy swept through Pepin. It was like missing your child's first step. "When?" he asked as Faolan helped him up.

"A week or so ago." They began the long walk through the mews.

Mild anger mixed with the other emotions and his tone came out sharper than he'd intended. "I was just here. Why didn't you tell me?"

Faolan looked at him sideways. "Pepin, you haven't been here for almost three weeks."

Though it was not said in condemnation, it nonetheless stung. Pepin's thoughts flew back to the past several weeks. He had spent a great deal of time going over the Mere Odain spring treaty with his father and Kyel. Then there had been the annual birthday celebration for all those adding a year that spring. That, and the fall celebration, had become tradition. It was just too hard to celebrate individually with families the size of those in Mayfaire and Lidgerwood. But what else had he done? Pepin grimaced. Pathetically little, while Faolan was here tending to the dragons and dragonlings, doing what the DragonMaster should have been doing - exercising them, drilling them, caring for them - watching them make their maiden flights. *Gods,* Pepin moaned to himself as he hobbled alongside Faolan, *he is the DragonMaster. I'm just a figurehead bearing the title.*

Well, that would have to change. Pepin knew what he had to do and the thought didn't sit well with him. He could think of few other places he wanted to live besides Aelfdene Valley. Mere Odain was definitely not one of those. Still, he needed to be close to the dragons, on a day-to-day basis, without suffering the time delay. Danns! He would have to move to Mere Odain. There was no other answer. He thought back to his father's parting words, can you postpone your move to Mere Odain until I get back, and realized that Treyas had known what even he did not.

Pepin slowed to a stop, leaning heavily on Faolan. The dragon mews were built with a large expanse of thick glass facing east to catch the morning sun. Its purpose was to warm the mews in the winter, but now with spring well in the air, it was stifling. Pepin wiped his brow. "You need to get these windows open. This is too hot for the dragons."

Faolan chuckled. "For the dragons, no. For someone suffering a broken ankle, yes."

Pepin bit off his comment. Faolan was right, he knew that. And it irritated him. He exhaled sharply and started forward once more. A few moments later, they left the mews and stepped into the grass outside.

The sun shone brightly over the land and, as always, Pepin was taken with Freyne's beauty. It was the only province in Mere Odain aside from Taithleach that held any appeal to him. Both had vast expanses of greenery and wildflowers. The only real difference was that while Freyne had its share of heavily forested areas, Taithleach did not. Which is why Taithleach was called The Dragon's Own. It was where they were born, where they took their first flight, where they laid their eggs, where they returned to die. Instinctively, Pepin looked west and his eyes narrowed. "There's a fleet coming in," he said.

Faolan nodded and kept him walking. "Ken's group is returning. The Queen sent them on a passover of Samia. The other fleets are drilling in Taithleach."

"Samia? Why? There's been nothing going on in the desert for years." Pepin frowned and looked Faolan in the eye. "Has there? Or did I miss that, too?"

Apparently Faolan didn't miss the sarcasm in the words. "Laith, Pepin, I didn't mean to chastise you. I don't know how you manage to spend the time you do here, what with your duties in Lidgerwood, too. But, to answer your question, no. There's nothing going on in Samia that I know of. I think Queen El'leigh just wanted to be reassured of that. No one has ever resettled those Standian villages that the Akuri destroyed and she seems to think they're an open invitation."

Pepin hesitated a moment before voicing his thoughts. "Fao, El'leigh said she thought Nydiri were involved in the Graybara attack. What do you think?"

A shudder ran through the Keltin, and Pepin was instantly assailed by emotions of terror, hate and rage. He brought up his shields as Faolan answered. "Graybara was destroyed, Pepin. Not by anything the Akuri could have done. You'll see when you go down there."

"Have you been there already?"

Faolan flushed. "Yes, but it wasn't authorized. I just wanted to see for myself." He lowered his voice. "Coals, Pepin, it's been almost ten years since we dealt with the Nydiri down there and it still makes my skin crawl."

"I know what you mean. After what Papay and the twins went through in Winze five years ago, I have absolutely no desire to get involved with Nydiri again. Of everything I would have to face in life, I think they're the worst." Pepin stopped again with a grunt of pain. "Gods, Faolan. I need to rest. Besides, I want to talk to Ken."

Faolan lowered him to the ground and they once more looked west. Where before the fleet had been but a dark patch in the blue sky, it was now discernible as five individual dragons, each with a green-skinned Foumen rider. Pepin's stomach fluttered in exhilaration and awe to watch the massive dragons in flight. They were incredibly graceful for their size and carried themselves proudly, their long, scaly necks and heads stretched into a tight line with their bodies. They were gliding now, preparing to land, their great wings folded close, their clawed feet extended. They were heading for the large, grassy meadow to the north of the palace, and Pepin shielded his eyes as Aleron, the lead dragon, opened his wings and backstroked, sending dust, leaves, grass clippings and dandelion heads flying through the air. A moment later, all of the dragons were down, their iridescent reds, blues, greens, yellows, purples and oranges creating a colorful display of muscular bodies against the green grass and blue skies.

Pepin rose and, at once, all of the dragon's heads turned his way. They began to call in the strange, throaty squawk that Pepin knew was a greeting and shuffled forward, throwing their riders, who were in the process of dismounting.

"Hold formation!" Ken ordered, waving his arms frantically. "Hold!"

But the dragons' desire to see the one they knew as DragonMaster was too overpowering. The best the four Foumen riders could do was to get out of the way. Pepin grinned at the dragons' loyalty and gave his own command, at once stilling the massive animals. The Foumen scampered clear, muttering to themselves about overgrown pets and walked wearily toward their quarters. Ken sighed and joined Pepin and Faolan.

"Welcome, Prince Pepin," the Foumen greeted and clasped his forearm. "You'd best go down and scratch a few bellies before the dragons storm you again."

"I'm afraid belly-scratching will have to wait a bit," Pepin replied. "Jevra stepped on my foot and broke it. I was just heading up to the palace to find Seker."

Ken's green face wrinkled in concern and he lowered his tall, thin frame down to inspect Pepin's foot. "Sit," he commanded.

Pepin obeyed out of both habit and respect. He owed a lot to Ken. Not only had Ken and his people been instrumental in defeating the Nydiri and Akuri ten years ago, the Foumen were kin of the elves and, as such, held magic. They were gifted healers, and Pepin surrendered his injury to Ken's gentle ministering.

He winced as Ken removed his boot, then probed at first his ankle, then his foot. Pepin yelped and jerked back reflexively. The dragons shuffled forward, obviously confused as to what was transpiring between their DragonMaster and their DragonKeeper. Pepin clucked his tongue at them and made an odd cooing sound in the back of his throat. Immediately, they calmed, though they didn't take their gaze off him or Ken.

"Laith, Pepin," Faolan said, his voice awed and just slightly frustrated. "How do you make that sound? I've tried and tried, but I can't do it. And look how it works!"

Pepin shrugged, regarding the dragons. They had stepped back and were blowing little puffs of smoke from their large nostrils, a sure sign that they were at ease and relaxed. They truth was, Pepin didn't know how he made that noise or where he had learned it. He had just done it one day when the dragons were young and had gotten into a squabble over a kill. He looked back at Ken. "Well?"

"You're right. It's broken. Three bones. Faolan, fetch Vashti would you?"

Faolan nodded and hurried away.

"So, you can mend it then?" Pepin asked.

Ken smiled and winked at him. "Of course, and it's better than being laid up with one of Seker's strange mending splints."

Pepin chuckled. "Any excuse to combine your magic with Vashti's, right Ken? When are you going to ask her to marry you?"

"When I'm sure she'll say yes. I despise rejection."

"Who doesn't?" Pepin mumbled.

Ken studied him. "I sense a story behind those words," he said quietly.

Pepin rubbed wearily at his eyes. "I guess I'm feeling sorry for myself." He paused and looked at Ken. "Ken, did I do the wrong thing in retrieving my title?"

Ken sat down in the grass opposite him and glanced at the dragons, before bringing his gaze back to Pepin. "Do you think you did?"

Pepin had followed his gaze and now regarded the beautiful and powerful dragons with love. "When I look at them, when I see them answer to my commands, when I speak with them, I don't think so. But what of my friends, my family?" He brought his gaze back to Ken. "Papay is upset with me for not telling him until now, and he's hurt that I would choose the dragons over him. Kyel is furious and questions my allegiance. Nila is scared, both of the dragons and of living here. El'leigh and Andison...well, I don't know what El'leigh is thinking. And Fao, what of him? He seems not to mind, but I wonder. Gods, Ken, everything is so confusing. I don't know what to do, or if I should do anything at all.

"And now, on top of all of my insecurities, Mere Odain is once more beset with problems. I can be honest with you, Ken, the Akuri Keltins and the Nydiri scare the hell out of me. Yet, it would seem I have to face both of them again." He looked up as Faolan arrived with Vashti, a strikingly beautiful Foumen healer.

Her skin was the same light green as Ken's, her eyes the same emerald color. On impulse, Pepin relaxed his empathic shields. At once, a smile crept across Vashti's finely boned features. She sat down near Ken, shot him a quick glance, then addressed Pepin. "Ken is quite old enough to ask his own questions."

Pepin grinned as Ken's face flushed a darker shade of green with embarrassment. His gaze darted to Pepin accusatorily but Pepin only chuckled. "Quite old enough to ask," he teased, "though maybe not to hear an answer."

"Pepin!" Ken admonished quietly and turned his attention on Pepin's injury. "Our young empath seems to have been in the way of Jevra's big feet. A pity it was his foot that suffered injury and not his mouth."

Vashti smiled at him. Her voice was soft when she spoke. "Faolan told me what happened. It will take but moments to mend. Provided, of course, we work together, Ken."

"I follow your lead, Healer Vashti," Ken replied quietly, his gaze on her.

Pepin and Faolan exchanged humored glances, then Pepin loudly cleared his throat. Ken and Vashti never even glanced his way but Pepin felt the distinct pull of magic. His foot began to tingle, then grew warm and warmer still, until the warmth became a fiery pain. Pepin closed his eyes and sought out his own magic to help with the discomfort. Moments later, as Vashti had predicted, the foot was healed and Pepin relaxed with an audible sigh.

"Is it healed then?" Faolan asked.

"You may expect some tenderness for a few days," Vashti told Pepin. "The bones, while set, are still weak and will be for several weeks. A splint, or a good stiff boot, will help stabilize it until it has time to heal properly. Do try to keep your feet from underneath the dragons."

Ken rose and extended a hand to Vashti. She accepted with a smile. Pepin carefully pulled his boot back on, then rose as well. He put experimental weight on his healed foot, winced slightly, then leaned on Faolan for support. He smiled at Vashti and Ken. "Thank you. Thank you very much."

"I hope," Ken said to Vashti, "that I didn't pull you from something pressing."

"Nothing more pressing than breakfast preparations," she replied, then looked to Faolan and Pepin. "I have more than enough. Would you all like to join me?"

Pepin was about to say yes when he caught the look in Ken's green eyes. "No, thank you, Vashti. You and Ken go on. I need to speak with Faolan and, as you can see," he gestured to the dragons, "there are still bellies to be scratched. But I would like to speak with Jibben, Ken. Where might I find him?"

Ken pointed westward and Pepin turned to see the other three dragon fleets headed toward home. Two were flying in a tight, well-balanced formation, while the third was obviously having problems. The lead dragon seemed not to be in control, varying both speed and distance between itself and its two wing-dragons. That, in turn, caused the wing-dragons to shift position, affecting the two rear dragons. In all, it looked as if a mid-air collision was imminent.

Alarmed, Pepin whistled once. Ken's dragon, Aleron, darted forward, lowering his head to the ground at the same time. Pepin quickly gained his back and the dragon shot into the air. Pepin drove Aleron forward, took a wide swing past the first two fleets and came up behind the faltering third. Aleron gained altitude, flew over the top of the fleet and took position above the lead dragon.

Pepin frowned. He knew that dragon. It was Teague. He belonged to Faolan and was one of the better trained in the entire fleet. Pepin couldn't understand what the problem was but didn't have time to dwell on it. He gave a series of short, guttural calls and veered off left. The four dragons behind Teague followed, and Pepin lead them down toward the landing pasture. He prayed Teague could come in safely on his own.

Aleron touched down lightly, the others following. Pepin leapt off and winced as his leg buckled. He righted himself and watched Teague make a hard landing, stumbling forward and careening into the other dragons that were already down. A chorus of confused, angry chirps went up from the dragons as they scattered out of harm's way. Their riders held on, waiting for the disturbance to end.

Teague's rider leapt from the dragon's back and snapped him soundly with a whip. Pepin gasped and surged forward but Faolan was faster. The Keltin reached the rider in three strides and backhanded him across the face, knocking him to the ground.

"You never," Faolan growled menacingly, "never take a whip to a dragon!" He hauled the Foumen up by the neck of his tunic, his face red with rage. "Nicabar, you are off fleet status! Your fine is six hundred golds. Go to your quarters!" He shoved the Foumen away.

Nicabar's face glowed with anger and he wiped blood from his mouth. "Your dragon acts like an unruly school child and you a parent overstepping your authority. I believe DragonMaster Pepin has seniority here."

Faolan's face went bright red, his fists tightened and he clenched his jaw, his gaze darting to Pepin. Pepin regarded him calmly, touching briefly at the Keltin's emotions. Anger, pure and hot, directed not only at Nicabar but at Pepin as well. Pepin drew himself up with a deep breath. "Master Faolan's decision stands," he said tightly. "In addition, you may consider yourself on mews' duty until further notice." He looked sharply at Faolan as Nicabar stormed off. "Since when has a reprimand included a physical attack?"

Faolan glared at him. "Forgive me, Master Pepin," he said, biting off each word. "I am a Keltin. Occasionally my warrior upbringing surfaces."

"I am fully aware of your background," Pepin returned, his own anger piqued by Faolan's tone. "See that it doesn't surface here again." He glanced at Teague, who stood head down, wings folded tightly, eyes half closed. "Your dragon needs attention, Master Faolan."

Faolan regarded him icily a moment longer, then gave a curt bow and strode away. Pepin watched as Teague lowered his head and nuzzled against Faolan's chest. He seemed relieved to have Faolan close. In fact, so did a number of the other dragons and more than half of the fleet followed Faolan and Teague further into the meadow, quite forgetting Pepin. Jealousy began a slow gnaw in the pit of Pepin's stomach and he turned away, looking to Ken and Vashti.

"Perhaps breakfast would ease the mind," Ken said softly.

Pepin grimaced, knowing all too well that his emotions lay upon his countenance. He changed the focus. "Who is Nicabar? I've never seen him before. Why was he drilling Teague?"

Ken paused, then offered his support to Pepin, urging him to walk. "You can walk and talk at the same time, can you not?"

"Just answer me, Ken," Pepin replied, nonetheless limping along, following Vashti to the palace.

"I do not know Nicabar personally. He does not come from my clan. Up until today, he has proven himself a worthy rider. Faolan gave him lead for two reasons. One was to test him, the other was because Faolan wanted to be here when you arrived. He has done an excellent job in your absence, Pepin. The men respect him and the dragons love him. He commands with patience, firmness and fairness. He expects adherence to duty. In all, Prince Pepin, you chose quite well in appointing Faolan as a DragonMaster."

"Then what did I just witness?" Pepin demanded.

"What you just witnessed, Prince Pepin, was Faolan's anger, nothing more, nothing less. I suspect you would have reacted quite the same had it been your dragon."

Pepin shot him a sidelong glance. The tone the words held invited no argument. In truth, Ken was correct, which only intensified Pepin's jealousy and he knew even as he said them that his next words amounted to nothing more than whining. "But then, I don't have a dragon anymore, do I?"

"If you are referring to Fayemera, that is true," Ken said. "If you are referring to your position, what is it you expected?"

Pepin balked, shrugging free of Ken's arm, and stopping short on the path. He glared at Ken, his emotions tumbling wildly. "What did I expect?" he repeated angrily. "I expected to be treated as the DragonMaster, not as an underling to Faolan! I expected my dragons to,"

"Come running to you," Ken interrupted. "To rejoice in your return, and immediately forsake the man who has cared for them for almost ten years."

Pepin gasped as surely as if he'd been struck. He opened his mouth to retort but Ken continued.

"Faolan was there when they were hatchlings. He raised them, was mother and father to them, gave them their first encouragement to fly, suffered with them when they failed and rejoiced with them when they succeeded. He trained them to accept riders and he trained the riders to accept them. Faolan,"

"Stop it!" Pepin snapped. "You have extolled Faolan's virtues to a fine point, Ken. But, what am I supposed to do? What the hell am I supposed to do?"

Ken sighed softly. "Is not what you have done enough? You have brought Keltin, Foumen and Merian together. You have allowed a semblance of peace to dominate Mere Odain for almost ten years. You have brought the continents of Glede and Mere Odain closer. What is it you want, Pepin?"

Pepin stared at him, confused, angry and unhappy. He threw his hands up in the air. "I don't know, Ken! I really don't know! I'm tired of this incessant struggle between Glede and Mere Odain, between my elfin half and my Merian half. I thought when I assigned Faolan as DragonMaster everything would be solved. But it wasn't. The dragons still pulled at me. I know I haven't been here as much as Faolan but, dammit, Ken, I was afraid. Afraid that Mere Odain would claim me. And now, it finally has. My world is coming unraveled around me. Gods! I just want to run away!"

"And give you a third land to which you don't belong?" Vashti asked softly.

Pepin looked to her and abruptly there were tears in his eyes. "What do I do?" he murmured. "Please, tell me, what do I do?"

Chapter Six

Jansson dropped his quill on the table and raked a hand through his dark hair. Afternoon Session had been canceled at Treyas' request and, while Jansson was highly concerned about Druce, he was equally glad he didn't have to face Kyel. He was still in a state of shock and disbelief at what Kyel had done. But what was even more disturbing was the lack of contact he and Kyel had had since arriving in Dalziel. It was almost as if Kyel were avoiding him. Jansson sat back in his chair with a frown, trying to think what he might have done to so incur the black elf's wrath. He once again touched gently at the MindLink he usually shared with the elf, and once again found it was gone. He sighed, shaking his head.

His gaze drifted toward the bed, which thankfully was empty. He had no idea who the girl was, nor how she had gotten there. The most he remembered from the previous night was having a glass of wine. Wine he hadn't ordered but that had been delivered compliments of the Dalziel officials.

Thoughts of the officials returned Jansson's mind to the parchment that lay before him and he scowled, his anger returning. He snatched up the quill and with one quick stroke, drew a long, black line through the agreement. He would not give up that much land to the Dalzielians. If Kyel wanted to give them land, let it be from Aelfdene.

He started at a loud rap on the door and rose. He halfway expected Kyel to storm in and punish him for destroying the agreement. He opened the door, surprised and relieved to see Thomlin standing there. "Uncle Jansson," the boy said quietly, "I need to talk to you."

Jansson motioned him in, empathically sensing fear and uneasiness. Thomlin shook his head.

"Could we walk?" he asked. "Outside?"

"Thoms, it's cold outside."

"Please, Uncle Jansson. It's...it's about Druce and Papay. I just want to be alone with you and your bardic skills. Please?"

Jansson hesitated, clearly reading the urgency in Thomlin's voice. And the deceit. He nodded and snagged his cloak, then followed Thomlin from the room, taking care to close the door securely. He had no desire to return and find company in the bed again.

Thomlin was quiet as he led Jansson down the hallways and stairs that would take them outside. Even then, he said nothing, but took Jansson past the maze garden and started up a narrow path.

"Thomlin," Jansson said softly, "for someone who wants to talk, you're doing very little of it. Where are we going?"

"Just up here a bit. Then I'll explain everything."

Jansson grimaced but followed him up the path, wrapping his cloak tighter against the cold evening air. He started violently as two more figures separated from the shrubbery to join them. "Firesass! Vans, Elecka! What in Tor's hell are you doing? You took years off my life just now."

"Sorry," Vantann mumbled. "It was Elecka's idea."

"So, what's going on?" Jansson asked.

"Not here," Elecka said. "Up there, in the field, where we can talk."

Jansson stood his ground. "We can talk here. What's going on?"

The three youths looked about uneasily, then Vantann sighed. "You tell him, Elecka."

Elecka drew a deep breath, her blue eyes wary. "Father isn't who you think he is," she said softly.

Jansson regarded her with slight humor. "He never is."

"Uncle Jansson, I'm serious!" Elecka snapped. "That man is not my father."

Jansson looked from her to the twins. Vantann merely shrugged but Thomlin gripped his arm, his face earnest. "I know it sounds odd," he said, "but I think it's true. Look at the way he's been acting, the thing with the land agreement, letting Elecka do what she pleases. That's not like Grandpapay."

Jansson was silent for a moment, then exhaled heavily. "He's under stress. We're all under stress. Alliances are not easy to generate. Especially when you're dealing with another dimension. Kyel is,"

"It's not him!" Elecka snapped. "I should know my own father! And if you really stopped and thought on it, you'd see it, too! You're as much his child as I am."

"Uncle Jansson," Thomlin put in, "how did Kyel know about that woman in your room?"

Jansson flushed, his gaze darting to the others. "Remind me not to tell you any secrets," he mumbled.

Thomlin ignored him and continued. "This morning, he said something about you being otherwise engaged while he had dinner with Neslin. How did he know?"

"How many bottles of wine did you order up?" Vantann asked.

"None!" Jansson replied defensively. "The house-girl brought me one. And I only had one glass. She said it was compliments of..." He stopped, his eyes going wide. "Neslin."

Thomlin frowned. "But this morning there were three bottles in your room. Enid said she only took up one."

"Who's Enid?" Jansson asked, very aware of the torrent of emotion rising off Thomlin.

"The house-girl," Vantann replied. "She works in the kitchen."

Jansson started at the feelings Vantann was throwing off. Perfect. Just to add to the confusion, the twins had to fall for the same girl. "So, what do you think is going on?" he asked.

The twins exchanged quick glances before Thomlin spoke. "Last night, Vans and I went down to the kitchen for some more dessert,"

"Ah," Jansson interrupted, "that explains first name basis with the kitchen help. Go on."

Vantann rolled his eyes and took up for Thomlin. "Two men came into the meeting hall. They were discussing how they were going to start a war. They said by week's end everyone would be so angry a war was imminent."

"And who were these men?"

"I don't know. We didn't see them. We were hiding behind the curtains," Thomlin replied.

Jansson's eyebrows rose. "Why were you hiding?"

Thomlin shrugged and Vantann answered. "Because we were afraid of getting into trouble. We weren't supposed to be down there."

"Then why were you?"

"Because of Elecka," Vantann retorted.

"Me!" Elecka cried. "What did I do to make you,"

"You went into the maze," Thomlin interrupted. "We saw you from our room. We wondered what you were doing so we thought we'd follow you.

But the door to the kitchen was locked and then those men showed up, so we hid."

"And what were you doing outside, Elecka?" Jansson asked.

Elecka scowled at the ground. "Getting away from that man posing as my father. He gives me the chills. I can't stand being in the same room with him."

Jansson sighed, everything he'd heard tumbling in a mind weary from stress and lack of proper rest. "Elecka, this is more than likely just your imagination. How could someone look, talk and act like your father? How would he know what to say? How would he know us?"

"Uncle Jansson," Thomlin said softly, "there's more."

"More?" Jansson threw his hands up. "I don't have time for this. Your Papay is expecting me to work with him tonight. I still need to come up with an alternative to Kyel's somewhat brazen and generous offer of this morning. You three will,"

"It's the Nydiri, Uncle Jansson," Thomlin interrupted.

Jansson started, his heart going to double-time, his gut forming into a tight knot. "Thoms Merripen!" he snapped. "That's not funny!"

Thomlin grabbed his arm and Jansson was nearly floored at the terror Thomlin held. "It's not a joke!" the boy cried. "I felt it. I felt their magic. Both Vans and Elecka saw the arrow disappear!"

"Arrow! What arrow?" Jansson demanded.

Thomlin's eyes filled with tears. "Someone tried to kill Vans! We were in your room and someone fired a crossbow quarral through the window. It just missed Vans and hit the wall. Then it disappeared. I felt the magic, Uncle Jansson. I felt it!"

Jansson swallowed hard, wanting to disbelieve yet not being able to so easily write off the terror-filled emotions rushing from Thomlin. Whatever the real truth, Thomlin believed what he said, and Jansson was not about to make light of it. He draped an arm about Thomlin's shoulder. "Thoms, maybe we need,"

"No!" Thomlin yanked away from him, his tears spilling over. "I don't need any bardic healing! I'm telling you the truth! Tobbar said the Nydiri can look and act like whomever they want to. I think they're doing it now. I don't know how that man can know intimate details or information about us, but I know that he is not grandpapay!"

Jansson stared at him, an uneasy feeling gnawing at the pit of this stomach. "Immix," he muttered.

Elecka gasped, her blue eyes going wide. Thomlin wiped his face roughly with the back of his hand and looked at Vantann.

"They could Immix," Jansson said quietly. "They would know everything, down to the last detail."

"But they couldn't necessarily act like the person, could they?" Vantann asked. "It's like Elecka said. They know all of the words, but not the tune. Gods, Uncle Jansson! What do we do?"

Jansson paused, his mind whirling. He wasn't quite sure if he believed all of this, but he decided to err on the side of caution. He had seen what the Nydiri were capable of. "We can't let them know we know. We need to find out what their purpose is. Vantann, you said they talked about starting a war." He hesitated, his eyes narrowing in thought, then he snapped his fingers. "Between the humans and the elves. That would be the single most dividing factor. Get the humans and the elves fighting, let Glede fall into a state of upheaval, then Dalziel steps in and takes over. Gods! That has to be it!"

"One of the men said something about revenge," Thomlin put in.

"Revenge?" Jansson repeated, then shrugged, not knowing how that fit in.

Vantann shuddered. "Maybe Dukker,"

"No!" Thomlin interrupted. "Dukker is gone! Herrick's coven sent him away. All of them!"

Jansson reached out, took his arm firmly and fed him some bardic comfort. "We need to come up with a special word or phrase that only we know. If these Nydiri are capable of both illusion and Immix, they could replace any one of us at any time."

Elecka abruptly burst into tears. "My father...where is he?"

Vantann gathered her close. "Hush. We'll find him, Elecka. And we'll find out what's going on. Don't cry." He looked at Jansson. "Can't you just MindLink with Grandpapay? Find out where he is?"

Jansson felt his cheeks grow warm yet again. "I think Kyel Blocked the MindLink. I would suppose it was because of his anger over this morning's incident. What about you, Elecka?"

Elecka stared at him in true horror. "I...I lost my MindLink at the Dimensional Border. I thought it was normal, that it always happened when crossing."

Jansson felt his stomach tighten further. He couldn't truly tell if his MindLink was simply Blocked or not there at all, which was puzzling and frightening in itself. Severed MindLinks always affected him poorly. Still, he sought to assuage Elecka's terror. "I still have the LifeStrandBond with him. He's not dead. It's just a question of where he is."

"And who's with him," Vantann added. "Tens, Uncle Jansson! How do we know anyone else is who they say they are?"

"For that matter," Jansson said, "how do we know each other is who we say we are?" The twins gasped and Elecka pressed closer to Vantann. Jansson gave a wry smile and continued. "We'll just have to trust that at least we four are the real thing. Anyone else is suspect." He thought for a moment. "Especially Elek. He's been very quiet, very reserved lately. In fact, I don't know that he's even visited Treyas yet. The real Elek would have been by his side immediately. Come to think on it, he never said a word about Druce's illness before we left Glede." His frown deepened. "We're just going to have to remember what Elecka said. Watch for those who seem slightly out of tune."

"Uncle Jansson," Thomlin said quietly. "I'm scared. I don't want to be alone."

"I'll stay with you at all times," Vantann assured him.

"Elecka." Jansson looked her way. "This is going to be hardest on you. Do your best not to let on. Try to make this Kyel think you believe he's your father."

Elecka shuddered but nodded. Vantann hugged her gently. "Thoms and I will watch out for you. We'll find ways to get you away from him."

"Good. Now, for the code words. Any ideas?" The three youths shook their heads and Jansson frowned, thinking. "I have an idea. This lack of a MindLink with Kyel may work to our advantage. Elecka, do you know how to MindLink?"

"Yes. Why?"

"MindLink me. I'll tell you the words, then you Link them to Vans and Thoms. You may say either word, the other person should answer with the opposite word. No one is to say the words out loud. Always Link them first before you begin a conversation. And always Link your conversation unless it's general information. Even if the Nydiri do Immix and get the code words, they can't MindLink them. Elecka?" Jansson waited, marveling at the ease with which she Linked him. She was definitely her father's daughter. He smiled fondly. ::Jvet:: he sent. ::Dekt.::

Elecka wrinkled her brow, puzzled, but turned to the twins. Jansson knew each of them had received the words by the looks on their faces. "All right," he said. "That's settled. I need to go speak with Treyas. Why don't you three plan dinner together in the twins' room?"

They nodded, and Jansson turned away. Thomlin stopped him with a touch on his arm.

"Uncle Jansson," he said, "what's wrong with Uncle Druce? Is he really sick?"

"Sick enough," Jansson answered vaguely. "He'll be better in a few days. Now, let's get back to the Session Chambers before we all freeze to death. I'll try to Link Kyel tonight when there's no distractions."

They agreed and the four of them walked back to the building. "Let's go in through the kitchen," Vantann suggested. "There's a back staircase that leads to the guest wing."

And Enid is probably in the kitchen, Jansson thought with a small smile. They stepped into the warm, aromatic room. It was busy with staff bustling about in dinner preparations but, as Jansson followed the others, a gasp went up. All talking and movement ceased and the entire staff either bowed or curtsied.

Jansson smiled his well-practiced diplomatic smile. "Carry on," he said and, after a hushed moment, the men and women resumed their work, though not their chattering.

"Enid." Thomlin beckoned to a sturdy looking girl near the bread table. She stared wide-eyed, then hurriedly began to brush the flour from her hands and clothes.

"That's Enid?" Jansson asked with a start. "She's not the one who brought the wine last night."

"But she brought it up from the wine cellar," Vantann whispered. "Thoms and I saw her. We saw her leave to take it to you."

Enid stepped close and gave a low, graceful curtsy. "Yes, Your Majesty?"

"Enid, this is," Thomlin began.

Jansson stopped him with a touch. "Do you know who I am, Enid?"

Enid went red, though she kept her eyes averted. "You...you're one of the visiting kings, Your Majesty," she stammered.

"Which one?"

Enid's gaze flicked up briefly to his face, then returned to the floor. "I...I..." Her voice cracked. "I don't know, Your Majesty," she whispered. "Please accept my apologies. I know I should be more well-versed in visiting,"

"Enid," Jansson interrupted, "look at me."

Trembling, Enid raised fear-filled eyes. Thomlin sucked in his breath. "Uncle Jansson, don't!"

Jansson exhaled sharply. He had wanted her to look at him fully so he could ascertain the truth behind her words. Now, that opportunity was gone. Enid apparently took his frustration as being anger directed at her. She blanched and fell to her knees before him. "Your Majesty," she said quietly. "I'm sorry! Please forgive me."

"Enid, no." Jansson brought her gently to her feet and touched at her chin, lifting her face. Jansson smiled. "I'm not angry with you. I do have a question, however." He lowered his voice, aware that the rest of the kitchen staff was listening and trying hard not to look like it. "Enid, I am quite fond of overlaced, buttered bread-ties. Do you know how to make those?"

"Y...yes, Your Majesty," she replied, confused.

"Would you do me this favor then? Bring them to my room as soon as they're out of the oven. I like them best when they're hot." Jansson released her and turned toward the stairs.

"Y...Your Majesty?" Enid's small voice stopped him and he turned, noticing at once the trepidation in the girl's brown eyes. "Your Majesty..." she swallowed hard, "I don't know which room you're in. I'm sorry."

Jansson smiled, assessing the sincerity of the statement, then had a sudden thought. "Thomlin will show you. He can wait here until the bread ties are done. And, Enid, I'd like you to be my nephew's guest at dinner tonight. The twins you've already met. This is Princess Elecka, King Kyel's daughter. She will join you as well."

Enid shot a quick, questioning glance to a sturdy dark-haired woman near the ovens, no doubt the head kitchen servant. The woman gave a curt nod and Enid looked back at Jansson. "Thank you, Your Majesty," she said with a curtsy, though she had gone pale at the mere prospect. "I would be honored."

Jansson smiled again, clapped a blushing Thomlin on the back and ushered Elecka and Vantann ahead of him up the stairs.

"Why did you let Thomlin stay?" Vantann whined. "I'm the one who..." He stopped, his gaze darting to Elecka.

Jansson grinned. "Because, my dear Vans, Enid is not the one for you."

"Well, how do you know?" Vantann cried as they emerged in the hallway of the guest wing.

"Because I,"

"Elecka!" *Kyel's* voice carried down the hallway and Elecka gasped.

"Remember," Jansson whispered, "he's your father." He had a sudden thought. Kyel, with his acute elfin hearing, would have heard those words. He wondered if this *Kyel* had.

"Where have you been?" *Kyel* demanded as he stopped before them.

"She was with me in the maze gardens, Kyel," Jansson replied. "You should see them. They're fascinating."

Kyel looked down at him. "I should think you have better things to do than run about the gardens."

"But, Kyel," Jansson protested jokingly, "they're really intricate. It's quite a mind-teaser. I've never known you to pass up a mental exercise like that."

The black elf stiffened slightly as if thinking on the words, then jerked his gaze back to Elecka. "I wanted to tell you that I would be dining with the Dalziel officials tonight. While I don't expect you to attend, I do expect you, Jansson. Treyas is emotionally unfit for such a dinner and will stay with Druce. Darosenim will join us as well." He held out two parchment scrolls to Vantann. "Your father requested that I give these to you and Thomlin. They are the minutes from yesterday's meeting. You will be expected to memorize them and recite back, not only their content, but their meaning. I trust you can get Thomlin's copy to him?"

Vantann grimaced but nodded.

"Good," *Kyel* continued. "Since your father is preoccupied, you and Thomlin will make your presentation to me tomorrow between Sessions. Please, be prepared."

"Father," Elecka said quietly, "since you're to be dining with the officials, would you mind if I ate dinner with the twins?"

"Not at all. But keep it short. The twins have a full evening of work. I will also be expecting a comprehensive overview of yesterday's Session from you. Jansson," he turned slightly, "dinner will be in two hours. Since you so vehemently disagreed with my choice of land, you should be prepared to offer alternatives."

"What about somewhere in Aelfdene?" Jansson asked.

"Aelfdene Valley is one-third the size of Odora Dava, Jansson," *Kyel* said tightly. "I do not wish to discuss it now, but think again. I will see you in two hours." He turned and strode away.

Jansson waited until he had almost reached the stairs, then muttered, "You think again, fool."

Vantann and Elecka gasped, their gazes flying to *Kyel*. But he never turned or slowed or gave any indication he'd heard the words. Jansson chuckled lightly. "Got you," he whispered, then looked at the other two. "Go on to your rooms. Keep a look-out for Enid. Oh, and Vantann, watch what you say at dinner. Try to get more information than you give." He started away, then stopped. "And save me some of those bread-ties."

Vantann nodded and Jansson hurried down the hall to Druce's room, making a quick stop for his lute along the way. The room was quiet, though laced with magic. Darosenim sat in a chair by the bed, his eyes closed, one hand on Druce's brow. Treyas was slumped in the other chair, fast asleep.

Jansson closed the door softly and waited for Darosenim to acknowledge his presence. When he did, it was with an epithet of frustration.

"Firesass! This magic is almost unworkable!" he muttered. "It's all overlaid with each other. Makes it almost impossible to sort out the Strands I need."

"What did you do to Trey?" Jansson asked, gesturing at the sleeping elf.

Darosenim rubbed at his neck and rose to stretch. "SleepSpell. He kept twisting the MagicStrands. I had to keep him quiet somehow."

Jansson nodded knowingly. "How's Druce?"

"He's actually doing better. He had a massive internal infection but he's fighting it now. I've put him in a MageSleep so his body can concentrate fully on his healing. I've also been giving him hourly treatments. He'll pull through this ailment."

Jansson sighed. "But what of the next?" He knew Yunyo's progress. It weakened the body so that other infections and ailments could take over. In fact, most people who had Yunyo didn't actually die of the disease itself, but of one of the interim infections.

"I don't know, Jans," Darosenim replied. "Druce has a lot going for him. He's got his Merian strength and Trey's HealBond. Still, it's going to be a rough road for Treyas and Brynne. That's why I asked for your help. Treyas needs you, Jans, not just as a bard, but as a friend."

"Just out of curiosity, has Elek been up?"

"Just once. Earlier this afternoon. But he wasn't much in the way of comfort. It was strange. He said all of the right words but they seemed to lack...I don't know...empathy?"

Jansson frowned. "So he doesn't know the tune either," he mumbled.

"What?"

Jansson paused, then found a piece of parchment and a quill. He motioned for Darosenim to keep talking while he wrote.

"But I suppose," the mage went on, "that Elek has a lot on his mind what with this alliance agenda. I can't blame him at all for being a little bit distracted." He read what Jansson had written, gave him a puzzled look but followed the instructions. "I'm going to try again with Druce's treatment. It shouldn't take more than ten minutes now that I have Treyas asleep and the Strands organized. Can you wait?"

"Certainly," Jansson replied. "Kyel said dinner would be in two hours. That will give me time to work with Treyas and get freshened up. Go ahead."

Instead, Darosenim stood, peering over his shoulder as he wrote furiously in Ginspeak, a secret code language he had invented years ago, though it wasn't much of a secret anymore. Treyas had always known it, Jansson had taught Dar, and Kyel had figured it out. But it wasn't likely that anyone else could decipher it. At least, not quickly.

Jansson gave Darosenim a brief rundown of his conversation with the twins and Elecka, stating their suspicions and what they intended to do. He started to write down the two code words, then hesitated and gave a Darosenim a quick, empathic probe. He met with outrage and hurt as Darosenim intercepted his wariness. The mage smacked him soundly on the upper arm, made a motion of chewing food, then opened his mouth. Jansson grinned and wrote down the code words, then pointed to both Druce and Treyas and made a big question mark on the parchment. Darosenim shrugged and shook his head. Jansson frowned and rose to feed the parchment to the fire.

"That's it then," Darosenim announced. "I think this treatment really helped."

"Good. Wake Treyas and we'll get started while you go and get ready for dinner."

"Be prepared," Darosenim warned. "Treyas is not going to be happy with me." He softly spoke the words that would recant the SleepSpell.

Treyas woke with a start and both Jansson and Darosenim gasped as powerful magic rolled through the room. It was apparent that Treyas had been attempting to break the Spell from the inside. Now, he surged out of his chair, turning a furious countenance on Darosenim. "You had no right to do that, Dar!" he fumed.

Jansson snagged him by one arm, already pulling bardic magic. Darosenim was right. The magic here was difficult to sort out and Treyas' rage was not making it any easier. "Trey, you know what you do to the magic when you're upset. Dar needed that magic. You want him to help Druce as much as he can, don't you?"

"Of course!" Treyas snapped. "That's why I'm not wearing the Triskelion. I didn't want to absorb all of the magic."

"So instead you just wanted to twist it into unusable clumps," Jansson retorted gently. He guided Treyas back into the chair. "Sit down. Let's talk."

"I'll see you later, Jans," Darosenim said, turning toward the door.

"Dar!" Treyas looked up at him. "I'm sorry. You were right." He looked to the bed. "How is he?"

"I'll tell you what I told Jans. He'll pull through this. He's on the mend, Treyas."

Treyas sighed and rubbed a hand over his face, his mis-matched eyes full of pain and grief. "From this, but not from Yunyo."

Jansson shuddered at the empathic emotional distress of his dearest friend. He picked up his lute, gave a slight nod to Darosenim and ran his fingers across the strings. Darosenim gave a small smile and quietly left.

"Treyas," Jansson said gently, "this will work better if we're MindLinked as usual."

Treyas looked at him, puzzled, and opened his mouth to question Jansson's statement. Jansson shook his head, put a finger to his lips, then to his head and continued to play.

Frowning, Treyas MindLinked him.

Chapter Seven

Pepin looked up from his book as a light tap sounded on the open library door. Surprise brought a quiet gasp from him. It was the last person he expected to see, especially in the palace. "Faolan! Come in."

Faolan stepped into the large room, his footfalls muffled by the thick blue carpet. He cast an uncomfortable glance about, as if he thought guards would appear from thin air to haul him outside. "Pepin," he said quietly, "I've come to apologize. I was out of line. I overstepped my authority in dealing with Nicabar. I'm sorry."

Pepin closed his book. "It's me who should be apologizing, Fao. I over-reacted." He rose, limping toward the bank of long, narrow windows that filled one wall. The afternoon sunlight was filtering through, and Pepin drew close to a window to bask in its warmth. "I wasn't really angry with you, Faolan. I was, I'm embarrassed to admit, jealous."

"Jealous? Of what?'

Pepin drew a deep breath and turned to face the Keltin. "Of you. Of your rapport with the men and the dragons. Of whom you've become."

Faolan regarded him, puzzled. "Who is that?"

"The DragonMaster, Faolan. You are the DragonMaster, not me." Pepin slouched into one of the many velvet, overstuffed chairs gracing the library. "I shouldn't even be here. This is no longer my place."

Faolan run a hand through his thick blond hair and slowly settled his muscular frame into a chair facing Pepin. "Pepin, can I speak candidly here? As brother to brother?"

"Of course."

"If I was to be honest," Faolan began, "I thought the same. That you weren't really the DragonMaster, that it was me who should bear the title. Until today. When I saw you take command of Aleron and bring in that fleet, when I heard the way you communicated with the dragons, saw how they responded...well, I was awed. And quite green with envy. I could never even attempt to ride Aleron. He would never allow it. Yet, he answered to your call as if he belonged to you instead of to Ken." He rose and moved to the windows, his back to Pepin. "Yes, I can instruct the dragons, I can run them through their training drills, I can touch any and all of them. But I don't command them, Pepin. Not like you do. You are the DragonMaster. It is your voice, your commands, your presence that the dragons yearn for." He faced Pepin. "There can't be two DragonMasters, Pepin. I know that. But staying here now that you've returned to claim your rightful place would be both confusing for the dragons and painful for me."

Pepin stiffened. "What are you saying?"

Faolan took a deep breath, drawing himself up tightly. "My father has offered me a place with him in Niavel. The only thing I request is that I be allowed to take Teague with me. I will understand if that is not possible, but I have grown quite attached to him over the years. It would be hard on both of us to part."

"No!" Pepin came to his feet, his heart thumping wildly. "No, Fao. I don't want you to go. If anyone leaves, it'll be me. This is your place, Faolan, as much, if not more, than mine. Mere Odain is your country, it always has been. Not so with me. We'll work it out, together. But, please, don't leave. I...I need you. Not just as a DragonMaster, but as a friend, as a brother."

Faolan stared at him. Pepin could empathically sense the confusion and pain raging through the young Keltin. It was not so much different than what he was feeling himself. He laid a hand on Faolan's shoulder, though to do so, he had to reach up, reminding him again of his small size. He should have gotten used to it. Although a lot of his family was small, the other elves at Lidgerwood were all taller than he was. Even his own wife was taller. And here, most everyone was. The Foumen and the Lushik Keltins towered over him and the dragons made him feel more like a sprite than an elf. He looked up at Faolan. "I can't stop you from going, Fao," he said softly, "but I beg you to reconsider. If the Nydiri are indeed involved in the attack on Graybara, I'm going to need your knowledge and expertise, both in regards to the dragons and to Kelta. We faced the Nydiri together before. Let us do so together again."

Faolan's shoulders sagged. "But, Pepin, what about our positions? I've been in charge so long that simple things, like discipline, have become second nature. I don't want to lose our friendship, or our bloodbrother ties, over jealousy and competition."

"You won't have to. I've done some thinking on this. My breakfast with Ken and Vashti was both delicious and enlightening. I would like you to continue on as you've been doing. Proceed as if I wasn't here. I'll no doubt be spending some time in council with El'leigh anyway. I don't know her entire plan, but I do know that she wants a post set up in South Kelta. That's your land, Fao. Would you like to head up that post?"

Faolan's face brightened. "I would," he answered enthusiastically, then frowned. "But I think Queen El'leigh wanted you to do it."

"Don't worry about El'leigh. I don't think she'll have any problems with me staying out of Kelta," Pepin replied. *And within her reach,* he thought with a grimace, then continued to Faolan. "I should think two fleets would be adequate to patrol Kelta but I wanted to ask your opinion on that. You are certainly more familiar with that area than I am."

Faolan nodded, sitting down. "Two would be sufficient for the southern region but it couldn't hurt to have something more central, say Wydrell."

Pepin pondered on that for a moment. "That leaves the north one fleet plus the dragonlings. What are they capable of?"

"They fly well, though I haven't tried them with a rider. I don't have anyone small and light enough. As far as their flame, I've yet to see any of them use it, though I believe they have the ability. I've seen smoke, just no flame. There is one thing I'm concerned about. It's their diet. They refuse to eat any source of meat. I'm not sure they're getting the nutrition they need but I don't know where to turn."

Pepin thought on that one a moment. "Perhaps the brownies could help," he mused, then snapped his fingers. "Dryads! They eat only plant matter. I know several of them personally. Brynne wouldn't be able to come because of the children, but Rusulka has no ties."

"Isn't she Thomlin's girlfriend?"

"Yes, but he's not in Lidgerwood right now. He went with Papay to an alliance meeting in Dalziel." He grinned. "Rusulka would probably love a diversion from mourning. I'll MindLink Nila and have her send Rusulka through the Portal."

Faolan nodded his agreement. "There is one other thing. I don't have anyone to replace Andison. I had hoped Nicabar would, but after what I saw today, I don't think so."

"I'm going to speak to Andison later," Pepin told him. "Maybe I can convince him to go to Graybara with you. A change of scenery might do him good."

Faolan was quiet for a moment, then spoke hesitantly. "Do you think that's a good idea? I mean, it'll leave you and El'leigh here alone."

Pepin flushed, the red creeping across his brown cheeks. "So?"

Faolan drew a deep breath. "So, it's no secret that she and Andison are having marital problems and that you're at the root of them."

Anger flashed through Pepin and he spun away from Faolan. "This is not my fault! I am above reproach here. I have done nothing to encourage El'leigh in any way."

"Maybe not," Faolan agreed. "But how will Andison see it?"

"How will I see what?" Andison had entered the library unheard.

Pepin whirled to face the man, while Faolan hurriedly rose and bowed. Andison waved the gesture away and approached the sideboard. He was pale, his eyes heavy with the last night's drink, though he had obviously bathed and cleaned himself up. He looked quite attractive in his silk tunic, leather hose and soft houseshoes. His dark hair was brushed back, revealing his still boyish features.

"Andison," Pepin greeted, "you look well."

Andison's eyebrows rose in humor. "Forever the diplomat, huh, Pepin? I look like hell and I don't feel much better. What did I interrupt?" He reached for the bottle of wine and a glass.

Pepin stepped forward and took it from his hands. "I think tea would be more appropriate," he said gently and rang for a servant before guiding Andison to a chair. "Faolan and I were just discussing the post El'leigh wants to set up near Graybara. We've decided that two fleets should go there while a third posts near Wydrell." He sat down and leaned forward earnestly. "Andison, I'd like you to go with Fao."

Andison grunted, leaned back and closed his eyes. "I already told you, Pepin, I'm no longer a rider. I resigned."

Pepin shot Faolan a quick glance, then looked back at Andison. "Have you seen your replacement rider yet? His name is Nicabar."

"No, but I've heard good things about him."

Pepin glanced over as a servant entered the room. He ordered up some peppermint tea for Andison, then returned his attention to the young king as the servant bowed and left. "Apparently you didn't hear this morning's news then."

Andison opened one eye to peer at him. "I'm listening. What happened?"

"Nicabar struck Teague with a whip," Faolan replied, his words edged with anger.

Andison's eyes snapped open and he sat upright. "He what! I hope he's off fleet status!" His gaze darted between Faolan and Pepin.

"He is," Pepin assured him. "And that leaves us a rider short. We could appoint one of the stand-bys, but I'd rather have you. The dragons know you, they're comfortable with you and, to be honest, I need your skills. Please, Andison, please reconsider."

Andison regarded him suspiciously. "What about you? Why don't you go with Faolan?"

"Because I plan to take the dragonlings to Taithleach. I want to run them through some training drills. If they can fly, maybe they can do other things, too. Anyway, I'd like to find out. We only have twenty-six dragons, none of which are at egg-laying age. We can't afford to have five of the fleet doing nothing more than eating." Pepin paused for a moment. "Andison, maybe some distance between you and El'leigh would help matters."

"It couldn't hurt," Andison mumbled. He exhaled slowly, then nodded. "All right, Pepin, I'll go with Faolan." He rose as the servant entered the room with the tea. "With any luck, I'll get captured."

Pepin gasped. "Andison! Gods, El'leigh is not..." He broke off, suddenly mindful of how his words might sound. He rose and laid one hand on Andison's forearm, once more sensing the man's emotional turmoil. "I could talk to Bard Webb about,"

"No." Andison took a cup of the tea and smiled. "Galen has already adopted me as a patient. In fact, I'm late for an appointment as it is. I'm quite surprised he hasn't called out the guards to find me. Let me know when we're to leave, Faolan." He gave a nod and left.

Pepin grimaced. He had a rider back, but in what emotional state? Faolan must have been thinking the same thing.

"Do you think he would be offended if I put Jibben in lead?" the Keltin asked.

Pepin shrugged. "I think that's a choice you'll have to make, Faolan. You might want to consult with Galen about it, too."

"I will. By the way, where did this idea to work the dragonlings come from?"

"From you. You got me thinking. Maybe we can't use them in fleet but we should be able to make use of them somehow." Pepin glanced at the clock. One thirty. El'leigh should certainly be up by now. And he had a few things he wanted to say to her. But first, he wanted to contact Nila. Even though that meant rousing her in the middle of the night. He smiled slightly just thinking of her deliciously warm body snuggled next to his.

Faolan caught the smile. "And who's on your mind right now?"

Pepin chuckled. "Need you ask? I'm going to try to Link Nila about Rusulka, see if she can come tonight. Then I need to go speak with our seductive Queen, whose only purpose in getting me here on such short notice seems to be personal." He glanced suddenly at the servant, who yet remained, standing quietly to one side of the room. Pepin motioned him his leave.

Faolan rose and headed for the door. "Then I'll leave you to your duties." He gestured at Pepin's foot. "How's it feeling?"

"Like I've been stepped on by a dragonling," Pepin said with a grin. "Actually, it's much better. Ken and Vashti are very gifted."

"I'm glad of that," Faolan returned, then smiled. "Tell Nila hello for me. And Pepin, watch El'leigh. I wouldn't meet with her in private, were I you. Rumors abound here."

"I'll keep that in mind," Pepin said and watched him leave. He sighed, took up a cup of tea and settled himself in a chair to attempt a MindLink with Nila. He wasn't sure he could accomplish that, given the distance, but he was determined to try. If El'leigh could do it, why couldn't he?

He had been told once that where one was born held the most powerful magic for that individual. Pepin had concluded a long time ago that he had been birthed right here in this very palace. His mother, Alita, had been one of King Be'an's concubines. Apparently his favorite, though Alita's SoulMate and only love had been Pe'pinlaidh. How that must have hurt King Be'an. Now, his daughter was hurting Andison through love. He shook thoughts of the Merian queen aside, took a deep breath and reached for the elfin magic, surprising even himself as the Link to Nila went straight through. ::Nila, beloved, wake up.::

::Pepi? Gods, Pepin! Where are you?:: Nila came awake with a start.

::In Mere Odain,:: Pepin replied, near giddy with the successful MindLink.

::Mere Odain? You're MindLinking me from Mere Odain? How?::

::I don't really know, to be honest,:: Pepin admitted.

::So, what's wrong? Has something happened? You're in pain! What's wrong?::

::No, Nila, nothing has happened. Really. Jevra stepped on my foot but it's been healed. I just wish other things were so easy to fix..:: Pepin briefly filled her in on the events of the previous evening.

::She's a vixen!:: Nila sent hotly. ::Just like her mother! You be careful around her, Pepin. Who knows what rumors she's liable to start.::

::I've been warned, myshay. A warning I take to heart. Thank you for understanding. Now, the other reason I contacted you. Faolan's worried about the dragonlings' diet. I thought maybe Rusulka could come over and help out with a dietary plan.::

::Good idea. She's done nothing but mope around ever since Thomlin left.::

::I thought as much. By the way, have you heard from anyone?::

::Not a word.::

::They're probably up to their eyebrows in paperwork,:: Pepin said. ::Anyway, have Rusulka come through the Portal tomorrow morning. I'll be here at least another day. I'm sending Faolan down to Graybara to oversee the post, but I'm going to take the dragonlings to Taithleach for practice.::

Nila laughed. ::Are you trying to escape the palace, beloved?::

Pepin grinned. ::You guessed, then? I'm not sure when I'll be home but I'll try to Link you every day.::

::Even from Taithleach?::

::No promises on that one.::

::Pepi, how's Faolan handling all of this?::

::He tells you hello. We have some problems to resolve but I think we'll be all right. Of course, it may mean you'll be seeing a lot more of me in the future.::

::Here or there?::

::I don't know at this point. I better go. You need to get back to sleep. Velouette will no doubt be up early.::

::No doubt,:: Nila agreed. ::Q'egoshay, Pepin. And keep your feet out of the way.::

Pepin chuckled. ::Q'egoshay, Nila. Good night.:: He dropped the MindLink reluctantly, wishing he were with his wife instead of in Mere Odain. He pushed himself to his feet, then fell back into it, reeling. Ok, so that use of magic cost him. He waited a few minutes, then tried again to stand. This time it seemed his legs would hold him. He took his tea and went in search of El'leigh.

He found her in the dining hall, staring absently at a platter of fruit and breads. She had bathed and changed into a pale green frock that almost matched her pallor. Her hair was in the process of being brushed out by her ladysmaid, Neala, an attractive young Merian woman. Pepin smiled at them both. "Good morning, El'leigh, Neala."

"Your Highness," Neala greeted, giving as much of a curtsy as she could being atop a stool and holding handfuls of dark hair.

"That looks good," Pepin said, gesturing toward the platter of food. "Mind if I join you?"

El'leigh moaned and pushed the platter toward him. "Have it all if you wish," she mumbled.

Pepin gave a small smile and sat down across from her. "Perhaps a lesson was learned," he said softly.

El'leigh glared at him, then snapped at Neala. "Ouch! Leave the hair in my head!"

"Yes, Your Majesty," Neala apologized, though she smiled at Pepin over El'leigh's head.

Pepin bit back his own smile. "I thought you might be interested in the plan Faolan and I have drawn up."

El'leigh waved her hand, indicating he should continue.

"You said you would like a dragon fleet posted near Graybara. I've decided to send two. Andison's and Faolan's."

El'leigh looked at him sharply. "I thought you were going to go. That's what I asked."

"I'm aware of that. I'm also aware of the fact that Faolan knows the area far better than I do."

"And why Andison?"

"Perhaps distance is a wise thing right now," Pepin replied.

El'leigh's dark face flushed. "Neala, that's enough! Leave us!"

"Yes, Your Majesty." Neala stepped off her stool and started for the door.

"Neala," Pepin said, stopping her, "would you send Del in with some tea and jam please? Mine's gone cold."

"Yes, Your Highness." Neala curtsied and slipped out.

El'leigh turned at once on Pepin. "I don't want Andison down there," she stated.

"Why not?"

"Because...he's not a fighter."

Pepin snorted, looking over the fruit and selecting a melon slice. "Don't be ridiculous, El'leigh. He's Armsmaster. He practices both sword and crossbow on a twice daily basis."

El'leigh paused. "He's also Charis' father. I don't want her to grow up without him." Her voice was bitter, no doubt recalling her own childhood. She had never really had a father. Be'an had died when she was but an infant. Pe'pinlaidh had cared for her for seven years before he, too, had died. Then there was Alinaena and Ashton, a Merian warrior woman and a white elf. But Ashton had been old and death claimed him as well. After that, El'leigh had been pretty much on her own, though both Galen and Avenal had watched over her. Pepin could feel the hurt and loneliness radiating off her now. And the love. There was no doubt in Pepin's mind that, despite her actions of the previous night, El'leigh loved Andison.

He finished off his melon piece as the kitchen servant brought out the tea and jam. "If you're adamantly against Andison going to Graybara, El'leigh," Pepin said, "I could assign him to Wydrell. That would probably be safer."

El'leigh hesitated. "What about you? Would you go to Graybara, then?"

Pepin watched Del pour the tea. "You don't mind me risking my life, then?"

"Oh, Pepin, stop it!" El'leigh snapped. "You have magic. Andi doesn't."

Pepin shook his head. "I don't have magic down there, remember? It's too far away from Lidgerwood. At least Andison has his sword and crossbow skills. Besides, I've made other plans." He dollaped strawberry jam onto a chunk of bread and took a bite.

El'leigh's delicate eyebrows rose sharply. "Indeed? And when were you crowned King?"

Pepin ignored her, swallowing. "I'm taking the dragonlings to Taithleach. I'd like to make them a contributing part of the dragon fleets."

"Why you? Why not send one of the Foumen?" El'leigh brushed aside Del's offer of tea.

"Because I'm the only one small and light enough to ride them, if indeed they can be ridden at all."

"And who stays here to guard the palace?"

"Ken and his fleet. That should be adequate. You'll have the stand-by Foumen as well. They all have magic. I shouldn't be gone long anyway, though when I return, I'll be heading to Wydrell and Graybara to check on the posts."

El'leigh frowned at him. "Then you won't be at the palace much?"

Pepin met her gaze evenly. "I came here to work, El'leigh, not to socialize. I would like to stabilize Mere Odain as quickly and as completely as possible."

"So you can return to Nila," El'leigh mumbled, then snapped her gaze to the servant. "Oh, honestly, Del! Will you stop hovering! Leave us!"

Del went white, murmured his apologies and backed out of the room. Pepin rose at once. "I have work to do, El'leigh. I need to prepare the dragonlings and myself. I hope to leave early tomorrow. I believe Andison and Faolan will choose to do likewise. You may want to speak to Andison regarding your concerns. Until later, El'leigh." Pepin gave her a slight nod, turned sharply on his heel and strode from the room, taking El'leigh's anger with him.

Chapter Eight

Thomlin watched *Kyel's* face carefully as Vantann finished reciting the Session minutes. The twins were both exhausted. They had stayed up half the night studying for this presentation, fearful of what this fake Kyel would do should they arrive unprepared. Yet, this Kyel didn't seem to be overly attentive to what they were saying, as if he really didn't care at all but had merely made a good show of demanding this presentation from them.

"Very good, Vantann," he now said, leaning back in the library chair. "I must confess, I did not expect you two to be so well-versed. I'm impressed, not only with your memorization skills, but your independent thought processes as well. There is one further question I should like to ask each of you." He rose and walked slowly to the hearth to stare down into the fire.

"As you know, King Jansson and I have had a difference of opinion on where Dalziel might establish a post in Glede. Vantann, as heir to the throne, what would be your suggestion?"

Vantann paused, darting a quick glance at Thomlin. He drew himself up and took a deep breath. "There are any number of places. Karsaba, Anrofia and Eltair all have vast stretches of unused, unsettled land that is in close proximity to Aelfdene Valley. If that was not a concern, there is also Kartonn and Euclea to consider."

"But not Odora Dava," *Kyel* said, then turned to look at Vantann. "Why not?"

"Be...because Odora Dava is one of the smaller provinces in Glede," Vantann stammered. "For that same reason, I wouldn't recommend Bailiwycke, Midway Vale or Kasal. Bailiwycke is highly populated and the other two lack hospitable conditions to give as a gesture of friendship."

Kyel studied him for a moment, then shifted his gaze to Thomlin. "And what of Aelfdene Valley? What are your thoughts on that, Thomlin?"

"Actually I suppose it depends on what sort of post the Dalziel officials are planning," Thomlin said. "If they're looking to establish a township, then I agree with Vantann. If, however, it is only a point of reference they seek, then I would propose a position on the Elfin Council."

Kyel inclined his head thoughtfully. "An interesting idea, Thomlin. It holds merit. Perhaps at this afternoon's Session, you two can present your ideas to the Dalziel officials. You certainly seem to be more on top of this than King Jansson is."

Thomlin's gut twisted into a knot. He shot a sidelong glance at Vantann, then started as the clock in the corner began to chime the noon hour.

"Well done, boys," *Kyel* said. "You're free to go have lunch. Session starts at two o'clock. Please be prompt."

"Grandpapay," Thomlin forced the word from his mouth, "could Elecka have lunch with us again?"

Kyel regarded them both carefully. "You three are spending quite a lot of time together. This is rather sudden isn't it?"

Thomlin took a chance. "No, not at all. We've always spent time together. I see no reason for it to change just because we're here."

Kyel's gaze shifted from one to the other. "Of course. You're right. I just thought you might be interested in expanding your friendships to include some of the officials' children. I believe there are several close to your age."

Vantann shrugged. "What's the point? We're not going to be here all that long."

"Still it would be a gesture of friendship," *Kyel* said. "I will arrange for you to meet with several of them. Perhaps they can show you around. For now, go to lunch."

"Thank you," Thomlin muttered and led Vantann from the room. He left the heavy wooden doors just slightly open.

Vantann started down the hall but Thomlin held him back, then leaned forward to peek through the crack in the doors. *Kyel* stood by the hearth, a weary look on his face. For just a second, his countenance seemed to shimmer as if he were too tired to continue to hold the Illusion. Then it stabilized, he straightened with a long intake of air and started toward the door.

Thomlin gasped in panic and desperately scanned the doors lining the hall. With a grimace and a prayer, he grabbed Vantann and dragged him into the first room they came to. Fortunately, it was empty.

"What?" Vantann whispered. "What did you see?"

Thomlin shuddered. "His face. It sort of moved, like the Illusion was failing."

Vantann leaned against the closed door. "We need to tell Uncle Jansson about this. It might be something we can use against them."

Thomlin closed his eyes, his heart thudding in fear. "Gods, Vans, all I want to do is go home."

"I know, me too. Come on, let's go find Papay and Elecka."

Thomlin nodded, opened his eyes, then the door. The hall was empty and they slipped into it, then hurried to the stairs and bolted up them. Once running, neither seemed to be able to stop. It was as if demons were hard on their heels and the twins wouldn't be safe until they were with their father. Jansson had filled Treyas in on everything, and told the twins he knew the code words as well. In the face of the uncertainty they all faced, with Nydiri once more surrounding him, Thomlin looked to his father as an oasis of calm. A calm he was desperately in need of now. He and Vantann stumbled into Druce's room, slammed the door behind them and leaned against it breathlessly.

Treyas came to his feet with a start. "What in Tor's hell...what's wrong?"

"N...nothing, Papay," Thomlin stammered. "It...it's just that..." He broke off trembling.

Treyas crossed the room and took Thomlin by the shoulders. "What is it, Thoms? What happened?" He brushed Thomlin's hair from his face and looked into his eyes.

"I...I just want to go home," Thomlin mumbled as tears trickled down his cheeks. Memories of the Nydiri, of the pain and terror they had inflicted on him threatened to overwhelm him. Seeking solace, he abruptly MindLinked his father. ::JVET.::

Treyas gave a small bitter smile. ::DEKT, Thoms. It's me. Don't worry. Now, tell me what happened.:: He drew Vantann into the Link.

::Nothing, really,:: Thomlin managed. ::It was just so hard to deal with that Kyel. He sounds so much like Grandpapay that I found I was questioning myself. Why is he trying so hard to be like Grandpapay? Why does it matter? Why doesn't he just--:: He broke off, wiping his face with a trembling hand. ::I'm scared, Papay. Can't we just go home?::

::I wish we could,:: Treyas replied. ::But I can't traverse a Dimensional void. It takes sorcery magic. Maybe Dar...I don't know. Gods! I wish I knew where Elek was. The real Elek.::

::Uncle Jansson wasn't able to reach Grandpapay empathically then?:: Vantann asked.

::No.:: Treyas replied, his face registering his own fears and despair. ::At least, not yet. But you know Jansson. He'll keep trying until he finds a route no one thought to Block. We'd better start talking, just in case anyone's listening.::

Thomlin nodded. "How's Uncle Druce?" he said aloud, as they walked to the bed.

"I don't know," Treyas replied with a sigh. "Dar still has him in MageSleep."

Vantann frowned. ::Are you sure it's Uncle Dar?:: he Linked.

Thomlin started, his gaze darting from Vantann to Treyas.

::Vantann, enough,:: Treyas sent. ::You're scaring Thoms and yourself. It's Dar.::

They all looked over, startled, as the door opened. Elecka stepped in, her eyes wide with alarm. "Where have you two been? I was waiting for you in my room like you said."

"Sorry," Vantann apologized. "We thought we'd come check on Uncle Druce before lunch."

Elecka joined them bedside. "How is he?"

"I think he's doing better," Treyas told her. "He's not pulling so hard at the HealBond. Still, it's exhausting." He sagged back into his chair. "Listen, you three, Dar and Jans are going to join me here for lunch. Do you want to stay?"

They exchanged quick glances, then Thomlin shook his head, although he had to take several deep breaths to steady himself before speaking. "No.

Enid is supposed to meet us in the field for a picnic lunch. In fact, she's probably waiting."

"Jansson told me about Enid," Treyas said. "Watch where you put your heart, Thoms."

Thomlin went red. "We're just friends, Papay. All of us," he added quickly.

"Likely story," Vantann mumbled under his breath.

Elecka rolled her eyes. "If you two are just going to fight over Enid, I think I will stay here."

The room suddenly felt incredibly hot to Thomlin and he ran a finger between his high silken collar and his neck, concerns about the Nydiri suddenly taking second to his feelings for Enid. "Vans and I are not going to fight over Enid," he said tightly. "She is only a friend. Like you are."

::Be quiet, Thoms!:: Vantann twin-touched hotly. ::Don't be putting those friend ideas into her head.::

::What?:: Thomlin could barely mask his surprise. ::You were serious about pursuing Elecka? I thought you were so in love with Enid.::

::Thoms!::

::All right, you two,:: Treyas said gently. ::What good is twin-touch when you carry your emotions on your face?:: Aloud, he said, "Go have your picnic. Just remember to arrive at Session clean and on time."

"You'll come to the picnic, won't you, Elecka?" Vantann begged and took her hand.

She hesitated, then laughed. "Oh, why not. I've never seen two men fight over a woman before. It might prove interesting." She pulled her hand free and stepped to the door.

"We're not fighting over Enid," Thomlin repeated.

Elecka laughed again and opened the door, nearly colliding with Jansson and Darosenim. Her smile faded and she regarded Jansson intently. Thomlin guessed they had MindLinked and resisted the urge to Link on. This was private, though he could tell by Elecka's sad expression that the news was not encouraging. Jansson squeezed her shoulder affectionately, then he and Darosenim stepped past the three youths into the room.

"We'll see you later," Treyas called softly.

Thomlin nodded and went with the others down the hall. ::Elecka,:: he Linked at the same time as Vantann, ::Uncle Jansson won't stop trying to reach your father. You know that.::

::I know, Thoms. I just miss him.::

::I never thought I would agree with that,:: Vantann teased.

Elecka shot him a sidelong glance. ::Maybe if you weren't constantly into trouble, you and father would get along better.::

Vantann grinned and draped an arm about her shoulders. ::But then, where would all of the fun be?::

Elecka shook her head in resignation. It didn't take the trio long to reach the grassy field where, as Thomlin had predicted, Enid waited. She had spread out a large blanket and placed a basket of food at its center. Thomlin felt a warm flush crawl over his cheeks. Enid was dressed in a simple coarsecloth frock of blue and white that dusted the tops of serviceable black boots. Thomlin took her in with one gaze, then once more settled on her face. Her cheeks were round and smooth, her small nose slightly upturned, her lips curved up slightly. Her large brown eyes held a sparkle and she looked like she laughed easily and often. Her wild brown tresses had been coaxed back into a thick braid that hung past her waist, though again numerous curly tendrils had escaped, to softly frame her face. Thomlin found himself wondering what she looked like with her hair loose, how it would feel to run his fingers through it, to touch her face, to kiss her.

Thomlin supposed there were more beautiful women than Enid - Rusulka was certainly one of those - but something about the Dalziel kitchen girl drew him, and suddenly he couldn't visualize his life without her at his side.

"Your Highnesses," Enid greeted with a graceful curtsy. "Your lunch is ready. If there is anything else you need, or if I've forgotten anything, please let me know right away." She took several steps away.

"Enid, wait!" Thomlin took her arm. "You're going to join us aren't you? You said last night that you had a lunch break at noon."

Enid flushed, her gaze darting to Elecka and Vantann.

::So, that's where you went last night after dinner.:: Vantann twin-touched. ::I knew you weren't studying in the library.::

Thomlin ignored him. "Please, Enid. Can't you stay for a while at least?"

Enid hesitated, then glanced back at the Session Chambers. "I suppose for a short while. I only have twenty minutes though."

"Twenty minutes!" Vantann cried, dropping onto the blanket. "Twenty minutes is not enough time to eat. Gods! One could barely get started in twenty minutes."

"Not everyone has your voracious appetite," Elecka pointed out, sitting down beside him.

Thomlin took Enid's hand and gently guided her to the blanket, where she sat next to him, nervously toying with her skirts.

"So," Vantann said, "what do we have here?" He reached into the basket and began pulling out food. There was a bountiful array of cheeses, breads, fruits and meats, plus a bottle of cider to wash it all down. "Ah, Enid! You have outdone yourself!" He leaned forward and planted a kiss on her cheek.

Enid went bright red and shot to her feet. Thomlin clenched his jaw and glared at his brother, then rose. "Ignore him, Enid. He's always like this. Come on, sit down."

"I...I'd better go," she stammered. "Besides, my twenty minutes...Oh! Madra of saints!" she gasped, her eyes going wide. The red blush rapidly faded from her face as she looked past Thomlin.

He whirled to see a tall, thin man dressed in a black uniform walking their way. The man's pointed face was set in a hard frown, his dark eyes hot with anger.

"Who is he?" Thomlin asked, though he seemed vaguely familiar.

"Pax," Enid whispered. "He's the new head servant. I'm in trouble."

Vantann and Elecka rose to watch the man storm up to them. He gave a stiff bow. "Your Highnesses," he greeted. "Is the girl causing a problem?"

"No!" Vantann answered quickly. "She made us lunch is all."

"I see." Pax looked at Enid. "And it takes you over forty minutes to deliver a lunch to a site within five minutes of the kitchen?"

"We were late in arriving," Thomlin cut in. "Enid graciously awaited us. I see no problem with that. Do you?"

The man turned an icy glare on Thomlin. "Certainly not, Your Highness. However, you are now here and the girl should be returning to her duties."

"But she hasn't eaten yet," Vantann protested.

Pax's dark eyebrows rose and he glanced at Enid. "Nor does she need to," he retorted sarcastically.

Enid flamed red and Thomlin drew himself up rigidly. "That is quite enough!" he snapped. "You need to temper your tongue, sir. Her name is not 'the girl'. It is Enid. And Enid will stay here to join us for lunch. It is our fault she missed hers and it will be our responsibility to remedy it. You may return to your station at once!"

Pax drew back, anger ripping across his face and in that instant, Thomlin recognized him. Killan! The Nydiri who had held the sacrificial daggers in Winze. Pure, cold terror rushed through him. He grabbed Enid, stumbled backward and frantically twin-touched Vantann all at the same time. ::Vans! It's Killan! Spell! Get us out of here!::

Vantann's eyes went wide and, without question, he threw his magic out. It connected with Thomlin's and swept the four youths up and away in a turbulent TravelSpell. Dirin magic slammed against the TravelSpell as Killan tried to drag them all back. The TravelStrand slipped, the magic faltered and Thomlin desperately sought more. He would not succumb to the Nydiri again. He would die first. Abruptly, powerful dark magic rushed into the Spell and the foursome was yanked free of Killan and sent hurtling out of control.

Thomlin clutched Enid's arm with both hands, cringing at the cold touch of the magic about him. The Spell seemed to last forever, pressing against Thomlin with a crushing force. But at last they were down, landing with a jolt in a dark bog. The ground was spongy, absorbing the impact but covering them with sticky, foul-smelling peat. The moist air hung hot and heavy, curling about thick, twisted vines that created a tangled mass of brown and green. Small pools of black water dotted the ground, vibrating and churning as if something lurked beneath.

Thomlin sat up with a moan, shaking his head as if that could rid it of dark magic. Vantann was far more verbal and turned on Elecka with a mixture of disbelief and rage. "Where did you learn that?" he demanded.

Elecka regarded him icily, her eyes a smoldering dark brown. Enid sat staring at the three elves, a look of shock on her mud-spattered face. "Where are we?" she whispered. "What happened?"

"I don't know where we are," Vantann retorted hotly. "As for what happened, maybe Elecka could explain that to all of us!"

"If I chose to," Elecka replied tightly. She rose and glanced about.

Vantann shot to his feet and grabbed her by the arm. "Then choose to!" he snapped. "When the hell did you start practicing dark magic?"

"It's in my blood, Vantann. Get used to it."

"Not a chance! Dark magic isn't instinct, Elecka. It's learned. I know damn well that your father isn't teaching it to you."

Enid abruptly turned and retched into one of the black pools, gaining everyone's attention. Thomlin grabbed at her to keep her from collapsing, then looked to Vantann and Elecka. "Let's save the argument for later. If it weren't for dark magic, Killan would have us right now. I'll take a hot, sticky bog any day over a damned Nydiri." He turned his attention back to Enid. "Are you all right now?"

She stared at him as if seeing him for the first time and suddenly tears flooded her eyes. Thomlin reached out to hold her but Enid moved away from his touch and came to her feet. "Leave me alone!"

Thomlin came to his feet at once. "Enid, please, don't be scared. Not of me, of us. We're elves. We have magic." He reached for her again and, again, she evaded his touch. Fear and anger shone in the brown eyes. *And why not,* Thomlin thought. She was just transported from her home into this smelly bog with the cold touch of dark magic. She probably viewed him as nothing more than a monster. Papay was right. He should have watched where he put his heart.

Vantann sensed Thomlin's despair and intervened. "Enid, we need your help. Do you know this place? Are we far from the Session Chambers?"

"I don't know," she replied tightly. "I've never seen this place before, Your Highness. Why did you bring me here?"

"I didn't want Killan to get you," Thomlin answered.

"Who's Killan?"

"The one you called Pax. He's a Nydiri."

Enid looked from one to the other. "Pax?"

Thomlin sighed. "I know this all sounds very odd, but Enid, it's the truth. Nydiri have taken the place of King Kyel and Elek. It appears they also replaced Pax."

"Have you ever even heard of the Nydiri?" Elecka asked tartly.

"Yes, Your Highness," Enid retorted. "I may be only a kitchen girl but I'm not stupid. There's a coven of Nydiri living in Dalziel. They're mostly healers and they don't practice dark magic. Unlike you."

"Gracious," Elecka seethed, obviously still harboring the effects of the dark magic. "You take the help away from their post and they quite forget who they are. Or whom they're addressing."

Thomlin caught his breath, his gaze flying to Enid. But instead of dissolving into tears, she narrowed her eyes and clenched her fists. "You come to your position by chance, Your Highness. There is really no more separating us than the luck of parentage. Fate alone dictated who bows to whom."

"That's enough!" Vantann snapped. "You're both reacting to the dark magic. Thomlin, you and Enid go over there. Elecka, you come with me."

The two girls glared at each other but separated as Vantann had ordered. Thomlin kept his distance from Enid as they walked along a boggy trail. "I'm sorry for getting you messed up in this," he said. "I should have let you stay behind. I doubt Killan would have done anything to you. My reaction was purely instinctual, but again, I'm sorry."

Enid glanced sideways at him. "What is your purpose with me, Your Highness?"

"What do you mean?"

She stopped and turned to face him. "Why me? Is this a game for you, M'Lord?"

Thomlin stared at her, aghast. "A game? What are you talking about?"

"Why are you pursuing me, M'Lord?"

Thomlin flushed. "Be...because I like you," he stammered. "I'll stop if you wish, if it makes you uncomfortable. I...I never meant to upset you."

Enid studied him for a long moment. "You're a prince. You're handsome, thoughtful, intelligent and kind. You could have your pick of women much more attractive than me, Your Highness. Why are you teasing me?"

But Thomlin had stopped listening after her first few words. "You think I'm handsome?" he asked. The mere suggestion that she found him so, lifted his spirits.

"You're very handsome, Your Highness," Enid murmured. "And you seem very sweet, but,"

"I am sweet," Thomlin interrupted with a shy grin. He reached out hesitantly and took both of her hands in his. "Enid, I can't totally explain my feelings. I don't know what will ever come of them. I just want to be with you. You make me feel...complete."

Enid attempted to pull back but Thomlin held fast to her hands, his heart thudding wildly. Then, before he could change his mind, he lifted both her hands and gently kissed the back of each, though to do so, he had to find a place free of the peat. She stared at him in astonishment. "Don't," she whispered. "Please don't toy with my emotions, Your Highness. It's unkind and it's unfair."

"I assure you, Enid," Thomlin replied, "it's not meant to be either. I can understand if you don't share the same feelings." He released her hands. "And I will honor that, though it pains me to do so." He drew himself up. "Come on. Elecka should be fine by now. We need to find a way back to the Session Chambers." He turned with heavy heart.

Enid stopped him with a light touch on his shoulder and he looked back at her. She opened her mouth as if to speak, then closed it again, but the look in her eyes brought him hope. He smiled and held out his hand. Slowly, she took it and they walked back the way they'd come.

Elecka and Vantann were waiting and Thomlin noticed with relief that her eyes were once more blue. Apparently, Enid noticed as well and she stopped so abruptly that Thomlin was pulled backward by her grip on his hand. "Her eyes," Enid whispered.

"I know," Thomlin said. "That's the way of dark magic for elves. To renounce its use is to have blue eyes, to use the dark is to have eyes as black as the magic itself."

"I'm sorry I frightened you, Enid," Elecka said. "I'm sorry I spoke to you the way I did. I guess I don't understand dark magic as much as I thought I did." She cast a glance at Vantann, then looked back at Enid. "I hope we can be friends."

"It is I who should apologize, Your Highness," Enid returned with a curtsy. "I was badly out of line. Forgive me."

Elecka smiled. "I will on one condition. You must stop calling me Highness and you must stop curtsying."

"I second that," Vantann put in. "From here on, we're equals."

Enid gave him a wry smile. "But, Your Highness, we're not. And we never will be." She gently released Thomlin's hand. "Fate has dictated our stations in life and we must adhere to that choice. I am a servant at the Session Chambers and that is all that I will ever be."

Vantann chuckled. "Don't bet on it."

Thomlin flushed and twin-touched his brother. ::Vans, I'm sorry. I know you liked Enid and I would never purposely intrude. You know that.::

::I know,:: Vantann sent back. ::Do you think she's your SoulMate?::

Thomlin couldn't hide a small smile as he glanced at Enid. ::Yes, I do.::

"Will you two stop it!" Elecka cried, then explained to a startled Enid. "They can talk to each other through their minds. It must be a pathetically limited gift."

Both Vantann and Thomlin gave her a sour look, though Enid giggled softly, then flushed with embarrassment.

"Well," Vantann said, looking about, "we need to get out of here. Papay was trapped in a place like this once and there were rotagillers there. I do not want to meet one of them."

"I've never heard of them, Your Highness," Enid said. "But I do know that bogs like this are home to the Segora."

"What's that?" Vantann asked uneasily.

"It's rather like a bird, M'Lord, but it can't fly. It lures its prey by using rhythmic movement as a spellbinder. The prey walks right up to it and is eaten."

"Gods!" Vantann cried. "Well, I say we get out of here before one of those finds us."

Enid frowned, looking at them. "Why don't you just use your magic to take us back, M'Lord?"

"What good would that do?" Thomlin asked. "We'd be going right back into a dangerous situation. One that I'm not willing to re-enter. Especially now that Killan knows we know."

"What about that coven of Nydiri you mentioned, Enid?" Elecka asked. "Do you know where they are?"

Enid glanced at Thomlin. "I thought you wanted to stay away from the Nydiri, M'Lord."

"Just from the dark Nydiri," Thomlin told her. "I know there are both, though to be honest, I don't know that I trust any Nydiri."

She looked away. "Well, I know where the coven is, Your Highness, but I don't know where we are. I may be able to tell you more tonight when the stars come out. Right now..." she shrugged.

Elecka frowned. "Should we try to MindLink your father or Uncle Jansson?"

"I don't know," Vantann replied, looking at Thomlin. "Nydiri can trace magic, can't they?"

Thomlin shrugged. "I don't remember. I mean, there wasn't any magic in Winze but it seems like they could. Anyway, I sure don't want to take any chances of them finding us. And I don't want to chance putting anyone else in danger."

Vantann sighed. "Me either. It looks like we walk."

"Which way?" Thomlin asked with a frown.

"I guess it doesn't matter. We just need to get out of this bog," Vantann replied, his eye on Enid.

Thomlin twin-touched him. ::What's wrong now?::

::I think she might know which way to go. I think she's just afraid to say because of her status with us.::

Thomlin glanced at Enid, who had turned to face north when Vantann made the suggestion of walking. "I think we should go north," he said aloud.

"Why north?" Elecka asked.

"It just seems right," Thomlin replied. He reached out and once more took Enid's hand in his.

Vantann grinned. "North it is then. Let's go and let's hope we can get back before those Nydiri cause any more problems."

Treyas paced frantically before the hearth, his hands clenched into tight fists behind his back. His gaze repeatedly wandered to the bed and Druce, who still lay in MageSleep. *Gods,* he thought, *I need you, Druce. I need you to wake up. I need your support, your strength, your wisdom.* His head snapped around as the door to the room opened. Jansson and Darosenim entered.

"Did you find them?" Treyas cried.

"No." Jansson answered softly.

"He means, not yet," Darosenim added. "We will. One of the servants is also missing. Neslin has half of the staff out searching."

"Neslin," Treyas repeated almost to himself. He wondered about Neslin, about an official who would take an advisor's word over a king's.

Today's two Sessions had been tense. *Kyel* and Jansson had been at odds over everything. Their words to each other had been crisp and almost hostile. If Jansson was trying to act toward this Kyel so as not to arouse suspicion, he was doing a poor job. As for *Kyel*, he had been furious over the twins' absence and had delivered a scathing lecture to Treyas about parental responsibility. A lecture well within the hearing range of the entire Dalziel alliance team. Treyas was sure the officials were beginning to view Glede royalty as both emotionally unstable and lacking in leadership. They were most likely beginning to wonder why Elek had even suggested becoming allies.

As for Elek - Treyas sighed with worry. Where were the real Elek and Kyel? And where were the twins and Elecka? He dragged his thoughts back to the fore. "Who was the last one to see them?" he asked.

"The kitchen staff saw Enid leave with a picnic lunch," Darosenim replied. "As for the twins, I guess we were the last."

Treyas looked at them both suspiciously. They caught his meaning at once and exchanged weary glances. Treyas sighed. "I'm sorry." He knew they were the real thing. He could sense their concern and worry. He rubbed his hand across his face, then looked to Druce, before returning his attention to Jansson. "Do you have any idea where they had planned to picnic?"

Jansson nodded. "I could take you there."

Treyas picked up his cloak and flung it across his shoulders. "Dar..."

"I'll stay with Druce," the mage interrupted. "It's almost time for his treatment anyway. I'll just give it to him early."

"We'll be back as quickly as possible," Treyas said and left with Jansson.

They gained the outside quickly, and Treyas drew his cloak tighter against the chill of the evening air. Jansson did likewise and led Treyas past the maze garden toward the grassy playing field. "They'd apparently met here before," he said. "Elecka seemed to favor the lack of shrubbery, if you get my meaning."

Treyas did. Lack of shrubbery meant lack of hiding places. His gaze traveled over the broad expanse of grass. It would be impossible for anyone to sneak up on them here. He slowly began to walk, instinctively probing the area for residual magic. Jansson watched warily and, when Treyas stopped abruptly, he hurried to join him. "What? Did you find something?"

Treyas stared at the ground in shock. "They TravelSpelled! From right here." He brought his gaze up to meet Jansson's. "Why didn't I feel it?" He began a StrandSearch, trying to sort out the confused tangle of magic. "Dark magic?"

"What!"

"There's dark magic. I didn't think Elecka knew that."

"Neither did I. Are you sure it was her?"

"Positive. It bears her Signature. The twins started the Spell...then...oh gods! Dirin!" Treyas had found the tight trail of Dirin magic laced with the others. His gut tightened in alarm and Jansson quickly clutched his arm.

"Trey, get control! Don't fuse the magic."

Treyas swallowed hard. He wished Kyel were here. He would be able to decipher the Strands, be able to tell if the twins had fled from the Nydiri or been taken by them. The best Treyas could do was guess. He looked back at the Session Chambers. Something didn't feel right but he couldn't put his finger on it just yet. He frowned and continued easing along the MagicStrands. He was tempted to pull a LocatorStrand to find out just where the twins were. At the same time, he worried about opening a path to them that another might follow. Gods! If only he knew which it was - had they fled or been caught? It was times like this that Treyas really valued Druce's ability to control his magic, to allow him to settle down and sort things out. His heart ached to think that a time would come when Druce would no longer be there for such a comfort. Thank the gods that Dar was along to help with the healing and... "Dar!" he cried aloud, suddenly aware of what was wrong.

Darosenim was treating Druce, using magic on him, yet Treyas had not felt a thing through either the SoulMate Bond or the HealBond.

"What about Dar?" Jansson asked uneasily.

Treyas turned on him, heart pounding. ::JVET:: he linked.

Jansson's face registered alarm. ::DEKT,:: he replied. ::What's wrong?::

::Were you away from Dar anytime today?:: Treyas sent.

::No. We had morning Session, then joined you for lunch, then went back to Session. Why?::

::Think, Jans. Anytime?::

Jansson hesitated obviously thinking back, then he snorted with annoyance. ::After lunch, we went to freshen up, him in his room, me in mine. I went to fetch him for Session but he was already gone. Firesass! They got him, too?::

::I don't know. He said he was going to give Druce a treatment but I haven't felt anything on the HealBond. Let's get back there.::

Together, they left the playing field and hurried back to Druce's room. Darosenim was sitting in a chair by the fire, browsing through a book. He looked up with a frown. "Did you find out anything?"

Jansson shook his head in answer while Treyas gently probed the room for magic. He sensed nothing. Slowly, he removed his cloak, anger and worry meshing together and he shot a quick glance to Jansson before addressing the mage. "Dar, could you bring Druce out of MageSleep now?"

"Why?" Darosenim seemed confused.

"I just want to talk to him," Treyas said, going to the bed. He regarded Druce's pale countenance worriedly. "Please, Dar?"

Darosenim rose and placed his book on the table. "I would rather not, Treyas. He's doing well. Why jeopardize it?"

Treyas sat down on the edge of the bed and caught up one of Druce's hands. It was cold and Treyas massaged it thoughtfully. "I don't want to jeopardize his healing," he admitted, "but he's been in MageSleep for twenty-four hours. That's a long time."

Darosenim gave him a weak smile. "People have been known to stay in MageSleep for three times that," he pointed out and laid one hand on Treyas' shoulder.

Treyas stiffened just slightly under the touch. "How long are you planning to keep him in it, then?"

The mage shrugged. "I don't know. We'll just have to wait and see. No more than seventy-two hours certainly."

"How did his treatment go?" Jansson asked.

"I didn't give him one," Darosenim replied. "I think he's strong enough to back off on the hourly treatments. He needs to be weaned slowly, though."

Without looking up, Treyas MindLinked Darosenim. ::DEKT.::

::JVET,:: Darosenim replied, confused.

Treyas whirled, relief surging through him. Darosenim looked down at him, puzzled. Slowly, understanding took hold and he backed away, hurt registering in his blue eyes. ::You didn't think it was me, did you?::

::I'm sorry, Dar,:: Treyas said. ::I was expecting you to use magic on Druce. When I didn't feel it, I got worried.::

Darosenim's gaze went to Jansson. ::Does he think that--::

Treyas pulled Jansson into the Link. ::I was wrong, Jans. It's Dar.::

::Firesass, Dar,:: Jansson sent with relief.

A small smile touched at Darosenim's lips. ::Hellfires, Jans.:: He looked to Treyas. ::We can't go on like this. It's too nerve-wracking.::

::What do you suggest?::

::I don't know.:: Darosenim sagged back into his chair. ::I just wish there was some other way we could tell. It's easy enough for you. You only need to MindLink, but what about between me and Jansson? We can't initiate a

MindLink and there are going to be times when you're not around. What then?::

::He's right, Trey,:: Jansson put in. ::I hate suspecting him every time he's away from me for five minutes. Gods! This whole situation is beginning to take its toll.:: He slumped into a chair and toyed idly with his wedding band. ::I want to go home to Zira. I want Kyel back. I want this Alliance Agenda to never have been suggested.::

Darosenim nodded glumly. ::Sounds good to me.::

Treyas regarded them both sadly. He knew how much they meant to each other. They were blood-brothers. They had come together at a desperate time in Jansson's life. They looked to each other for support, friendship and assistance. And now they were being pushed apart by a power of evil that had no right to do so. Treyas wished he could just Spell them all away, find someplace safe where they wouldn't have to worry about who was who. His gaze returned to Druce. The man couldn't travel, that was obvious, but Treyas would never leave him here alone.

And what of the twins and Elecka? Kyel and Elek? Where were they? How were they? He once more Linked Jansson and Darosenim. ::I need to find my children, but I don't want to leave Druce here alone to do so.::

::Nor will you go off alone,:: Jansson retorted at once.

Treyas grimaced. ::I doubt I'll be alone. This fake Kyel will most likely want to tag along to keep up appearances.::

::If you think for one minute that you and that Nydiri will ride off together, think again,:: Jansson told him.

::I agree with Jans,:: Darosenim put in. ::Druce can't travel. I'll stay here. Jans will go with you.::

Jansson's gaze swung to his friend. ::Dar, I can't leave you here alone!::

::I won't be alone. I have Druce and he needs me.::

::I don't want to leave him here either, but I see no choice,:: Treyas admitted. ::I need to get away from the Session Chambers if I'm going to pull a LocatorStrand to the twins. Hopefully, the Nydiri masquerading as Kyel won't want to leave here.:: He had a sudden thought. ::Maybe he can't. Maybe he wouldn't be able to maintain the Illusion if he got too far away.::

::It's worth a chance asking then,:: Jansson replied. ::But you're still not going off alone.::

Treyas rose from the bed, ignoring Jansson's last statement. He would worry about the overprotective Bard later. ::I guess it's time to go ask then. Wish me luck.:: He drew a deep breath and left the room.

It was a short walk down the hall to Kyel's room and Treyas hesitated only briefly before knocking. *Kyel* answered at once and ushered Treyas inside. "Have the children been found?"

"No, not that I've heard. Kyel, I'm going to look for them. I know that this will disrupt the Sessions and I apologize in advance, but I,"

"No need to apologize, Treyas," *Kyel* interrupted. "I can quite understand your position. Now, I hope you can understand my position. I cannot accompany you on this search as much as I would like to. I must stay here and continue with the Session meetings."

Treyas turned away, hoping his face didn't show his annoyance. The real Kyel would have canceled the meetings immediately to search for his daughter. "Perhaps Elek can,"

"I don't think so," *Kyel* interrupted. "This Agenda was arranged by him. Neslin expects him to be in attendance. Treyas," he laid a hand on Treyas' shoulder, "I trust you to find them, to bring my daughter back."

Treyas nodded, and turned to face *Kyel*, slipping free of his touch. "Have you MindLinked her yet?"

"No." *Kyel* turned away. "We lost the MindLink at the border. I did try to reinstate it but was unsuccessful. They may no longer be in magic."

Treyas started. "Then Dalziel also contains areas void of magic?"

"From what Neslin has told me, yes. In fact, the major concentration of magic is right here, around the Session Chambers. Apparently, the farther out one goes, the weaker the magic. There may be none on the coasts."

Gods, Treyas sighed. *If I leave here my HealBond with Druce may be broken. Unless...unless I can keep it intact with naiad magic.* Or if Neslin's information was wrong. It didn't take much in the way of elfin magic to keep a HealBond intact. It wasn't the same as pulling magic for the SoulMateBond or for Spells. "Has Neslin told you much about Dalziel's topography? It would help to know what I'm heading into."

Kyel returned his gaze to Treyas. "Not really. I do know that most of Dalziel is farmland, one of the key reasons for considering it as, if not an ally, at the least a partner in trade. We are hoping to be able to trade Glede's abundant resource of wood for Dalziel's ability to grow citrelles."

Treyas nodded. He knew of citrelles. The tangy, aromatic fruit needed long seasons of warmth to grow properly. There were several small orchards in the province of Pendorelle to the far south of Aelfdene Valley but they could not provide enough to satisfy the need in Glede. And just getting to them was a hazard since the valley trolls frequented the area. It would indeed be welcome to have a more reliable source but Treyas wondered about that being enough of a reason to form an Alliance Team and have this agenda. Also, from what he had witnessed of Dalziel, it was none too warm. He wasn't even sure if citrelles could grow here, and chastised himself soundly for not questioning the reasonings of this alliance before he'd even left Glede. Then again, he had had no reason to question it then.

His thoughts went back to the lost children. They were at the mercy of Dalziel's cold nights, and Treyas doubted that they had any more clothes than those on their backs. As the twins had pointed out numerous times, silken formal wear was not exactly warm. He brought his mind back into focus. "Do you think Neslin will allow me the use of a horse and some supplies?"

"I would think so," *Kyel* replied. "Are you intending to go alone, then?"

"No. Jansson has volunteered to go with me."

"Jansson!" *Kyel's* voice held irritation. "That is not possible, Treyas. Jansson's input into the Session agenda is vital. He cannot afford the luxury of an adventure."

"This is hardly an adventure," Treyas pointed out, his voice tight and controlled.

"But you know as well as I that Jansson is viewing it as such. No. I am afraid that this time he cannot go. Nor can Darosenim. The provinces must be represented."

"They're hardly represented, Kyel," Treyas said. "Anrofia, Eltair, Pendorelle and Kartonn did not send an emissary. Nor did quite a few others."

"They were asked. They declined. It was their choice. We must do what we can with what we have."

Treyas pondered both his words and *Kyel's*. It hadn't even dawned on him before now, but the only provinces actually represented were Karsaba, Odora Dava and Aelfdene. He frowned. "Is this alliance for the betterment of Glede or the elves?" he asked.

Kyel glared at him. "I would hope both. However, I am growing somewhat weary of the humans' sense of complacency. They seem to view the elves as the caretakers and military strength of Glede. I believe it is time for them to stop relying on our empire and our magic and start relying on themselves."

A chill ran through Treyas at the words. "I believe the humans have done well with or without our magic. I would hate to see the two races alienated."

"Perhaps that is because your wife is a human," *Kyel* pointed out.

Treyas stiffened. "My wife's heritage is not at question here. Maintaining peace in Glede is. I would hope that would be as high a priority for you as it is for me."

Kyel eyed him coldly. "Peace," he said, "will be up to the humans. War takes two sides, not one."

"War?" Treyas repeated, aghast. "Since when has war ever been a consideration?"

Kyel abruptly chuckled and clapped Treyas on the back. "I assure you, it is not. I am tired, Treyas. My mind is wandering. Forget my words." He guided Treyas toward the door. "Go find your children, Treyas. I will deal with things here."

Treyas searched his face, noting the exclusion of mentioning Elecka, then nodded and left. *I'll bet you'll deal with things here,* he fumed. *But don't expect Dar or Jans to fall into your pathetic little trap.* He returned to Druce's room where he found Darosenim alone with the Merian. "Where's Jans?" he asked immediately.

"Right here." Jansson came out of the bathroom, still toweling his face. "I thought I'd freshen up a bit before we leave."

Treyas frowned. "It's not going to be 'we', Jans. Kyel insists that you stay here. He says it's vital to the Agenda."

"Too bad," Jansson replied. "That doesn't change my mind."

"Actually, I agree with him," Treyas replied, then MindLinked them both. After giving and receiving the code words, he continued. ::He's going to do something drastic. He's talking of war between the humans and the elves. He seems quite eager to get me out of the way. You have to stay here, Jans. You can't let this Kyel sway the alliance.::

::Then I should give my land?:: Jansson asked in annoyance.

::No. I didn't say that. But maybe you and Dar can keep the Dalziel officials on task and away from any more thought of war.::

Jansson frowned and tossed the drying towel onto a chair. ::Then if I'm not going with you, who will?::

::I don't know. You were right about this Kyel. He doesn't want to go. Neither does Elek.::

::Then Kyel be damned,:: Jansson seethed. ::I'm going with you and there's nothing he can do to stop me without exposing himself for who he really is.::

They all looked over at a light tap on the door. Treyas answered it, admitting *Kyel.*

"Forgive my intrusion," the elf said. "I wanted to speak with Jansson. When he wasn't in his room, I guessed he might be here. Jansson?" He motioned the bard forward, then left the room.

Jansson shot a quick glance at Treyas before following *Kyel.* He could do nothing else.

"Easy now, Jevra," Pepin murmured, stroking her under the neck. He slowly flipped the strap across her back.

She started, then looked down at him, her pale yellow eyes questioning. Pepin cooed soothingly, reached around and snagged the free end of the harness. It wasn't an elaborate piece, just a single length of leather hooked loosely about her neck. Its only purpose was to give the rider a handhold. On the dragons, it was often unnecessary. Pepin remembered how easily and securely he had fit into the hollow at the base of Fayemera's neck. Controlling her movements had been as simple as touching her scales on either the right or the left. Pepin had found out early on that a dragon's neck scales were extremely sensitive, as were their horn fans. He had always found it amazing that if a dragon could clear an opening with its horn fans, the entire body could follow.

The dragonlings, however, didn't seem to have that ability, even though their horn fans were quite small compared to the dragons. Both Pepin and Faolan had at one time or another been forced to back a dragonling out of a place it thought it could fit.

"All right, Jevra," Pepin said. "It's time you learned a purpose. Head down."

Jevra obediently lowered her head to the ground, one yellow eye fixed on Pepin. He gripped the leather harness with his left hand and, with a deep breath, swung astride her back. He had spent the entire day watching the dragonlings fly. He had observed both their take-off and the way they landed. He had studied the position of head, neck and tail as they soared about the pasture. He didn't expect Jevra to fly the first time she had a rider. She would need to get used to the shift in weight, to learn to be aware that she held another life, that the playful dips and rolls that she and the other dragonlings engaged in, weren't something she could do while in service.

Pepin pulled back gently on the harness. "Head up," he ordered, then adjusted his position as she complied. He was surprised at the ease with which he could sit. Though Jevra didn't have the same neck hollow as the dragons, her strong, bony wing bases came together in such a way as to provide a shelf-like seat. "All right, M'Lady," Pepin murmured, "step three. Let's try walking a bit, just to get used to me being here."

Jevra snorted, small puffs of smoke curling from her nostrils. She took two hesitant, lurching steps, then shot upward into the air, her small wings beating powerfully.

Pepin caught his breath and tightened his grip on the harness, heart pounding. He expected that at any moment, Jevra would lose her balance and come crashing to the ground, or worse yet, toss him from his lofty perch. Instead, she continued to gain altitude, then streamlined her body and glided out across the meadow as if carrying a rider was something she'd done every day.

The other five dragonlings excitedly joined her, fanning out behind like a flock of geese. Pepin exhaled sharply with relief, and experimentally pressed his knee against her right side. Jevra turned gracefully, accepting his unspoken command, winging silently toward the palace. Pepin shook his head, amazed, then caught a glimpse of El'leigh in one of the courtyards. A sense of mischief welled up in him. She had scoffed at his idea to train the dragonlings, had forbidden him to go to Taithleach with them. Well, let her scoff at this.

Pepin gave a series of high-pitched whistles and glanced over his shoulder. The dragonlings repositioned themselves, forming a straight line behind Jevra. Obviously they had been studying the larger dragons, listening to the commands issued. With a triumphant grin, Pepin returned his gaze to the palace and El'leigh. "Come on, Jevra," he murmured, "let's show our Queen just what we can do."

He drove Jevra down on a silent, gliding approach at El'leigh's back, the five other dragonlings following. El'leigh abruptly stopped, then whirled. Her dark eyes went wide and she flung herself to the ground with a shriek as Jevra soared no less than ten feet above her head. One by one the dragonlings copied the pattern, the wind from their passing whipping El'leigh's long blue skirts and her dark tresses into tangles. Dust and debris swirled around her in a mini-cyclone and she covered her face with both hands. Pepin laughed giddily, brought Jevra into a wide turn, called the rest into a V formation and headed back to the pasture. He was sure to get a dressing down for his actions but shrugged it off. The look of surprise and disbelief on El'leigh's face had been worth it.

Jevra landed as easily and expertly as she had flown. Pepin regained the ground with a whoop of success, ignoring the twinge of pain that shot through his foot. "Perfect Jevra!" he cried, then greeted each dragonling as it came in. "Shann, wonderful job! Pias, Oreb, beautiful! Miele, splendid! Tam, outstanding! All of you! You should be proud! I am." He moved amongst them, scratching bellies, patting lowered heads, rubbing behind horn fans.

The dragonlings hissed and snorted in pleasure, puffing smoke and creating a grayish-white fog around Pepin.

"Prince Pepin!" A strong voice penetrated the noise and smoke. A voice holding condemnation.

Pepin grimaced and sidled behind the nearest dragonling, big red and gold Miele. The dragonling snorted, twisting his long neck to nudge Pepin affectionately. "Hush!" Pepin whispered, putting a finger to his lips.

"Pepin Merripen! At once!" The man's voice now held anger.

Resigned, Pepin stepped around Miele to stand before Galen, El'leigh's Merian Captain of the Guards. He forced a smile to his face. "Good evening, Galen," he said innocently.

Galen ignored the greeting, his dark eyes flashing his disapproval. "Would you care to explain what I just witnessed?"

"They were wonderful weren't they?" Pepin gushed. "The way they responded, the way they carried themselves. They've never even,"

"Enough!" Galen interrupted hotly. "You know what I was talking about, Prince Pepin. Just what was the purpose in scaring our Queen half to death?"

Pepin cringed at the thought of El'leigh being called his Queen. "All right," he conceded, "it was an error in judgment. I just wanted to show her what the dragonlings could do."

Galen was quiet for a moment, in which a sparkle of amusement flashed across his face. "Could I venture to suggest that there might have been a better way to showcase the dragonlings' talent?"

Pepin shrugged. "Perhaps," he said, then grinned. "But it probably wouldn't have been as much fun."

Galan shook his head with a sigh of resignation. "I've known you since you were seven years old. Sixteen years, Pepin. In that sixteen years, I can count on one hand the number of times you and Queen El'leigh have been civil to each other."

"That often?" Pepin teased, then withered under Galen's glare. "All right. I'm sorry. It's just that she can be so damned...annoying." He turned to remove Jevra's harness.

Galen watched him thoughtfully. "I understand Queen El'leigh sent for you with some urgency," he finally said.

Pepin nodded, pulling the halter away from Jevra. "She did. She wanted me here within the hour." He began to coil the harness, his gaze on his brown hands and the white leather slipping against them. "I didn't even have time to say goodbye to my daughter. And for what?" He brought his gaze up to meet Galen's. "So El'leigh could try to seduce me in my own quarters. With her husband two doors down the hall, no less. She claims she wants someone in Kelta, yet she won't allow Faolan to go. She acts as if she no longer desires Andison as husband, yet keeps him close. Coals, Galen! Sometimes I really question El'leigh's state of mind."

Galen sighed. "She's confused right now. Much the same way you are."

Pepin looked at him sharply. "How so? She has no question about her title, about her allegiance, her heritage. Her father was Mere Odain's king."

"And her mother was a concubine who practiced dark magic," Galen put in.

"So what?" Pepin snapped. He didn't want to be reminded of El'leigh's mother. The woman had caused him nothing but grief. Treyas had almost died because of her. Fayemera had. Pepin whirled toward the dragonlings. "I need to stable the fleet," he said curtly.

Galen took his arm, stopping him. "El'leigh is not Irida," he said softly.

Pepin stiffened at the mention of the name. "But she carries the same blood," he replied tightly.

"Your wife also practiced dark magic," Galen pointed out. "In Reyuann's camp. The same camp that Irida lived in."

Pepin jerked away from him. "My wife has renounced necromancy!"

"And Queen El'leigh has never practiced it!"

"Never? That's all she knows, Galen! Her magic is as dark as any follower of Reyuann. The sad part is, she revels in it. She enjoys using it. Especially on me!"

"Pepin!" Galen's word held a warning and Pepin clenched his jaw, biting back any further words.

For a moment, the two men stared at each other, each holding his own anger and the reasoning behind it. Pepin well knew of Galen's devotion to not only his duty as Captain of the Guards, but to El'leigh, Queen of his country. He and his SoulMate, Avenal, had taken over parental responsibilities of El'leigh after Ashton had died. Not that it had always gone smoothly. There were numerous conflicts between the three of them over the years. More than once Galen had been ready to throw up his hands and walk away. But his love of Mere Odain and his insatiable thirst for peace had always won out. As Pepin was sure it always would.

In some ways, Pepin felt just a little chagrined that his own love for the continent didn't run as deep. He supposed that as DragonMaster it should. Still, he had been raised in the elfin way and his heart remained there, no matter his words or his title.

He willed his anger away. "I'll apologize to her," he told Galen.

Galen nodded. "An apology is a start," he said, then looked past Pepin to the dragonlings who had wandered off to graze. "They do fly well. Andison told me of your plans to run them through some training drills. Do you have any thoughts about riders?"

"No, not really. The Foumen are too tall, the Merians and Keltins too heavy. El'leigh is the only other Merian-elf who I know of."

"Perhaps a Belfourian halfling would suffice," Galen said.

Pepin glanced at him, surprised. "Avenal?"

"He's not much bigger than you."

"True, but I thought Avenal preferred to stay close to home," Pepin said choosing his words carefully.

Galen chuckled. "We both know that's my preference, not Avey's."

Pepin smiled. "So, after sixteen years you're finally going to loosen the reins a bit?"

"Even I can change," Galen pointed out. "As long as I don't have to bear witness to another near fatal stabbing."

Pepin winced at the emotions rolling off the Merian. He remembered all too well how Avenal had almost died in Winze only five years ago. Would have died but for Jansson's quick thinking and determination in keeping him alive. Now, Pepin gave a smile of reassurance to Galen. "We're only training. I shouldn't expect any daggers to come within a thousand leagues of Avenal."

Galen nodded absently. "I'll send him round in the morning, then. See what you two can work out." He started away, then stopped. "And, Pepin, no more dragonling runs on the Queen. Period."

"I promise," Pepin returned. "I'll be good."

Galen regarded him suspiciously, sighed and walked away.

Chapter Ten

"Jansson?"

The familiar voice filtered into Jansson's mind, bringing both fear and joy. He opened his eyes to see Kyel hovering over him, blue eyes concerned, black face set in a hard mask of anger and frustration. Jansson prayed neither emotion was directed at him. "Kyel?" He murmured the name with more of a question than he'd intended.

"It's me, Jans. Are you all right?"

Jansson sat up slowly, taking in his surroundings. He was in a cavern of some sort. Torchlight flickered against jagged gray stone walls, casting eerie shadows across the dirt floor, and sending acrid smoke curling upward to the high domed ceiling. There were several piles of what looked to be blankets and a stack of wooden crates along one wall. Other than that, the cavern was empty. Jansson looked back at Kyel questioningly.

"You tell me," Kyel said, anger evident in his voice.

Jansson hesitated, unsure if he was with the Nydiri-Kyel or the real Kyel. He started as one of the blanket piles suddenly moved.

"Is he awake yet?" Elek boomed from amidst the fabric.

"He is," Kyel replied, glancing over. "Though he doesn't seem to be as talkative as usual." He returned his gaze to Jansson. "Do you remember what happened to you, Jansson?"

Jansson thought back. He and *Kyel* had left Druce's room and gone toward Jansson's. He remembered opening the door and stepping inside. Then...he frowned, concentrating...then...he caught his breath. The Immix! Someone had Immixed him. Forcibly and against his will. Which meant...he groaned in dismay. He had been replaced by a Nydiri. "Dar," he mumbled.

"Dar?" Kyel repeated, puzzled. "What about him?"

"He's alone..." Again Jansson hesitated, looking from Kyel to Elek and back.

Kyel abruptly shot to his feet, his face contorting in frustration. He took several steps first one way, then the other, then stopped and flung his hands up. "Firesass!" he finally raged, his voice echoing from wall to wall.

Jansson stared at him in shock, then leapt to his feet and gave Kyel a fierce hug. Kyel started in surprise but returned the embrace with obvious relief.

"Gods, Kyel!" Jansson cried. "I've been worried sick about you! How long have you been here? How did you get here?" He paused. "Where is here?"

"Where is Treyas?" Elek asked, rising.

Jansson exhaled slowly. "He went looking for the twins and Elecka."

Kyel drew a small breath. "What happened to them?"

"Treyas thinks they TravelSpelled. Probably to get away from the Nydiri."

"Nydiri?" Elek cried, storming toward them. His red sorcerer robes billowed out behind him making him resemble an approaching dragon.

"I think you'd better start at the beginning," Kyel said calmly. He reseated himself, drawing Elek with him.

Jansson looked at the two before him. "How long have you been here?"

"This is my fourth day," Kyel replied. "Elek has been here,"

"Two weeks!" Elek interrupted. "Two weeks without my magic!"

Kyel laid a restraining hand on the sorcerer's arm. "Please, Jansson, tell us what happened. We know only that someone has held Immix with us both."

Jansson nodded, although his insides trembled at the mere thought that a Nydiri had Spelled everyone to Dalziel in the first place. "It's the Nydiri again, Kyel. They're impersonating both you and Elek. And from what I gather, it was a fake Elek who set up this Alliance meeting in the first place."

"That much I know!" Elek boomed. "Kyel told me."

"Elek, please, let him finish," Kyel said quietly.

"Obviously it was a trap from the beginning," Jansson said. "You, Kyel, must have been snatched at the crossing of the dimensional void, which makes sense now. Both Elecka and I lost the MindLink with you. I just thought it was because you were angry with me."

"Angry?" Kyel shook his head in confusion.

"It seems to be the Nydiri intent to stir up hard feelings between the humans and the elves. Apparently, they'd like us to go to war. I guess I'm here because I know too much, though it was actually Elecka who figured everything out. She knew it wasn't you from the onset."

Pride flitted through Kyel's eyes before his gaze resettled on Jansson. "How long did it take you to figure it out?"

Jansson flushed. "I didn't. There were too many other strange things going on." He related the story of the wine, the woman in his bed, and the fact that the Nydiri-Kyel had signed over a hefty chunk of Odora Dava to the Dalzielians. Kyel looked hurt and just a little angry.

"I would never do that, Jans," he said. "You are the Davan king, not me. Besides, if the Dalziel officials wish to establish an outpost in Glede, there are far larger, less populated provinces to consider."

Jansson grinned and reached out to grip Kyel's forearm. "Gods! It's good to be back with you."

"Tell me something," Kyel said. "How did you know I was the real Kyel? That this was not just an elaborate illusion and I with it?"

"Easy. It was your language. The real Kyel wouldn't say firesass unless he was completely at a loss for words. So, it wouldn't have been something that would have carried over in the Immix. The Nydiri-Kyel wouldn't say it either, then. But you said it here. Since the Nydiri-Kyel can't think for himself without giving himself away, I knew you had to be the real Kyel. Simple."

Kyel stared at him in bewilderment. "So, you knew it was me because I said something that I would never say?"

"Exactly."

Kyel's eyebrows rose in surprise, then he shook his head. "I'm afraid your sense of logic escapes me, Jansson. Tell us what else happened."

"Well, after the twins and Elecka convinced me, I told Treyas and Dar. Then the twins and Elecka disappeared. Treyas did a StrandSearch but he couldn't tell if the Nydiri had taken the children or if the children had fled from the Nydiri. They also took one of the servants with them, a kitchen girl named Enid. I'm pretty sure she's Thomlin's SoulMate, too."

Kyel and Elek exchanged startled glances. Jansson shrugged. "It happens. Treyas has already warned him about the possible consequences but it looks to me like we're going to have to pursue an alliance with Dalziel for real." He paused. "One other thing. Druce has Yunyo."

Kyel sighed. "I'd guessed as much. Does Treyas know?"

Jansson nodded. "Unfortunately, yes. And you know Trey. His heart is on his sleeve. He's a mess. He's HealBonded to Druce and, despite Dar's warnings, he refuses to drop the bond. Dar's put Druce into a MageSleep and he gives him round the clock treatments as well." Jansson started, a sudden thought occurring to him. "Kyel, what about the magic? Why haven't you just Spelled out of here?"

Anger settled in the blue eyes. "Because, Jansson, this entire mountain we're imprisoned in, contains iron in its purest form. I don't even have enough magic to MindLink."

Jansson frowned. "Then it's gone? Not Blocked? Why don't I feel anything bad, then? Usually I do."

Kyel laid a reassuring hand on his shoulder. "After our ordeal in the Caves of Challenge, I MageProtected our MindLink."

"What does that mean?"

"It means," Elek answered, "that you won't have a pit of despair in your little brain every time the MindLink is compromised."

Kyel flashed him a sour look. "It simply means, Jansson, that you will not notice a severed MindLink."

"What if I want to notice?" Jansson demanded. "What if I don't want my MindLink MageProtected?"

"Why wouldn't you?" Kyel asked in surprise. "You are always telling me how uncomfortable it is to have,"

"But, Kyel," Jansson interrupted, his voice tight with annoyance, "if I hadn't been MageProtected, I would have known that you weren't really you the minute you appeared!" He frowned, not sure what he had just said. "Anyway, I like knowing when our MindLink has been compromised! It's...it's reassuring. Somehow."

Kyel eyed him, obviously confused. "Very well, then. I thought I was helping. When we return to magic, I will remove the MageProtect and you can once more suffer."

"Thank you," Jansson replied, just as confused as Kyel. He looked about the cavern. "So, how do we get out of here?" He rose and began to explore.

"If I had my magic," Elek seethed, "I'd blow the top clear off this mountain!"

"But you don't," Kyel said. "Continually wishing for something you don't have is pointless."

Elek glared at him. "You're too damn pragmatic. All of you black elves are! Hellfires! It's a wonder you accomplish anything at all. Sitting around discussing things to death instead of just doing."

Kyel regarded him calmly. "A plan well thought out is a plan well executed," he said. "You're just upset because you don't have magic. And might I point out that you went a good many years without it before."

"By choice," Elek growled. "Not by force."

Jansson had ignored most of Elek's and Kyel's squabbling as he investigated the stacked crates, which he found were filled with food and drink. He knew their bickering to be lacking in true animosity. The sorcerer and black elf had been friends for decades, ever since they were young. They were both powerful with their respective magics, both used to having it at their command. Jansson didn't doubt their irritability and, instinctively he directed a bit of calming bardic magic their way.

Elek was on his feet at once, while Kyel gasped openly. Jansson dropped the tin of tea he'd picked up from a crate, and looked to Kyel in alarm. "What's the matter?"

"Magic!" Elek answered. "You have magic!"

"Well, yes," Jansson mumbled. "For all the good it'll do. It's only bardic."

"But that may be enough," Kyel said rising.

"Enough for what? It's not like I can TravelSpell."

"No, but I can." Kyel studied him thoughtfully. "If you could gather enough magic to Ward me against this iron, I might be able to pull enough magic to cast my own TravelSpell."

"I don't know how to Ward," Jansson pointed out.

"It's not too unlike your empathic shields," Kyel told him. "You learned how to do that. You can learn how to do this."

"But I don't know how to gather magic either," Jansson protested weakly, guessing accurately what Kyel's response to that would be.

"Again, you can learn," the black elf said.

"It'll take a lot of time," Jansson countered.

"Do you see anything more pressing for us to do?" Kyel asked with just a trace of amusement showing in his eyes.

Jansson acquiesced. "All right, all right. But, Kyel, please promise me one thing. Remember that I am your adopted son. I have no elfin blood. My magic is limited to bardic. I may not be able to do this."

"Are you asking for my patience, Jansson?" Kyel mused.

"That and your understanding."

Kyel draped one long, sinewy arm across Jansson's shoulders. "When am I not patient and understanding, Jansson?"

Jansson drew a deep breath and rolled his eyes. "When you're without your magic, when you're excessively worried, when you're,"

Kyel silenced him with a gentle squeeze. "First, let's have some breakfast. Then, I want you to tell me everything that has transpired since your arrival in Dalziel. Then, we'll start our lessons."

Jansson groaned softly in resignation.

Thomlin woke stiff, sore, wet and irritable. The little group had been forced to spend the night in the bog and his silks were soaked through. His tunic clung to him like a thing alive and he stripped it off with a grimace, hampered by the tunic belt binding his left wrist.

His gaze traveled along the belt. It was wrapped securely about Enid's right wrist, then tied into a strong knot with Vantann's belt. His belt in turn bound him and Elecka. In this way, none of the four could succumb to the Segora's hypnosis without alerting the others.

Thomlin trembled, his ears picking up the strange clicking noise made by the Segora. Enid had pointed it out to them the previous evening and Thomlin had been half awake the entire night listening. This one sounded close and Thomlin's gaze darted about the dark, misty bog. So far, none of the Segora had been seen, though their calls had gone on all night, starting just after sunset.

Thomlin untied his wrist and shook the tunic free, then rose. Still, there was no sign of the flightless bird, though standing had reminded him of morning bodily functions. He glanced down at the others, then sought out a place to relieve himself away from them.

That accomplished, Thomlin turned back toward the others, then stopped. Something out in the mist was glowing red. He hesitated, then took several steps toward it, trying to make out what it was. He was only vaguely aware that the clicking noise had increased in intensity. He walked slowly, squinting against the gray morning light, and finally realized that the two red spots were eyes. Bright red eyes set in a feathered black face. The creature was no more than a big, round ball of black with long spindly legs, the feet hidden beneath the slimy waters. As Thomlin watched, the creature began to sway from side to side, its red gaze locked on Thomlin's. He frowned, puzzled at this strange behavior and moved closer to investigate.

He noticed that he had left the path and was almost knee deep in muck, but the overpowering urge to see this creature up close took precedence and he continued on. He had almost reached it when something heavy plunged into the water near him, showering him with smelly, black water. The creature, startled, fled, flapping its useless wings and sending more of the brackish water over Thomlin.

He blinked and shook his head dizzily, then gasped as hands closed about his arm and yanked him backward onto the path. He whirled and looked into the terror-stricken faces of his companions.

"Gods, Thoms!" Vantann cried, still gripping his arm. "What in Tor's hell were you doing?"

"I... I was just..." Thomlin stammered, not exactly sure what he had been doing. He looked at Enid. "That was a Segora, wasn't it?"

She nodded.

"And you were almost its breakfast," Elecka put in. "If Enid hadn't wakened us, you might well have been."

Thomlin's heart skipped a beat and his knees suddenly felt weak. He clutched Enid to him in a hug of gratitude, noticing that she was trembling almost as hard as he was. "What did you throw at it?" he asked Vantann. "I didn't see anything you could have used."

"I didn't throw anything," Vantann said. "Enid did."

Thomlin glanced at her in question. She blushed and lifted her skirts slightly. One of her boots was missing. "I couldn't think of anything else, M'Lord," she said.

"Effective," Thomlin said with a hesitant smile, "but not very practical. I'll see if I can find it for you." He waded back into the water and felt about with his foot. It took some searching but at last he found the boot and hefted it from the water, then sloshed back to Enid.

She accepted it with a grimace and poured muddy water out, then sighed and put it back on. Elecka handed Thomlin his tunic, which she had been clutching. "You'd better put this back on, too, unless you prefer being eaten alive by insects."

"Besides," Vantann teased, "no one wants to look at your scrawny little chest."

"How do you know?" Thomlin asked, glancing at Enid. She went bright red and Thomlin chuckled, pulling on his tunic. "Gods! I'm hungry."

"Me, too," Vantann agreed. "But I don't see anything to eat here. We'll just have to,"

"There's a lot of food here," Enid said, then hastily added, "M'Lords."

"Enid, stop," Thomlin pleaded. "Just call us by our given names or so help me, I'll give you a title."

She looked at him, startled and Vantann quickly picked up on the idea. "He's right, your Ladyship. We're equals here. So, if you insist on calling us Lords, then by rights, you'll be a Lady."

"N...no," she breathed, obviously appalled. "You...you can't, M'Lord." She looked wildly at Elecka. "Tell them, M'Lady, tell them!"

Elecka gave a sly smile. "Tell them what, M'Lady?"

Enid caught at her breath, her face flaming. Her gaze darted from one to the other and abruptly there were tears in her eyes. "You tease me," she murmured, anger edging her voice. "For what reason?"

"Enid, we're not teasing you," Thomlin said softly. He reached out and pulled her closer, surprised that she allowed it. "Why can't you see that? We like you. We want to be friends."

"You don't call your friends M'Lord and M'Lady do you?" Vantann asked.

"No," Enid admitted, "but my friends are not royalty, Your Highness."

Elecka smiled and laid a hand on her arm. "They are now."

Thomlin kissed the back of Enid's hand. "Now, suppose you tell us just where all of this food is."

Enid paused only briefly, then reached into her dry boot and pulled out a dagger.

Thomlin drew back with a gasp. "Do you always carry a dagger in your boot?"

Enid glanced at the wickedly sharp blade. "Not always, Your Highness," she admitted. "Just since the Nydiri arrived with their dark magic."

The twins exchanged startled looks. "You knew about them?" Vantann asked.

Enid ignored the question and turned to the bog. She knelt down and plunged her arms into the fetid water. Eventually, small white tubers popped to the surface. These she gathered, swished as clean as she could, and handed up to Thomlin. She moved to another spot in the bog and used her dagger to cut the unripe, green heads of several cattail, which she handed to Vantann. Next, she again reached beneath the waters and came up with a handful of bulbs. "Now," she said, "if we can get a fire going, we can eat, Your Highnesses."

The three elves stared at her in amazement. Enid eyed them, shrugged and walked away. They followed silently. Finally, Enid stopped, put down the bulbs and began to stack branches and reeds into a tight pile. Thomlin laid the cattail heads aside to help, though he had no idea what Enid would use to start the fire. When the fire pit was done, Enid chose a long, dry stick and walked to a thick pile of rotting material. She shoved the stick deep into the smelly mess and began to roll the exposed part rapidly between her palms.

The others watched curiously, then all three gasped as Enid yanked the reed out of the muck and it burst into flame. Quickly, she fed it to the material in the fire pit and, in just moments, had a pleasant fire going. Thomlin was thoroughly astounded.

"So, what do we do with these?" Vantann asked, gesturing at the foodstuffs. "And *don't* call me Highness."

"The tubers we roast," Enid said, after a moment. "The cattails as well. The bulbs will provide us with water since we can't drink the water here, Your..." She broke off, flushing.

Thomlin grinned at her. "You're learning," he teased.

"Speaking of learning, where did you learn all of this?" Vantann asked, as they waited for the food to cook.

Enid shrugged. "My father. He loved the land and living off it. He used to go out for weeks at a time with absolutely no supplies just to prove he could do it. Of course, whenever he took me along, he was careful to pack well. Still, we lived with what we found for the most part. It was fun." She sighed heavily, sadly. "I miss him."

"He's dead, then?" Elecka asked softly.

Enid nodded. "He was quite advanced in age when he sired me. He died of old age on one of his trips. The gods willed that I was with him to lay him to rest as he had wished. Buried beneath the earth that he so loved." She exhaled softly, as if purging herself of painful memories and handed around the cooked cattail heads.

"Enid," Elecka said, "tell us what you know of the Nydiri."

Enid drew a deep breath. "I suspect their arrival has something to do with Anwyl. He's an old sorcerer who lives in northern Dalziel. He likes to visit other dimensions, and I think he just went to the wrong one."

Thomlin chewed thoughtfully on his meal, his gaze on the girl. It was apparent that not only was she self-sufficient, she was also well-learned. And once told to refrain from using titles, she seemed to find it easy to comply. In fact, very easy, as if using titles was a strain she was not wholly accustomed to. Not common traits of a simple kitchen-girl who had been raised to obey without question. He began to wonder about her background.

"At any rate," she continued, poking at a tuber with a stick, "they're here. From what you've said, I take it they're capable of impersonating other people. That would explain a lot. Here." She passed around several hot tubers apiece.

"How would that explain a lot?" Vantann asked.

"People have been acting strange," Enid replied. "They are and they aren't the same. I don't know. It's hard to explain."

"You don't need to," Thomlin said with a grimace. "We understand completely. Elecka's father and our grandfather have been replaced by Nydiri."

Enid looked at Elecka with empathy. "I'm so sorry for you."

"I'm going to find him," Elecka said. "Wherever he is, I'm going to find him."

Enid drew a slow breath, her gaze traveling over the others faces. "I would ask that you refrain from magic use. I think the Nydiri can detect it. It would be like sending up a smoke signal to our whereabouts."

Vantann swallowed his bite and regarded her suspiciously. "You seem to know a lot about the Nydiri all of a sudden."

"Vans!" Thomlin chastised.

"Well, it's true!" Vantann protested. "Back at the Session chambers, she acted like an empty-headed farm girl. Now, she's suddenly able to pull food from swampland, handle a dagger and spout information like a...a..."

"Person with a brain?" Enid snapped. She came to her feet, anger racing across her face. "Just because I work to survive doesn't mean I don't have a thirst for knowledge. I suppose it would surprise you to know that I can read, that I've read over half of the books in the Chamber library. I can also speak in several different languages and I've begun teaching myself advanced healing. I'm only sixteen, yet I've helped deliver over a dozen babies, both in my village and in neighboring ones. While it's true that I've not dealt with royalty before, I've certainly had my share of dealing with ambassadors and lords from many different areas. And if I came across as an empty-headed farm girl, it was because I chose to. Your Highness!" she added testily.

The three elves stared at her in astonishment, then Thomlin broke into a wide grin, his blue eyes awash with awe and delight. He didn't care one bit that she suddenly seemed so much more than a kitchen girl. He didn't even care enough to be suspicious or wary. He rose and swept Enid into a giddy embrace. "You're wonderful!" he cried. "Gods! I've never met anyone like you. I never will. I love you!"

"Thoms!" Elecka gasped.

"Oh, tens!" Vans mumbled.

Thomlin released Enid as if he had been stung. His gaze darted from her to Vantann, to Elecka and back to Enid. She was staring at him, her face expressionless. Thomlin drew a deep breath, took hold of her hands and squeezed them gently. "There," he murmured, "I've said it. I love you, Enid. Make of it what you will."

Chapter Eleven

Treyas shielded his eyes from the afternoon sun and once more looked east. He could clearly make out two riders pursuing him. With a soft curse, he guided his horse farther upward into the rocky, brushy hills. It was the wrong direction. He knew that, knew that the four youths he was searching for were south of him. Yet, he dared not go in that direction.

He had pulled a LocatorStrand just hours ago, sure that he was far enough from the Session Chambers for it to go undetected. Apparently, he was wrong. The mysterious riders had appeared less than an hour later and were fast closing the gap. *Well,* Treyas thought, *let them come. They won't find me easy to catch.*

He had already tested Dalziel's magic. Out here it was unstable. Heavy on the sorcery, practically non-existent on the elfin. There had been barely enough for the LocatorStrand. There certainly wasn't enough to TravelSpell or put up a good fight. Or to keep the HealBond intact. That perhaps bothered him the most - losing the HealBond with Druce. He prayed that Darosenim could take up the slack.

He urged his horse around a rock outcropping, following a hunch, and smiled at what he saw before him. A small lake lay nestled in gray rock, its placid waters sparkling in the sunshine. Though Treyas much preferred working with river magic, the lake would do. He dismounted and led his roan down the gentle slope to the lake's edge. He hunkered down and dipped his hand into the water. It was bitter cold and he sucked in his breath, resisting the urge to pull back.

The naiad MagicWeb appeared and Treyas grimaced. It was just as unstable and confusing to him as the elfin magic was. Using it to cast a TravelSpell would be extremely risky, yet what choice did he have? The only sure methods to slay a Nydiri were fire, drowning and donkey hair, none of which he had at his disposal. Scowling, he straightened and un-strapped his pack from the horse. It carried food, drink, blankets, his cloak, a dagger and a flint. The latter two he took out. He strapped the scabbard to his side, and secured the flint in his tunic pocket. The cloak went across his shoulders, as did one blanket. The food he ignored, words of bewitched meals ringing in his memory. Tobbar, the little boy rescued from Winze's dark coven, had claimed the Nydiri put Spells on their food to make their captives compliant. It wasn't something Treyas wanted to experience first hand. He took out the waterskin, emptied it of the Chambers drink and refilled it from the lake, then slung it across his shoulder. Satisfied that he would have everything he needed, he hunkered down and once more plunged his hand into the water.

The naiad web appeared and he began to reassemble the MagicStrands to something workable, praying all the while that he could come up something before his pursuers arrived. The sound of horse hooves on stone told him he'd failed. He was about to wade into the water to gain easier access to the magic when one of the riders called out. Treyas whirled, astonished and confused. Darosenim and Druce rode toward him.

"What in Tor's..." Treyas started, then caught at Druce as he slumped in the saddle. "Dar, what are you doing?"

Darosenim leapt from his horse and helped Treyas lower Druce to the ground. "MindLink me," he ordered.

"I can't," Treyas replied. "There's not enough elfin magic."

Darosenim frowned, then sought out a small stick and scratched the code word in the mud. Treyas sighed and did likewise. Druce watched them in puzzlement.

"What's happened?" Treyas asked.

"They've got Jans," Darosenim replied glumly. "They must have taken him last night after he left us. I...I just couldn't stay there. After morning Session, I woke Druce, stole some horses and left." He sagged to the ground beside Druce, his face weary and unhappy. "I know I should have stayed. I've probably tipped them off but, baerns, Treyas, I felt so alone. So painfully alone."

Treyas sat down and laid a hand on the mage's shoulder. "It's all right, Dar. I fully understand." He looked to Druce, who still had not said a word. "How are you feeling?"

Druce met his gaze. "Like hell, to be honest. I suppose Dar told you about the Yunyo?"

"Yes. I would have preferred the news from you though."

"Coals, Trey, how could I tell you? You're my SoulMate. I couldn't hurt you like that."

"Druce," Treyas said softly, "it was going to hurt no matter when you told me. What I want to know is, how did you keep it from me? Why didn't I sense it on the MindLink or through the SoulMate bond?"

Druce cringed. "I asked Darosenim to Block it for me."

Treyas' gaze shot to the mage, who merely shrugged and averted his gaze.

"I'm sorry, Trey," Druce mumbled. "I'm sorry I have to put you through this. I wish I could,"

"Sorry? Druce, please." Treyas draped his arm about the Merian's shoulders. "Don't apologize for something that isn't your fault. I'm sure you don't want this anymore than I do." He gave Druce a gentle squeeze. "We're going to beat this, Druce. You and I together. I promise."

"Trey," Darosenim cautioned gently.

Treyas looked over at him, his face firm. "It'll happen, Dar. I just know it. Somehow, it'll happen."

Darosenim searched his face sadly, then shook his head. "With your persistence, I have no doubt it will." He glanced about them. "Where do we go from here? They're going to be after us as soon as I don't show up for afternoon Session."

Treyas glanced at the sun. "Another hour then? That is, if no one checks Druce's room."

"They won't. I told them I would be working with Druce and that I needed complete isolation from any other magic. And I locked the door."

"How did you get Druce out, then?"

"He shoved me through the window," Druce grumbled. "I had to climb down some sort of trellis with very spiny bushes."

Darosenim half-smiled. "That was all I could think of." He shrugged. "I panicked."

"Well, no matter," Treyas said. "You're here and I can't say I'm completely unhappy about it, either. How are you going to take to traveling, Druce?"

Druce eyed him warily. "That all depends. Are we speaking of horses or magic?"

Treyas sighed. "Horses. The magic here is very different. Have you noticed, Dar?"

"I should say so. It takes me a good fifteen minutes to reorganize it to workable levels." He regarded Treyas with frustration. "It's really me, Treyas. You don't have to keep testing it."

Treyas rose and walked closer to the water, his back to the others. He wished he knew for certain. As far as the code word, a Nydiri could know that if he'd Immixed Darosenim. And what of Druce? With no magic, Treyas couldn't even be sure of him. And, if he wasn't sure, absolutely sure, he would not seek out the twins and Elecka. He would not willingly lead the Nydiri directly to them. Yet, that had been his sole purpose for leaving the Session Chambers. He stared thoughtfully at the water shimmering before him and wondered if he could stabilize the magic well enough to MindLink. He guessed he would have to try. It was pointless to ride around in circles accomplishing nothing.

And if these two men with him were Nydiri? What then? How could he avoid capture? He had no weapons he could use against them. They could possess him easily and completely. No. The only thing he could do was to continue to treat them both as the real thing, wait for a good opportunity to verify it and have a well-planned method of escape if he couldn't.

He squared his shoulders and looked back at Darosenim. "I didn't mean to test you, Dar. I just wasn't sure if the sorcery magic was as confused as the elfin. Apparently, it is. Which means, looking for the children is going to be like looking for a copper in a wheat field. Where do we start?"

"I don't know. Can't you use your naiad magic to pull a LocaterStrand?"

"I've tried," Treyas lied. "I suppose I could try again, but that water's damn cold. There's no telling how long I'd have to stand in it to reassemble the magic."

"Maybe this will help then." Darosenim pulled a scroll from his tunic and handed it up to Treyas. "It's a map. At morning Session I got the topic turned around to the possibility of establishing our own outpost in Dalziel. Neslin provided the map to show why it wouldn't be possible. Baerns, Treyas, you should have heard Jansson and Kyel going at it. Jansson tried to pull me into siding against the elves. I'll tell you one thing, if those Nydiri impersonating Kyel and Jansson return to Glede, there will be a war. We have to find the real Kyel and Jansson before that happens."

Treyas had unrolled the map to study it but now looked to Darosenim, startled. He had not thought about the fake Kings going to Glede. It suddenly became a very real threat. He swallowed hard and returned his attention to the map, though his mind was whirling so fast, he wasn't really seeing it.

This had to be the real Dar, he thought. *A Nydiri wouldn't relay information like this, wouldn't be so worried about finding the real Kyel and Jansson. Unless...unless it was part of the plan to lure me into trust.* Gods! This circle of doubt was not only frustrating, it was frightening. He glanced up briefly to find Darosenim watching him, his face taut, his mouth drawn into a firm white line.

Abruptly, the mage leapt to his feet, anger ripping across his face. Treyas stumbled backward into the water as Darosenim's dagger appeared in his hand. Druce was on his feet at once, his pale face alarmed.

"You don't believe me, do you?" Darosenim cried. "Maybe this will convince you of who I am!" He drove the point of the dagger into his finger. Bright red blood spurted out and Darosenim waved his hand in Treyas' face. "Do you see it? It's red, Treyas! Do Nydiri have red blood?"

Treyas gaped at him, his memories overwhelming him. He remembered now, remembered seeing the Nydiri fall during the battle in Winze. He had thought it a trick of the orange moonlight that night, or his imagination, but the Nydiri blood had been pink. Pale, frothy pink, as if it were missing the key element that would make them human. He shuddered, looking at the blood that ran from Darosenim's finger to drip in the water at his feet.

"Baerns, Treyas!" the mage went on in a softer voice. "If you don't believe I am who I say I am, then I'll leave. But I won't go back to the Chambers." Tears gathered in his blue eyes. "I can't stand to see Jansson and know it's not really him. I feel lost, Treyas, lost and alone. I don't know what to do."

Treyas reached up and took Darosenim's bloody hand between both of his. "Dar," he whispered, "I'm so sorry. Forgive me."

Darosenim nodded, the knife slipped from his fingers and he bent his head to weep. Treyas held him close, his own heart aching. Druce slowly retrieved the dagger, then brought his gaze up to meet Treyas'. "I think we need to be sure all around," he said softly and before Treyas could stop him, he, too, drew blood from his finger.

Darosenim pulled away from Treyas to stare at Druce in disbelief. The Merian gave a half smile, shrugged and handed the dagger to Treyas.

"Oh, tens," Treyas muttered and winced as he, too, pierced his finger.

Darosenim chuckled wryly. "This is just great," he said. "If we have to do this every time we wake or are away from each other, we'll either bleed to death or die of infection."

Treyas couldn't help but laugh at the irony of it all. He held up his bleeding finger. "Why don't we make good use of it then? Blood brothers?"

Druce grinned. "Why not?"

The three of them pressed their fingers together gently, meshing blood of elf, Merian and Karsab. And, as they did, Treyas felt a surge in the naiad magic. He gasped, his gaze flying to Darosenim. "Dar! Your magic! I can use it to supplement the naiad!"

Druce groaned, dropping to soak his finger in the cold waters of the lake. "Does that mean a TravelSpell, Trey? Because I don't think I'm up to that just yet."

Treyas looked at him with a small smile. "No, Druce, no TravelSpell. The Nydiri would probably trace it anyway. It just means that we're not completely helpless, that we will have some magic at our disposal. As for how you're feeling - should we go on or not?"

Druce nodded. "I can manage for a few more hours." He straightened with a weary smile. "But I'd love to have that HealBond back."

Treyas gave his shoulder a gentle squeeze, then looked to Darosenim. "Ordinarily, I'd ask for a spark of magic to heal these wounds, but I think we'll just have to make do with wrapping them."

Darosenim nodded, then laughed again. He shook his head at his own desperate act and went to get some bandaging material from Treyas' pack.

Pepin stopped outside the dining hall doors. El'leigh was in there and Pepin hadn't quite worked up the desire to confront her. Yet, he had told Galen he would apologize for the afternoon's prank with the dragonlings. He would have to do it. He reached for the heavy, silver door handle and it turned under his touch. El'leigh's maid-servant slipped out, carrying a writhing, squalling little girl.

"Charis, sweet thing," Pepin said, his face relaxing into warm smiles.

The little girl stopped her wailing and turned large, innocent brown eyes on Pepin. She had El'leigh's slight build but Andison's coloring with her dark curls tumbling about a face as pale as the moonlight. "Pin!" she squealed, reaching for him. The maid-servant eagerly relinquished the squirming child to Pepin's waiting arms.

"So, what's Charis all mad about?" Pepin asked the little girl.

"I don't go to bed," Charis cried, wrapping her tiny little arms about his neck.

"Oh, I see. You think you're not sleepy, don't you?"

Charis nodded, her dark curls bobbing. Pepin grinned. "But what if I can find sleepy on you?" he asked.

Charis giggled. "Not on me," she proclaimed.

Pepin looked at her through narrowed eyes, his signal that the little game he played with both Charis and his own daughter was about to begin. "We'll just have to see, won't we?" He touched her satin-clad feet. "No, no sleepy there." He felt her knee beneath her velvet gown. "No, no sleepy there." He rolled his eyes and Charis laughed, covering her tummy with one hand, while hanging onto his neck with the other. "No fair!" Pepin told her in mock seriousness. She yanked her hand away, then giggled happily when he touched a finger to her stomach. "No, no sleepy there."

His voice softened, and the game proceeded slowly, moving to her shoulder, her elbow, her hand, each finger, her mouth, ears and nose, until, finally, Pepin lightly touched each drooping eyelid. "Ah," he whispered, "I found the sleepy." He gave her a gentle kiss on each smooth round cheek. "Goodnight, Charis." Carefully he handed her back to the maid-servant, who flashed him a smile of gratitude, then took the drowsy child away.

Pepin watched them go, his heart aching for home. With a heavy sigh, he squared his shoulders and entered the dining hall. El'leigh looked up at him from where she sat near the hearth. She was dressed in the same pale blue velvet as Charis, her hair braided to one side. She held a half empty glass of wine and her brown cheeks were flushed, though Pepin wasn't sure if it was from the heat of the wine or the fire. He approached her slowly, once more caught off guard by her fragile beauty. She said nothing, but fixed her dark eyes on him. Pepin stopped before her.

"I owe you an apology," he said. "My actions this afternoon were childish and unnecessary. I'm sorry if I frightened you." He paused, but she remained quiet and he went on. "I'll be leaving in the morning for Taithleach, El'leigh."

"What!" she snapped, anger flashing across her face. "I told you that,"

"I know what you told me," Pepin interrupted. "But, as DragonMaster, I feel it's in the best interests of Mere Odain to fully use the dragonlings. They need to run through drills. To do that, they need space, the open spaces that Taithleach offers."

"They seemed to have adequate space this afternoon!" she said tightly.

A flush crept over Pepin's face but he chose to ignore her words. "I shouldn't be gone long. The dragonlings have apparently been,"

"No!" She interrupted and rose. She drained her glass and set it down hard on the small table. "You will not be taking the dragonlings to Taithleach. You will not be taking the dragonlings anywhere!"

"Why not?" Pepin countered, his own anger surfacing. "I see precious little reason to stay here. My calling to Mere Odain involves handling of the dragons, not you!"

El'leigh's hand flew out, striking him sharply across the cheek. Pepin caught his breath in pain and fury, his hands closing to fists at his side. "I apologize," he said through a clenched jaw, chastising himself for allowing El'leigh to rouse his anger so.

El'leigh glared at him. "Mere Odain's strength does not lie in some scrawny halflings," she seethed. "It lies with the true-bred of the country, those of power who are loyal to the crown. I suggest, DragonMaster, that you would do well to remember that and put your energies where they belong." She whirled and strode from the room.

Pepin stared after her, rage burning in his chest. He had not missed her double meaning, comparing him to the dragonlings. Well, he fumed, perhaps we are both halflings and small of stature, but we're both powerful in our own right. And I'll prove it. He stormed from the room, his angry steps taking him outside the palace and toward the dragon mews.

The sun had set, plunging the land into chilly darkness and Pepin found himself longing for the pleasantly warm springs of Aelfdene. Gods! I hate this place! I've always hated this place. Nothing good had ever come out of his time in Mere Odain. First, there had been his desperate search for Fayemera, the agonizing pain of sharing her injury. That was when he was still LifePledged to her, before his own experience had shown him the risk of such a pledge.

Then, Irida had shown up and tried to convince Pepin and El'leigh that her place was the throne, and his, at her side. Fayemera, his beloved Fayemera, had died stopping Irida. Pepin trembled, amazed that after all of these years, thoughts of Fayemera's death could still bring tears. He brushed them aside and stumbled into the lamplit mews, his feet automatically turning him toward Aleron's stall.

He was Fayemera's kin, that much Pepin knew, though just how he knew was unclear. Aleron had the same coloring, the same graceful build, the same way of peering at him with slightly tilted head. The only difference aside from their respective sexes, was Aleron's eyes. His were as green as Taithleach's meadows. Fayemera's had been blue as the summer sky.

Aleron lifted his head at Pepin's approach and puffed smoke gently from his nostrils.

"Good evening, sir," Pepin murmured and reached out to stroke the dragon's snout, watching the lamplight flicker on Aleron's iridescent scales.

Aleron cocked his head just slightly to peer at Pepin through one enormous green eye and abruptly Pepin was weeping. He laid his forehead against Aleron's neck, feeling again the pain of seeing Fayemera die. Sometimes he wished he had never known about her, about Mere Odain, about Pe'pinlaidh. Life with Sarben and his adopted family in the north territory of Karsaba had been good. Days filled with lessons and swimming in the hot springs, nights with pleasant dreams in a safe, warm environment.

And then Treyas had shown up. Much as Pepin loved him, he sometimes wished that meeting had not taken place. He had gone with Treyas and Kyel, left the only home he had ever known for a life of uncertainty and clashing emotions. Now, here he was, once again leaving a home he loved, people he loved, for something frightening and unclear. He wondered if he would ever find a place he belonged, a place he could stay and live out his life.

"Pepin?" Ken's voice reached him, surprised and questioning.

Pepin hurriedly dried his face on one sleeve as Ken stepped into the stall. Aleron greeted him with an affectionate hiss, and Ken rubbed the dragon's snout, his gaze on Pepin.

"Ken, I...uh...I was..." Pepin sniffed, keeping his face turned away, facing the shadowy darkness of the stall.

"I'm sorry, Pepin," Ken said softly. "I didn't mean to intrude."

"No, you're not. Intruding, I mean." Pepin shrugged. "Aleron's your dragon." He took a deep, shaky breath to compose himself, one hand absently stroking Aleron's scales. "What are you doing out here, anyway? It's late."

"Aleron's been restless as of late," Ken replied. He was quiet for a moment before continuing. "When's the last time you went for a moonlight flight?"

Pepin turned to him, startled. "It's been months. Why?"

"I think someone is asking to go." Ken smiled and gestured to Aleron.

The dragon had his head down in the position he'd been taught to allow a rider easy access to his back. His gaze was on Pepin and he fairly quivered with excitement. Pepin looked from Aleron to Ken. Ken took a heavy riding cloak off its peg. "Go," he said. "I'm getting tired of singing him to sleep every night. Maybe this is what he's been waiting for." He held the cloak out to Pepin, who took it slowly.

"Are you sure that,"

"Yes! Go!" Ken gave him a gentle push toward the door, then clucked at Aleron, who immediately shuffled after him.

Once outside, Pepin tied the cloak securely about his shoulders and climbed into the hollow at the base of Aleron's neck.

"Good flight," Ken said with a smile.

Aleron tensed, waiting for Pepin's command. When it came, the great dragon seemed to go straight up with just three powerful beats of his wings, then veered northwest, away from the palace and Mere Odain.

Jansson trembled, turning his gaze once more on Kyel. The black elf and Elek were seated not far from him, enjoying a meager dinner of tea and hard biscuits gleaned from the storage crates. It had been a long, uncomfortable day for Jansson. Though he was extremely glad to once more be united with Kyel, he was concerned about Darosenim. The mage was alone at the Session Chambers, surrounded by Nydiri going about their business of starting a war. Jansson wondered how long he would hold up under the stress, how much longer he could isolate himself with Druce. And Jansson also worried about Druce, how he was recovering, what would happen once he did? Would he accompany Dar to the meetings? Would he offer any input? Or would he simply find a horse and go after Treyas?

And what of Treyas? Where was he? Where were the twins? And Elecka? Who was Enid? Really.

"Jansson?" Kyel's voice broke into his jumbled thoughts.

"Argh!" Jansson cried, as the Strands of bardic magic he'd been holding, slipped away.

Kyel frowned. "Concentration and focus," he reminded.

"I was concentrating!" Jansson snapped. "Until you interrupted."

Elek grunted. "You looked like you were about to give birth," he mumbled.

Kyel shot him an exasperated look, then returned his attention to Jansson. "Holding MagicStrands should be subconscious. You should be able to carry on as you would normally. If those around you are aware of what you are doing, you defeat the purpose."

Jansson sighed, anger, frustration and fatigue clawing at his mind. "I'm not an elf," he reminded Kyel. "I'm a bard. We pull magic and feed it directly into song. Holding it is unnatural."

"Empathic healing is unnatural for most bards," Kyel told him. "Yet you do it." He paused, eyeing Jansson. "Come. Get something to eat. Then we can try again."

Jansson groaned softly and joined them. "What about sleep, Kyel? Or will we work all night?" He well knew of Kyel's adherence to duty. The elf had foregone sleep many times over the past years when he felt the situation had demanded it. Jansson, however, wasn't of the same mold. He needed his sleep to function properly, to keep his mind and reflexes sharp and alert. If Kyel began denying him proper rest, he would be one very irritable bard in one very short time. Fortunately, Kyel seemed to know this.

"No," he replied with a slight chuckle. "But the evening is yet young. We have a few more hours before you need your beauty rest."

Jansson glared at him, chewing absently on a biscuit. "How do you know what time it is? It could be the middle of the night for all we know. Gods, this place is starting to get to me. It's just too damn familiar." Though he had tried to keep his thoughts from going there, they nonetheless had returned him to Karsaba and his imprisonment in a cavern just such as this. At least that time there had been several small holes in the rock admitting light and air. Here, though the air was fresh enough, there was no light save from the three torches mounted on the rock walls. He had wondered early on why the torches hadn't burned out. Kyel had told him there they were the work of Dirin magic. If Jansson cursed the Nydiri for everything else, he was immensely grateful they hadn't left the cavern-prison in darkness. That would have been more than he could handle.

He tossed his biscuit back into the sack it had come from. "Isn't there anything else to eat? That's like chewing on a rock."

"There are some meat sticks," Kyel replied. "But go easy on them. I don't know how long we'll be here or if the Nydiri are planning on replenishing our food supplies. It may be that we have only what is here and when it is gone, it is gone."

"I don't plan to be here that long," Elek grumbled.

Kyel tossed him a wry smile. "Elek, when will you accept the fact that without your wristlet as a conduit, you have no magic?"

"That's another thing!" Elek retorted. "I'm tired of relying on a conduit to access my magic. This little incident proves how inadequate that is."

"And you would suggest what?" Kyel asked.

"Making the conduit a permanent part of my body," Elek told him. "If it was inside of me, no one could remove it."

"Unless they chose to remove that part of you containing the conduit," Kyel mused.

Jansson grimaced. "Please, if you two are going to discuss dismemberment, do it elsewhere and in quieter voices. I'm eating."

"Jansson, if we discussed things only when you weren't eating, nothing would ever get discussed," Kyel said dryly.

"Oh, ha, ha, Kyel," Jansson retorted. "Gods, it's bad enough being held prisoner here. Don't make it worse with your questionable humor."

Kyel chuckled softly, then returned to his conversation with Elek. "Although I can't think of any solution at the time, I quite agree with your assessment of a conduit being somewhat of a burden. Those many years I safe-guarded your wristlet left me unable to access sorcery magic."

Elek looked at him, startled. "You never told me that!"

Kyel shrugged. "It was unimportant."

"But what about now?" Jansson asked. "Why can't you access sorcery magic now?"

Kyel sighed and downed the last of his tea. "I had only begun my lessons of sorcery magic when I became caretaker of Elek's wristlet. It was not a great loss at the time. Once Elek's magic was restored to him and elfin magic was freed, I began again my studies. But, since I am an elf, sorcery magic is not an easy fit. Therefore I tied its use to elfin magic. As long as there was elfin magic, I could supplement it with sorcery." He glanced at Elek. "While you are pondering on how to conduct your magic without a conduit, perhaps you could also find a way for elves to override iron."

Elek grunted in frustration and settled down in his blankets, one arm flung across his eyes.

Jansson sat back against the wall, his thoughts spinning. He knew of iron and elves. Iron had imprisoned Pepin and Nila, had felled Ken, had almost brought about an Akuri stronghold in Mere Odain. Each time, another magic had worked its way past. Most notably naiad. Jansson wondered if Treyas could Spell him, Kyel and Elek from the mountain. But, how to reach Treyas? He couldn't MindLink. Neither could Kyel. Not here, at any rate. Unless, of course, there was a way to Ward him against the iron. Jansson sighed wearily. He knew Kyel was counting on him to do it. If using sorcery was not an easy fit for an elf, holding magic was not an easy fit for a bard.

Especially this bard, Jansson thought. He closed his eyes and yawned, his mind drifting.

For just a second, his empathic Gift touched at another and he started, his eyes popping open. Kyel regarded him with curiosity and question. Jansson remained still, trying again to connect empathically with whoever had touched him. But the path was gone, either Blocked or...most likely just his imagination.

"Shall we try again to gather some magic?" Kyel asked.

"All right, but not for much longer," Jansson agreed. "I'm spent, and you know how cranky I can get." The truth was, he wanted to explore his surroundings a bit more thoroughly with his empathy.

He settled back and reached for the bardic MagicStrands. Again, he felt the fleeting touch of an empath. Abandoning the MagicStrand, Jansson reached out with an EmpathicLink, something he knew would have repercussions later.

::Who are you?:: a startled voice connected. ::Go away! Leave me alone!::

::No! Wait!:: Jansson cried. ::I...I need your help. Where are you?::

::Leave me, demon voice!:: It sounded like a young boy.

Jansson sensed a short, hastily said prayer. ::I'm not a demon!:: he sent, his head beginning to reel from the strain of the Link. Pain shot through him, pain he tried unsuccessfully to keep to himself.

::Madra of Saints!:: the boy cried. ::You torment me! Go away!::

Jansson thought quickly. ::I will leave you for now,:: he sent, hating his next words, ::but you would do well to stay where you are. I will contact you again and if you are not there, it will be the worse for you.:: Another surge of pain ripped through Jansson and he heard the boy gasp.

::I will stay, demon,:: the boy said quickly. ::But release me from this pain, I beg you.::

Jansson let the Link go. He had no other choice. Kyel had guessed at his actions and now gripped his arm in anger and concern. "An EmpathicLink, Jansson? With whom?"

Jansson hesitated. If he told Kyel the truth, the black elf would forbid him to Link again. Twice he had almost killed himself by doing an EmpathicLink. He averted his gaze. "No one," he lied. "I just thought I would try. I thought maybe I could reach someone who could help us."

Kyel studied him for a long moment, then relaxed his grip. "I will not accept help at the risk of losing you," he said quietly, then added, "Perhaps we have done enough work for one day. Get some sleep."

Jansson didn't argue with him, but snagged some blankets and stretched out near the small campfire, his thoughts on the boy. He sounded young. Jansson hoped that he wasn't too horribly frightened by the 'demon'. It was one thing to spend the night alone in the dark, it was quite another to spend it alone and in terror. *But then,* Jansson thought, *how do I know he's alone? He may be with his family or his clan. I hope so. I would hate to think he's sitting out there shaking in his boots.* Guilt pressed against him and Jansson glanced at Kyel.

The elf had leaned back against the crates, obviously reluctant to touch the iron-ore laden walls of the cavern. Elek looked to be asleep as well. Jansson pulled the blankets close and once more hooked up empathically with the mysterious boy.

At the edge of the swamps to the south, Enid sat up with a gasp. "Ranen!"

"Enid? What's the matter?" Thomlin looked over at her from where he sat dejectedly against a large boulder. His proclamation of love for Enid had done nothing more than further alienate them from each other. Enid simply couldn't accept the fact that he, a prince, would have any interest in her, a servant. She continued to believe it was nothing more than a game, meant to humiliate and disgrace her. There didn't seem to be anything Thomlin could say to make her change her mind and they had spent the day in uncomfortable silence. Now, he wondered if she would even answer his query.

Enid rose, her gaze north across the dark, empty fields. The little group had finally reached the ends of the swamp just as the sun began to set. They were all exhausted, not to mention mud-coated and reeking, and the sight of the vast fields stretching before them had been welcome. That is, until the sun was well down. While the bog had been almost uncomfortably warm, here the air held a chill that crept through their wet clothes and into their bones.

They had been forced to retreat to the edge of the bog and had kindled a fire using the same method Enid had used earlier. Still, it did little to ease their discomfort and nothing to ease the pain of rejection in Thomlin's heart. He looked at Enid, standing swathed in moonlight. "Is something the matter?" he asked again, not really expecting an answer, surprised when he got one.

"It's Ranen," she whispered. "He's frightened."

"Who's Ranen? Where is he?" Thomlin got slowly to his feet, his heart racing. He glanced at Vantann and Elecka, who slept nearby, wondering if he should wake them.

"He's a friend," Enid replied. "He must be fairly close. I can't usually sense him over long distances." She looked to Thomlin earnestly. "I have to go to him. He needs me."

Thomlin studied her face, wanting to touch it, forcing himself not to. "Then go," he said. "We'll be fine. You said the Session Chambers were north of us, so we'll go that way."

"What! You can't go back there! You said so yourself!"

Thomlin frowned. "We don't have anyplace else to go, Enid. I just want to find my father and the others and go home. Dalziel seems very cold and unwelcoming suddenly. You go. We'll be fine." He turned and walked into the tall field grass, both wanting and dreading her departure.

He supposed it would be best if she just went her own way. This Ranen person sounded very special to her. Thomlin had never even stopped to consider that Enid might have another man. He had been so sure of himself, so giddy with his newfound emotions, that he had just assumed she would respond in like. *But that's not going to happen,* he chastised himself. Gods! Why hadn't someone told him that the SoulMate bond didn't always run both ways! That the love might not be shared or reciprocated. He would have been a lot more careful with his heart. Tears pricked at his eyes and he brushed them away bitterly.

"M'Lord?" Enid's voice was soft and close.

Thomlin didn't turn around, afraid that if he did he wouldn't be able to stop the tears. "It's all right, Enid, really. I never should have gotten you mixed up in this in the first place. If you have a chance to walk away from it, you should do so."

"What of you? Vantann and Elecka? I can't just leave you out here. Not if I can help you."

"You have already helped us, Enid. We couldn't have survived the bog without your knowledge. And we wouldn't know which way to go now if you hadn't been able to read the stars. In all, it is we who owe you. Let us repay you by giving you the opportunity to,"

"M'Lord." Enid touched his shoulder lightly, interrupting him.

"Enid, please," Thomlin murmured, his heart torn with pain. "It would be better if you left. I," He started when she placed her hand against his cheek, and he turned to face her. She was close, very close and he caught his breath, steadying himself, checking his impulse to gather her into his arms.

"I didn't mean to hurt you, M'Lord," she said softly, "yet it is obvious that I have. I still don't understand this. Why would you be interested in me? I'm just a kitchen-servant, not even much to look at and,"

"You're wrong!" Thomlin interrupted. "You're beautiful. You're also smart, resourceful and incredibly kind. All of the things a man could ever want in a woman." He paused and drew a deep breath. "Ranen is very lucky."

Enid started, then suddenly grinned and flushed. "Ranen is ten years old," she said. "He's a friend, just like I said."

Thomlin went red. "Oh," he mumbled. "I...I thought when you...well, I..." He gripped her hand, his heart going wild in his chest. "What do I do, Enid? I may only be fifteen but I know what I feel in my heart and in my soul. I love you and I want to be with you. Tell me now if that can't be. Please."

Enid was quiet for a long moment, her brown eyes locked on his blue. Finally, she spoke, her voice soft and choked with emotion. "I don't understand any of this. I only just met you, M'Lord. Just days and yet...somehow...somehow I feel that if I let you walk away from me, I would regret it for the rest of my life."

Thomlin studied her face, then hesitantly leaned forward, expecting her to draw back. She didn't, and their lips met in a gentle kiss that sent Thomlin's soul soaring and his heart racing. When they parted, Enid's face was flushed. Thomlin swallowed hard, hoping she wouldn't feel him trembling. For long moments they merely stared at each other, then Thomlin cleared his throat a little too loudly. "This boy, Ranen," he said, trying to return to business lest his volatile fifteen-year-old hormones get the better of him, "you said you could sense him. What do you mean?"

Enid drew a deep breath as if trying to calm her own emotions. "He's an empath. I'm a healer. I can pick up on emotions of empaths, especially him. He's sort of like a little brother to me. Right now, he's terribly frightened. I don't know what he's doing out here. Probably looking for me."

"Can you tell how far away he is?"

"No, but it can't be too far. Like I said, I can't sense him over great distances. Quite honestly, I'm surprised at how strongly I sense him now. Thomlin, I really do need to go to him."

"Then we'll come as well," Thomlin said. "My Uncle Jansson is an empath, too. He's done an EmpathicLink several times in the past. Maybe Ranen could do something like that and we,"

"No. He's only a little boy," Enid interrupted. "But as soon as we get to Landis, you and the others will be able to contact your family."

"Why? What's Landis?"

"He's not a what, he's a who. He's the coven leader of that Nydiri clan I told you about. He's my friend."

An involuntary shudder ran through Thomlin and he forced himself to remember Herrick and Anyar, the two Nydiri who had helped him and Vantann escape from Dukker. Thomlin knew there was such a thing as a good Nydiri. Still, the thought of walking right into a coven sent chills racing up and down his spine. He took Enid's hand. "We'd better wake Vans and Elecka then. We need to find Ranen."

Enid smiled, nodded and walked with him back toward the camp, where Thomlin stumbled to a stop, a gasp of astonishment escaping his lips. Vantann and Elecka were locked in a tight, passionate embrace and now hastily parted, embarrassment evident on both of their faces.

::Not a word, Thoms!:: Vantann twin-touched, glaring at him.

Thomlin choked back his smile and entered camp, not daring to look at Elecka. ::I hope this was mutual,:: he sent to his brother.

Vantann glanced at Elecka. ::It was.::

"Stop it!" Elecka snapped, startling everyone. "Why don't we just put everything out in the open here?"

"Fine," Thomlin agreed. "I love Enid. What about you two?"

There was a moment of silence before Vantann rose. He extended his hand and helped Elecka to her feet. They looked into each other's eyes, then both grinned awkwardly. Thomlin laughed and stomped out the fire. "One of Enid's friends is close by," he said. "His name is Ranen. He's an empath and Enid picked up his emotional web. He's scared and we need to find him." He looked at his brother. "Enid's going to take us to a coven of Nydiri. She says they can help us."

The grin faded from Vantann's face and he swallowed hard. "How?"

"They may be able to Ward you so that you can MindLink your father," Enid replied, then sighed. "M'Lord, please don't look so surprised every time I say anything with an ounce of sense in it. Forget how I acted back at the Session Chambers. I was only a servant, you, visiting dignitaries. What purpose would there have been to be anymore than an 'empty-headed farm girl'? I certainly never thought any of this would happen."

"Who are you?" Vantann asked. "As long as we're laying out our cards, I'd like to know a little more about you before I follow you into a coven of Nydiri."

Thomlin glanced at him sharply, ready to protest. But Enid nodded. "That is fair," she said. "But could we walk while I talk? I'd like to get to Ranen as soon as possible. You have my word that we'll not go to the coven until you're ready."

"We have your word," Vantann said. "Do we also have your dagger?"

"Vantann!" Thomlin cried, anger surging through him.

"It's all right," Enid said, though her face furrowed in puzzlement. She pulled the dagger from her boot sheath and handed it to Vantann. "Perhaps sometime you can tell me where the roots of your fear of the Nydiri lie."

Thomlin glared at Vantann and took Enid's hand. "There'll be plenty of time for that," he said. "When we get home."

::Lidgerwood!:: Vantann twin-touched.

::Of course!:: Thomlin retorted. ::I love her. I'm not leaving her here.::

::Have you asked her opinion on this? Maybe she won't want to go. And what about Rusulka?::

Thomlin ignored him, though his questions burned uneasily. He turned and began to walk, Enid at his side, the others trailing.

"So, M'Lord," Enid said to Vantann, "you wanted to know of my background. My mother was no more than a herdsman's daughter. She had no money or property but she was rich beyond most people's dreams. She was loved by everyone who met her, respected by everyone who'd heard of her. She was sweet, kind and giving and I miss her very much. She died when I was only eight. Too young to lose one's mother.

"My father was a scholar and scribe. From him I got my love of learning. He tried to fill the void left by my mother's death, but his own grief was too overwhelming. I truly believe that killed him more than his age. He just couldn't go on without her." She trembled and Thomlin put his arm about her shoulders.

"Have you no other family, then?" he asked softly.

"No. I was twelve when my father died. I was quite old enough to begin services. I stayed with Landis until I was thirteen, then went to work at the Session Chambers. It's been a pleasant enough place, up until the Nydiri came. No one could really figure out what they wanted. Landis and his coven have been watching them for a year now and are still no closer to understanding. It's been giving him fits to have me working there." She eyed the twins thoughtfully. "Somehow, I think you and the Nydiri are involved."

Thomlin started but Vantann only grimaced. "War," he said.

"What?"

"The Nydiri are trying to start a war between the elves and the humans."

"Why?" she asked.

"Divide and conquer, I guess," Vantann answered.

Thomlin frowned. "But what about revenge?"

"Wouldn't revenge be exacted by a war?" Elecka asked grimly.

"I suppose," Thomlin agreed. "But he made it sound personal."

They were quiet for a moment, each mulling it over, then Elecka spoke reflectively. "Let's look at who came to Dalziel. My father, your father, Jansson, Darosenim, Druce, us and Elek, who supposedly set this whole alliance up."

"You say supposedly," Vantann said. "You don't think he did?"

"I don't know. If Elek had set this up, don't you think he would have insisted on representatives from Glede's other provinces?"

"They were asked," Thomlin pointed out. "They refused to come."

Elecka frowned. "So I've heard. You two know King Prytel of Pendorelle and King Greyson of Anrofia. Would they refuse?"

The twins exchanged worried glances, then Vantann shook his head. "Probably not."

An uneasy feeling began to gnaw at Thomlin's gut. "Revenge?" he murmured. "Killan said revenge. If the Nydiri seek revenge, it would be against us and Papay." He stopped walking, sudden terror stilling him. His gaze locked onto Vantann's. "Dukker. It's Dukker. He's come for us, Vans. For us and Papay. And if we don't find Kyel and Elek, he'll have us."

Chapter Thirteen

Treyas held Druce's hand loosely in his, his face set in a mask of concern. Druce's finger, the one he had cut open to prove himself to Treyas, was red, hot and swollen. Darosenim had already pulled a spark of healing magic but it had seemed to have no effect. Now, Treyas looked once more into Druce's face, his eyes begging for the truth.

"Trey, really," Druce said again, "it doesn't hurt. I know it looks like it should, but it just doesn't. In fact," he glanced over at Darosenim, who was crouched near the lake, sword in hand, "I feel better today than I've felt in a long time." His gaze returned to Treyas. "Really."

Treyas frowned and sat back, then rubbed wearily at his face. He had re-instated the HealBond using naiad magic, but doubted that it alone was giving Druce much strength. "I don't understand this," he murmured, then started as Darosenim gave a whoop of success.

"I got one!" The mage held up his sword. A large, silver fish was impaled on its tip.

"Yum," Druce teased. "Fish."

"It's a damn sight better than nuts and roots," Darosenim pointed out, as he pulled his dagger to gut the fish. "Or any of that bewitched food at the Chambers."

The words brought Treyas' thoughts back to their predicament. He was sure that by now someone had been sent to look for them. He was reluctant to leave the lake and the magic it offered but, at the same time, knew he had to. The twins were south of them, far south. It would take days of riding to reach them and who knew where they would go in the meantime. *I could MindLink them,* Treyas thought with a grim face. *And lead the Nydiri right to them, most likely. And what of us? We're nothing more than targets. We're too damn close to the Session Chambers. Yet, the only way to put sufficient distance between the Nydiri and us is to TravelSpell. TravelSpell creatively, confusing and overlapping the MagicTrail so it wouldn't be easily traced. But to where?* Treyas didn't know this land. He could put them into more peril than they were in now. He picked up the map Darosenim had supplied, unrolled it and perused it once more.

There was a lot of boggy land to the south, land that Treyas had located the children in. Treyas' finger tapped lightly at the mountain range to the north of the Session Chambers. That was where he, Druce and Dar were. In between the bogs and the mountains were the vast farmlands the fake Kyel had remarked on. Nothing for cover there, and no rivers, just small streams and lakes. Treyas followed the mountain range with his finger. It ran south, paralleling the coast, though a number of leagues inland. *If we follow it,* Treyas mused, *we have adequate cover and it would take us west of the bogs. Plus, according to the map, there was a wide river that cut a path through the mountains and emptied into the wetlands. A river meant magic, the type of water magic Treyas was most comfortable with. Still, the route south was a long one. Who knew where the twins and Elecka would be by that time. *So, a TravelSpell then. To take us into the mountains, cutting the time in half.*

Treyas glanced at Druce, who was helping Darosenim cook the fish. He did look better, Treyas had to admit that much. But well enough to take part in a complicated TravelSpell? Treyas wasn't so sure about that. He frowned and looked back at the map, his gaze once more drawn to what appeared to be a large mountain standing alone just south of the Session Chambers. He wondered about that mountain, how it came to be there with no foothills. Perhaps it was only drawn that way. He sighed and re-rolled the map.

"So, what have you come up with?" Druce asked. "Which way do we go and how?"

Treyas chuckled softly. "You know me well, Druce. The twins are south of us, in the bogs. They'll probably head north since that's the driest route. I'm also hoping Enid will have some knowledge of her land and be able to help."

"Well, that's half of the answer," Druce said. "How do we travel?"

"I don't know. If we continue on with the horses, they'll catch up to us easy enough. But if we TravelSpell, we'll be on foot. And," he hesitated, eyeing Druce, "I'll have to overlay the TravelStrands if we're to avoid leaving a trail."

Druce grimaced slightly and Darosenim groaned. "That is not something I look forward to," he grumbled. "This fish will most likely end up right back,"

"Dar!" Druce interrupted. "I know what will happen. I don't need it explained." He turned his gaze on Treyas. "Do what you have to do, Trey. I'll be fine."

Treyas regarded him with a small smile. "You always say that and look at you now."

"Let's eat, then get moving," Darosenim said quickly.

They did as he suggested, polishing off the fish in a matter of moments. Afterward, as if by some unspoken agreement, they stripped their gear from the horses and prepared individual packs. Darosenim had been lucid enough to bring his and Druce's packs along, as well as some weapons. There were two swords, plus a dagger apiece. Treyas insisted Druce and Darosenim hold the swords.

"There's a river that runs through these mountains," he explained. "I intend to set us down near it. That way I can access the magic if need be. You'll have to hold tight. This may be a bit rocky."

"I have a better idea," Druce said and took up the length of rope hooked to Treyas' horse's saddle. "I'm not about to get separated like we did in Winze." He tied a loop about his waist, then looped it around Treyas and finally Darosenim. "Wherever we go," he said, "we go together."

Treyas grinned and led them into the water.

"Baerns!" Darosenim cried. "Make it fast, Trey. This water is like ice!"

Treyas frowned as the MagicWeb appeared before him. "I'll do my best, Dar, but this is going to take some time to reorganize."

Druce abruptly gripped his arm. "Reorganize later! We have company!"

Treyas looked up with a gasp. *Kyel* and *Elek* were guiding their horses through the rocks toward the lake.

"Treyas!" *Kyel* yelled. "It's us! Thank the gods we've found you."

"Hold on," Treyas whispered and grabbed at the naiad magic, whipping it into a TravelStrand.

"Treyas! No!" *Elek* cried. "It's really us!"

Treyas hesitated for only a split-second, then cast the Spell. It sucked them up like a tornado, spinning them crazily first one way, then another. Treyas tried desperately to direct the Strand but each time he thought he had it, it was snatched away. Strong Dirin magic swirled around them, trying to pull them back. In panic, Treyas sent a stinging GrayBolt hurtling back along the Dirin Strand. It was just enough to startle the two Nydiri, and their magic scattered. The rebound spun Treyas and his companions out of control. For a brief moment, Treyas saw the rushing river deep in the canyon, then inexplicably his TravelStrand was seized and he, Druce and Darosenim were dragged rapidly north.

Treyas felt unconsciousness beckon and he fought against it. He had a need to know where he was going and to whom. He knew he couldn't override whatever magic had claimed him, but maybe he could arrive in fighting shape.

A moment later, he was down, landing with bone-jarring force in a sea of tall grass, but landing on his feet. Druce staggered against him and fell, pulling Treyas with him. Darosenim followed and the three of them ended up in a pitiful, helpless heap.

"I'm so sorry!" A man's voice reached them. "I'm so very sorry! Are you hurt?"

Treyas struggled free of the others, coming to his knees, prevented from standing by the rope about his waist. He peered up at the aged, balding man. His thin, wrinkled face was flushed beneath a white beard, his blue eyes filled with concern. He reached out gnarled hands to help Darosenim, who immediately recognized the pale green robes the old man wore. "A sorcerer," he whispered to Treyas, as he unlashed the rope. "Level Three."

"Yes, yes," the old man agreed. "My name's Anwyl. You're the elf from Glede aren't you?"

Treyas started, his hand straying to his dagger.

Anwyl's eyes went wide and he held up his hands. "No, no!" he cried. "I want to help you. It's my fault those Nydiri are here. We need to send them back where they came from."

Treyas hesitated, exchanging a wary glance with Darosenim. Druce moaned softly, then turned to retch. Treyas was at his side immediately, supporting him, pulling the rope away from him.

"Gods, Trey," Druce murmured. "So much for feeling better."

Treyas looked up at Anwyl, reluctant to trust him, but seeing no alternative. "Do you have a place where my friend can lie down?"

"Certainly!" Anwyl replied. "My cottage is right here. It's in Illusion." He stepped forward to help Druce stand. The moment he touched him, he started. "Yunyo!"

"How did you know?" Treyas gasped.

Anwyl shrugged. "I'm a healer. I can read illness with a touch."

"Can you also cure with a touch?" Darosenim asked.

"No." Anwyl gave a small smile. "But often I can cure with magic. Come."

He led them toward a small grove of oak trees. The cottage appeared before them and again Treyas was surprised. "Brownie Illusion?" he asked, studying the thatched-roof and field stone cottage.

"Benefits of friendship," Anwyl explained. "Come inside."

They followed him into the cottage, and Treyas' gaze went immediately to the hearth. An aged female brownie dressed in a simple brown coarsecloth robe was stirring a large pot of vegetable stew. Her wiry gray hair was fastened in a knot at the nape of her neck and she greeted Treyas with the by now familiar phrase, though it was said with more humor than animosity. "Ack! Elf!"

Treyas couldn't help but smile. "I'm Treyas Merripen. These are my friends, Druce Sinclair and Darosenim Quartermane."

The brownie grinned, revealing a set of flawless white teeth. Her blue eyes twinkled. "You know your brownie legends well. I am now bonded to aid you. My name is Glenna."

"His friend here needs help," Anwyl said, assisting Druce into the only bedroom and bed.

Glenna set down her spoon and followed Anwyl. Treyas trailed after her. Glenna perched on the side of the bed and laid one small hand on Druce's brow, as Anwyl fetched a quilt to cover him. "Yunyo," the brownie murmured with a frown of puzzlement. "And yet..." She began to explore Druce's exposed skin with the tips of her fingers. When she reached his hand and his swollen finger, she gave a small gasp of surprise. "What happened here?"

Treyas flushed and shot a quick glance at Darosenim, who stood in the doorway.

"My fault," said the mage. "I was trying to convince Treyas that I wasn't a Nydiri. I cut my finger to prove it and Druce did the same."

Glenna was silent for a moment, her brow furrowed in thought. "And that is all you did?"

"Well, not exactly," Treyas replied. "I cut my finger, too, and since we were all bleeding, we decided to become blood brothers. I know it was a stupid thing to do considering Druce's illness but,"

"Incredible!" Glenna interrupted, her gaze flashing to Anwyl. "This supports my theory!" She bent to examine Druce's finger carefully, probing at it gently. "Does this hurt?"

"No," Druce replied, casting a confused look at Treyas.

Glenna looked up at him. "And how are you feeling generally since this blood sharing?"

"Actually better. Or at least I was until that wild TravelSpell."

"The Nydiri tried to retrieve them," Anwyl told her, almost apologetically.

Glenna turned a sharp eye on Treyas. "There were Nydiri that close? Palls! Curse this old body! If I was fifty years younger I'd have read that Brownie Spell on you the moment you entered this dimension."

"Fifty..." Darosenim echoed. "How old are you?"

"One hundred and thirty five. Why?"

Darosenim stared at her, agape. "One hundred thirty..." His words trailed off and he staggered to a chair, sitting down in a daze.

"He's married to a brownie," Treyas explained. "I...don't think he knew how long they lived."

Glenna grunted. "If I know your wife, she's already adapted herself to your lifespan."

"What do you mean?" Darosenim asked.

"Where do you hail from?"

"Karsaba. Why?"

"Karsab, huh? And a mage? You'll be expected to live ninety five to a hundred years. Your wife will, too. Brownies adapt to the culture they live with. If you were an elf, she'd live one hundred eighty to one hundred ninety years. If you were Standian, sixty might be all."

"Baerns," Darosenim whispered. "She never told me."

Treyas sat down and changed the subject. "Anwyl, you said it was your fault the Nydiri were here. How so?"

Anwyl shifted uncomfortably, his gaze settling on Glenna. She grimaced. "Anwyl, our friends could use some tea. Peppermint would help ease their stomachs. Go along with you." He mumbled something unintelligible and shuffled out of the bedroom. Glenna watched him away then answered Treyas' question. "He's not all that young himself. Fancies himself quite a sorcerer. At one time, he was. But age has a way of slowing you down. Anwyl likes to visit other dimensions. Usually it's not a problem." She chuckled lightly. "Goodness, he's outrun some fairly nasty demons in his time. Anwyl always managed to close the dimensional void before they could cross over. But the Nydiri...palls! They're another story. They came across with a vengeance. Almost killed poor Anwyl. Anyway, they're here now and we have to find a way to send them back." She studied Treyas thoughtfully. "Any idea why they're so interested in you?"

Treyas sighed heavily. "I've dealt with them before. Both in Mere Odain and Winze. Mere Odain was almost ten years ago. The Nydiri were helping the Akuri Keltins in their bid to rule Mere Odain. My son...my adopted son, is DragonMaster. The Nydiri and Akuri seized him and tried to make him command the dragons to their benefit. I inadvertently destroyed most of a coven in trying to rescue him.

"Then, five years ago, the offspring of the original coven attempted to bring their members across the dimensional void. They..." he drew a deep shaky breath, the memories still raw and painful, "they almost sacrificed my twin boys to accomplish that. Fortunately, we had some help from two Nydiri. My boys wouldn't be alive today if it wasn't for Herrick and Anyar." He looked up at Glenna. "But as to what these particular Nydiri want,"

"Treyas!" Darosenim interrupted. "It's Dukker's coven! It has to be!"

Treyas felt the color drain from his face. "No!" He rose stiffly. "No, it's not! Another coven has,"

"Trey!" Druce's voice was soft, yet commanding. "Think on Dar's words. What would another coven want with you? Dukker, on the other hand, has ample reason for revenge."

"It's not enough just to go after you," Darosenim put in. "He's going after Glede as well. You imprisoned his coven. He plans to imprison Glede."

"And what of the twins?" Treyas cried, his heart racing. "If I believe Dukker is behind this, then I also need to believe he'll kill Vans and Thoms if he gets the chance! No! This isn't Dukker's coven. It can't be! It can't!" He leaned against the wall, burying his face in his arms. Terror consumed him. He fought against Druce and Dar's words, yet knew them to be true. Who else but Dukker would do this? Would seek to destroy everything that Treyas held dear?

I should have killed him, Treyas thought. *I should have killed Dukker when I had the chance*. Dimensional imprisonment didn't work. It never had. Rugan and Vaalde has both escaped to wreak havoc, to prey upon him and his loved ones. Now, Dukker had done the same thing. *Only this time*, Treyas seethed, *this time it will be different. Dukker won't live to return and plague me again. Not this time, not this time.*

Pepin woke with a start, his mind fighting to make sense of his surroundings. Slowly, it came to him, along with a simmering anger. He was still hunched in the neck hollow of Aleron, who was silently winging his way west. The flight had started off well with Aleron obeying every command almost before it was spoken. But then, about an hour into the ride, Aleron had turned west, and no amount of commanding, yelling, coaxing or threatening had turned him back. Pepin didn't know what to make of it, and around two in the morning, had fallen asleep, exhausted. At least, he thought it was sleep. He couldn't tell judging by how his head reeled.

He straightened and peered down at the passing land. Jagged mountain slopes with heavy growths of evergreen trees were directly below and at his back, while ahead stretched a vast ocean that glimmered in the rising sun. Pepin had no idea where he was. "Aleron, come on," he begged. "You've had your fun. Now, let's go home. Please?" he added, then gasped as Aleron abruptly plunged toward the ground.

The great dragon landed easily, gently upon a white sandy beach and lowered his head, indicating Pepin should dismount. He did so slowly, warily, his dark gaze dancing across the beach and the jagged cliffs to the east. "Yes," he mumbled to Aleron, "it's quite beautiful, but why are we here?"

"Pepin!" The call rang out across the sands, startling Pepin so badly he stumbled backward and sprawled across Aleron's snout. The dragon snorted, emitting a great puff of smoke that sent Pepin into a sneezing-coughing fit.

"Pepin! Laith! It really is you!" Faolan pounded up to him and hauled him up and away from Aleron.

"Fao!" Pepin managed, before sneezing again. "What in Tor's hell are... Rusulka!" He stared at the dryad in shock, then swung his gaze back to Faolan, who went red. Pepin shook his head, almost overwhelmed by the emotions coming from Faolan. "I'm confused. Where are we and what's going on?"

"We're west of the P'lay Mountains," Faolan answered. "On Mere Odain's western coast."

Pepin glanced at the towering mountain range, the tallest in the entire world. Just east of them was the Samia Desert and the province of Taithleach. As far as Pepin knew, no one had ever been on the west side of the P'lay's. He looked back at Faolan. "Why?"

Faolan shrugged. "I guess you'd have to ask Aleron and Teague." He gestured to where Teague lay curled up, basking in the morning sunshine.

Pepin hadn't even seen the gray-brown mottled dragon against the rocks. "How long have you been here?"

"A few hours," Faolan replied. "I took Rusulka up for ride last night to watch the sunset. Then Teague took a silly notion to fly west. He wouldn't listen to anything."

"Same as Aleron," Pepin said, an uneasy feeling churning in his gut. He turned to the dragon. "All right, Aleron, we're here. Now what?"

The dragon hissed and prodded Pepin forward with one clawed forefoot. The Merian shrugged and followed Aleron's guidance, Faolan and Rusulka trailing. Around a narrow ridge of rock, a wide beach lay, its sparkling sands stretching up to an enormous cave. Pepin and Faolan exchanged wary, confused glances, then went forward, urged on by Aleron's anxious hiss. Rusulka clung to Faolan's arm, her small face pale and frightened. Pepin wondered what was going on between the dryad and the Keltin, but set that aside to concentrate on his footing.

The cave was not as dark as Pepin had expected, though it was deep. Light filtered in from strategically placed holes, coming to rest on what looked to be a pile of rocks. Pepin took a step closer and gasped as recognition hit. Eggs! Dragon eggs!

"Laith," Faolan whispered. "How..."

"What is it?" Rusulka asked.

"They're dragon eggs," Pepin replied, bending to examine them. "It looks like there's twenty, twenty-five."

"But not all are developing," Pepin said, then rocked back on his heels. He ran one hand across a smooth gray shell. "This one's dead. So is this one. They look close to hatching. I wonder how long they've been here."

"I wonder how they got here."

"Do the dragons want you to do something with them?" Rusulka asked.

"Take them back I suppose," Pepin told her.

"But as eggs or hatchlings," Faolan mused, then straightened. "Coals! This is really bad timing. Despite what Queen El'leigh says, we need to get to south Kelta. We can't be waiting around here for eggs to hatch."

Pepin looked over at him. "When were you planning to leave?"

"This morning. Andison is probably looking everywhere for me. I hope he doesn't go off alone. In his state of mind, he's liable to start a fight just to get himself killed."

Pepin rose. "Maybe the dragons would let one of us leave. It's worth a try at least."

Faolan nodded his agreement and followed Pepin back out to the beach. Aleron had curled up next to Teague and both dragons were half-asleep, little puffs of smoke coming from their nostrils. Aleron opened his eyes at Pepin's approach and lowered his head expectantly. Teague yawned widely and flopped to one side.

"Well," Faolan said, "I guess that's our answer."

The dragons' decision chafed at Pepin. It seemed they preferred Faolan's handling over his. "If Aleron didn't want me to stay," he grumbled, "then why did he bring me here?"

"Because you're the DragonMaster," Faolan said. "You needed to see your new fleet. Now it's up to your assistant to help them hatch out and get home."

Pepin frowned. "Fao, you are no more my assistant than I am the DragonMaster." He climbed into Aleron's neck hollow and pulled his cloak tight, then looked to Rusulka in question.

She shook her head. "I'll stay with Faolan," she said quietly.

Pepin wasn't surprised. "What'll you do for food and water? I'll have to send someone back."

"No, we're fine." He stepped closer to Pepin, lowering his voice. "We have a basket of food. We were going to have a sunset supper before Teague pulled this one us."

"Fao, I..." Pepin stopped, glancing over his shoulder at Rusulka.

"I know!" Faolan interrupted. "I know she's Thomlin's girlfriend. Laith! It's been on my mind constantly. But I can't help myself, Pepin. I like her. A lot. And...and I think she likes me. I won't say anything to Thomlin until I know for sure and then I'll speak to him personally. I promise."

Pepin could well feel the sincerity of Faolan's words. He could also feel warm emotions harbored not only in Faolan, but Rusulka as well. It seemed Thomlin would soon be dealing with heartbreak. Pepin gave a wry smile. "Love isn't always fair, Fao. Nor is it always painless. I'm sure Thomlin will survive. I'll see you soon."

Faolan nodded and stepped back beside Rusulka. She gave Pepin a hesitant smile, which he returned before giving Aleron the command to fly. *So*, he thought, as they turned east, *more eggs*. He couldn't begin to imagine how they'd gotten there. As far as he knew, none of Mere Odain's dragons were of breeding age. But then, how much did he know of dragons? Really? He only knew what he sensed, what the elders of Mere Odain had told him. He wondered if Pe'pinlaidh had kept journals of any kind. Up until now, Pepin had resisted researching his father's life. He felt somehow that it was an affront on his relationship with Treyas. Now, however, it seemed to beg to be looked into. He sighed and settled further into his cloak as the air began to chill. They were gaining altitude, getting ready to top the P'lay

Range. It was a little harder to breathe here and Pepin became very aware of his ability to draw air. His head again reeled, and it dawned on him that he had most likely fainted the previous night. A few moments later, Aleron was across the peak. He drew his wings close and soared down the mountainside toward the Samia Desert.

Pepin had never been there but he knew there were several abandoned townships. Townships that the Akuri Keltins and a few elfin necromancers had laid waste to. Townships like Andison's home. Andison's grandparents had come to Mere Odain from Standforth, seeking land of their own. Instead, they had found death.

Andison had already had a hard life. He'd lost all but one younger sister, and she'd returned to Standforth to raise her children. Andison had only been able to visit her twice in the last ten years. El'leigh and Charis were all the family he had and now that was being threatened, too. Pepin scowled into his cloak. Well, it wasn't going to happen. El'leigh was not going to destroy everything because of an infatuation with Mere Odain's DragonMaster. *Gods,* Pepin thought, *it probably isn't me at all. It's just the title, the fact that she believes the Queen and the DragonMaster belonged together.*

He sat up a little straighter, a sudden idea beginning to gel in his mind. Maybe DragonMaster was a title and only a title. Yes, the dragons responded to him, but they also responded to Faolan. Pepin had felt all along that he was no more than a figurehead, someone to give the dragons focus. Faolan was the real master, the one who had trained and cared for the dragons all of these years. And it was painfully obvious that the dragons still considered him as such even though Pepin was now on-site.

A smile formed slowly on his face. This plan might just work. And maybe, for once, everyone would be happy.

Chapter Fourteen

Jansson shivered and pulled his blanket closer, casting a wary glance at Kyel. The elf was busy brewing tea but had enough time to glare at Jansson. "I said I was sorry," Jansson mumbled. "What else do you want me to do?"

Kyel stopped his work. "Listen," he said. "I want you to listen."

"I was only trying to help."

"You would be helping if you would do as I ask," Kyel retorted, returning to his work.

"Ease up, Kyel," Elek said calmly, as he rummaged in the crates for breakfast fare.

"Ease up?" Kyel snapped. "He could have killed himself!"

"He didn't," Elek pointed out.

Jansson gave Elek a grateful smile, then shivered again and moved closer to the fire. He knew Kyel was right. He shouldn't have done an EmpathicLink in the first place. It was far too draining. But then to do a second one without adequate recovery time, that was pure foolishness. Jansson had not only lost the Link, he'd lost consciousness as well. Since he had been huddling beneath his blankets feigning sleep, it wasn't until early morning that Kyel had noticed something wrong.

By that time, Jansson was precariously close to slipping into twilight sleep, a sleep just one small step from death. It had taken Kyel many minutes to bring him back and even now, hours later, Jansson could still feel the effects. He was thoroughly chilled, his head reeled and his stomach churned. Still, he had gathered some information.

The boy's name was Ranen. He was ten years old and had been searching for his sister. Jansson had finally managed to convince the boy that he was not a demon but rather a fellow empath who desperately needed his help. Jansson had explained who was with him and how they were trapped. Ranen had promised help and the Link had ended with a sense of hope.

Until the aftereffects of the EmpathicLink had occurred. Jansson was terrified that Ranen had also suffered and wanted to contact the little boy. But with Kyel hovering nearby, he supposed there was little chance of doing that.

"Hoi!" Elek exclaimed, pulling out a square tin box and key. "Pickled herring!"

Jansson gagged involuntarily and hunched further into his blankets. "I'd rather chew on a biscuit."

"Suit yourself," Elek replied, sitting down. "But you don't know what you're missing."

"I do, however," Kyel put in. "Would you kindly take that offensive smell elsewhere?"

Elek grunted but complied, moving to the far side of the cavern. Kyel handed Jansson a mug of steaming tea and a hard biscuit, then sat down next to him. "I don't mean to be punitive, Jansson," he said quietly. "It's just that without my magic, I feel a trifle helpless. If I had not noticed your condition when I did, I might not have been able to waken you at all. That frightened me."

A pang of guilt assailed Jansson and he glanced sideways at Kyel. The stress was evident in the black elf's face. He had been incarcerated here for almost five days now. It was no doubt the longest imprisonment he had ever had. Jansson was amazed that he wasn't a lot more volatile than he was. *I've only been here two days and I'm ready to climb the walls,* he thought.

Climb the walls...his gaze drifted upward to watch the thin trail of smoke curl toward the ceiling. It was being vented out somehow and fresh air vented in. But from where? The ceiling was a mass of jagged, protruding black rock, as were some of the walls. Jansson appraised it thoughtfully, noticing the numerous hand and toe holds the coarse rock afforded. Though he wasn't a boy any longer, he still maintained a lithe, supple form. And he was small. Climbing the walls wouldn't pose much of a problem. Kyel, on the other hand, might.

Jansson nursed his tea along, all the while scanning the rocks for an easy path. At last, he believed he'd found one. He finished off his tea, set the mug down and rose unsteadily, still somewhat dizzy from the previous night's catastrophe. Kyel watched him carefully. Elek shot him a questioning glance and downed another pickled herring.

"Have you ever wondered how big the vents are?" Jansson asked of no one in particular. "They move air well. It seems they would have to be fairly large to do that."

"What are you thinking?" Kyel asked warily.

Jansson walked to the wall and reached out to grip a handhold. The rock was coarse, abrasive. A fall would be painful. "I'd like to see just how large the vents are. Maybe I could squeeze through."

"And what would you do then?" Kyel asked.

Jansson shrugged. "I could at least survey the surrounding lands. Who knows? Maybe we'll get lucky and there'll be a sympathetic village nearby."

"Or the Session Chambers," Elek put in. "I think we're fairly close. We'd have to be for the Nydiri to maintain their Illusion."

Kyel looked over at him. "Explain that."

"I'm guessing, but the fact that we're still alive suggests that the Nydiri need us. And about the only thing they would need us for is the Illusion. I think they're bouncing their magic off us. We can't feel it because we're both rather compromised right now."

"Then why can't I feel it?" Jansson asked.

"It's not usual for you to feel other magics," Kyel reminded him. "And if we are close to the Session Chambers, you can't expect a lot of help there."

"But what about Dar and Druce? They're not here yet, so the Nydiri obviously aren't impersonating them yet."

Kyel was silent for a moment before he spoke. "I doubt that Darosenim and Druce stayed at the Chambers. Druce wouldn't want to be too far away from Treyas. Darosenim wouldn't want to be around a fake Jansson."

"Anyway," Elek said, "you couldn't just go marching into the Chambers. They already have a Jansson, remember?"

Jansson frowned. "All right. All of that is true. But I still want to see how big the vent is. Who knows? Maybe you two could get through it, too."

Elek grunted. "If I could climb those rocks, I'd have done it by now."

Jansson surveyed the wall before him. "It doesn't look that hard." Without another word, he began to climb, scampering up the rocks like a squirrel in a tree.

Kyel shot to his feet, his blue eyes wide. "Come back down!" he snapped.

Jansson ignored him, concentrating on the next hand and foot hold, pulling himself around a sharp outcropping.

"Jansson! Come down!" Kyel ordered. "I don't have magic to heal!"

"You won't need it," Jansson called back, steadying himself and craning his neck to find the vent. He grinned as his gaze settled on a gaping black hole. "I think I found it, Kyel!" he called and began to creep toward it, already feeling the air movement on his face.

He reached it in a matter of moments, and peered into a long, dark tunnel. It was quite large enough for him to crawl into, but he hesitated. He couldn't see daylight at the other end and had no torch. It was hard telling how long the tunnel was or if it maintained its width all the way to the outside. Jansson had no desire to get halfway there and become trapped. The very thought gave him chills. He didn't like caves or tunnels. Too many bad things had happened in them. With a heavy sigh of resignation, he turned and began to climb back down. More than once, his toe slipped and he was forced to grip the rock harder than he wanted. His hands bled from numerous small cuts, and he grimaced. He was sure to hear about this from Kyel for hours on end.

He was pulling himself around the stone outcropping when disaster struck. The entire mountain shook violently, rumbling deep within itself. Jansson was knocked off balance, his feet missed a step and he grabbed frantically for a handhold. But the mountain seemed intent on shaking him free and he fell, striking the wall several times before landing in a pitiful, bloody heap. Pain roared through his head and one arm. He rolled onto his back with a groan of agony, Kyel's cry of alarm ringing in his ears, as the mountain calmed and was still.

Kyel and Elek were at his side in seconds.

"Damnation, Jansson!" Kyel raged. "I told you not to do this! When will you ever listen!"

"Calm yourself, Kyel," Elek said quietly. "Just get some water and a cloth."

Kyel hesitated only a second, before surging to his feet and storming away.

Jansson shuddered, allowing his face to contort in pain once Kyel was out of sight. "Gods, Elek," he whispered, "what happened? What was that?"

"I don't know. Maybe an earthquake. Lie still."

"My head,"

"Is cut wide open," Elek interrupted. "We'll fix it. Does anyplace else need attention?"

"My arm. I think it's," Jansson broke off as Kyel returned, his black face set in a hard frown of anger and concern.

"Broken?" the elf finished curtly. "I shouldn't wonder!" He handed the wet cloth to Elek, then once more walked away.

Jansson winced as Elek cleaned the head wound. "Is it bad?" he ventured.

"It needs closing," Elek replied, then patted Jansson's shoulder reassuringly. "You've got long, strong hair. We'll tie the wound shut. It'll heal in no time. Maybe you could help yourself a bit with the pain."

Jansson wearily closed his eyes and reached for his magic. This was getting to be habit. It seemed he was always in need of healing. Maybe Kyel was right. Maybe he did need to listen better. He frowned and concentrated on his arm, directing the magic there as Elek deftly wove his hair into tight little knots over the head wound. He wondered where Kyel had gone, when his anger would calm. Jansson hated having the elf irate with him. His magic faltered as his attention wavered and pain raced through his wrist. He gasped involuntarily just as Kyel once more came to his side. Though Jansson tried to put on a mask of comfort, it was impossible and he simply looked up to Kyel, his eyes begging forgiveness.

Kyel exhaled slowly, shook his head and offered Jansson some pain-killing willow powder. Jansson accepted gratefully. "It wasn't my fault, Kyel," he said. "I was doing just fine until the mountain moved."

"It rarely seems to be your fault," Kyel said, sitting next to him. "Yet your body holds more scars than a man twice your age. To look at you, one would think you were Captain of the Guards as opposed to King of the Guards."

"Really?" Jansson asked with pride.

Kyel groaned and Elek chuckled. "That one backfired, Kyel," he said, then sat back. "There. Done. Now, let's see that arm." He reached for Jansson's arm, then abruptly, he disappeared.

Vantann dropped down wearily in the chest-high grass. "I have to stop," he said.

Thomlin exhaled with fatigue. "I agree. I'm exhausted." He caught up Enid's hand, looking into her brown eyes. He saw worry there. Worry and fear.

The group had walked all night, wading through the tall grass, following Enid's lead. Still, Ranen was nowhere in sight and Enid's uneasiness had grown with the coming of morning.

"Come on, Enid," Elecka said. "You'll do him no good if you collapse from exhaustion. Let's rest a bit before we go on."

Thomlin squeezed her hand gently. "Please?"

Enid's shoulders sagged but she nodded and joined Vantann and the others.

"I'm starved," Vantann grumbled.

"Here." Enid bent several grass stalks down and shook them hard. Small, dark brown seeds flew through the air, pelting Vantann.

He drew back with a quiet oath, then picked up a seed. "You can eat these?"

"Of course. This is Ajana grass. We use the seeds for all kinds of things. Flour, breads, cereal. You can roast them or eat them raw."

Vantann tasted one, then raised his eyebrows in surprise. "They're not bad. I bet they taste even better roasted with some salt."

Thomlin gathered up a handful, popped several in his mouth, then offered some to Enid. She refused and Thomlin sighed. She had not eaten since their desperate flight from the Session Chambers, though she had found and prepared various items for the others. Thomlin wondered if Killan's callous remark about her size had anything to do with it. *But then,* Thomlin mused with happiness, *Killan has never held her like I have.* That wasn't fat on her bones, but muscle. She was strong, like a warrior, and Thomlin suddenly wondered if she knew swordplay. *If she doesn't, I'll teach her when we get home,* he thought, then grimaced as Vantann's words came back to haunt him. What if Enid didn't want to leave Dalziel? Didn't want to become part of the royal family? And what of Rusulka? Thomlin didn't want to hurt her. He cared for her. Just not the same way he cared for Enid. He hoped desperately that leaving Dalziel wouldn't mean leaving Enid as well. Shaking the unpleasant thought aside, he once more held out some of the seeds. "You need to eat something," he said quietly. "We're relying on you for help. You can't do that if you're passed out from hunger."

"I'm not hungry," Enid replied, then abruptly rose and walked off through the grass.

"What's wrong with her?" Vantann asked, as he harvested more of the seeds.

"I don't know," Thomlin said, getting to his feet. He watched Enid walk about thirty paces away, then drop down in the tall grass. "Elecka, help me out here. Should I go after her or leave her alone?"

"What does your heart tell you to do?" Elecka asked.

Thomlin gave a small smile. "If I did what my heart told me to do, I could be in trouble."

Vantann chuckled but Elecka shushed him with a quick, hard thump on the head, before looking back at Thomlin. "Don't confuse want or lust with love, Thoms. That would be unfair to both of you."

Thomlin blushed. "You're right, Elecka. And Vans, you would do well to listen to those wise words." He walked away, ignoring Vantann's startled response.

He followed Enid's path through the grass, then stopped and called to her softly. "Enid? May I join you?"

"I suppose," she replied.

Thomlin found her huddled on the damp ground, her arms wrapped about her muddy skirts, her forehead resting on her knees. He sat down next to her and hesitantly smoothed her wild curls. "Do you want to talk?" he asked.

She was silent for a moment, then spoke without looking up. "This is wrong, M'Lord. You and I. It can't work."

Thomlin felt as if his heart had dropped to his gut. "Why not? I told you how I felt about you. Why won't you believe it?" She remained quiet and he went on anxiously. "Enid, I love you. And you said,"

"I know what I said," she interrupted. "And I shouldn't have said it."

Thomlin regarded her sadly. "Then you didn't mean it?"

"I...I didn't say that," she stammered, then raised her head to look at him. Her brown eyes were full of tears, her dirty face streaked with them. "Look at us, M'Lord. It can't work. There's so much you don't know about me. You're an elfin prince. I'm a servant. It doesn't matter how smart or well-learned I am. I'm from a whole different class than you are."

"That doesn't matter to me, Enid, and it wouldn't matter to those I call family."

"But it will, M'Lord. Someday it will. Besides, you're a prince. You could never stay here."

"Then come with me," Thomlin said. "Come back to Lidgerwood with me."

Enid shook her head. "I could never belong there, Thomlin."

"You could. If you wanted to. But maybe," he rose, "maybe you don't want to. I know I'm asking a lot of you. I'm asking you to leave your home, your friends, your way of life. Maybe that's not fair. Maybe I have no right to ask, to put you in this situation. I love you, Enid. Because I love you, I'll accept whatever you decide." He turned away, drawing a deep breath to check his tears. He had thought to leave her alone there, to let her think in solitude, but he could not bring himself to actually move. So he stood, while silence pressed against him, while his stomach grew tighter and tighter, while tears blurred his vision. Finally, he heard Enid sigh. She rose and came around in front of him. He brought his gaze up to meet hers. He didn't know what to say, how to convince her of his love, so he did the only thing he could think of. He kissed her.

It took only a second for Enid to recover from the shock, then she wrapped her arms about him, and delivered her own passion into the kiss. Thomlin pulled her down into the grass. Unmindful of the filth covering her skin, he kissed her cheeks, her forehead, the tip of her nose and again her lips, his heart racing, his hormones keeping pace.

She stroked his cheek lightly and played her fingers through his hair. He chuckled as she caught at a tangle. "I'm not usually in such a mess," he apologized.

She smiled. "I don't imagine I'm looking so good myself."

"You're beautiful," Thomlin told her, brushing her hair from her face. He kissed her again, then wrapped his arms about her securely, reveling in her softness, her warmth. He wanted this moment to never end. "Enid," he breathed in her ear, "will you marry me?"

Enid started, and drew back to look into his eyes. "M'Lord! We've only just met! And...and I shouldn't even..."

"I know that," Thomlin interrupted, fearing he had spoiled the moment. He could see true alarm in the brown eyes, and wanted only to chase it away. "But I also know we belong together. Doesn't this feel right? As if it should be?"

Enid didn't answer, stammering out another point. "You...you're just close to sixteen! You're a very long way from getting married."

Thomlin paused, chewing on the inside of his cheek. "I...um...I guess I should tell you the truth there. I'm not close to sixteen. I just turned fifteen. I'm sorry I lied."

"Fifteen?" The word came out in a whisper. "And you're speaking marriage?"

"I didn't say it had to be right away," Thomlin said quickly. "I just want to know. Would you marry me?"

She stared at him, then suddenly laughed. "Ask me again, then, in three years."

"In three years, then," Thomlin told her, not missing a beat. "And every month in between until you say yes." He started to kiss her again but their lips had barely touched when Enid gasped and jerked away from him. He sat up, staring at her in confusion. "What? What did I do?"

"The Nydiri!" she breathed. "The coven just attacked the Session Chambers."

"How do you know?" Thomlin cried, his gut tightening into a knot.

"I felt it. The magic." She scrambled to her feet, Thomlin close behind. "Landis is looking for me. Saints! I have to stop this. Thomlin, help me!"

"How?"

Enid clutched his arm in panic. "Send me to Landis. Do your magic and send me there."

"I can't. There's not enough elfin magic here."

"But you brought us here," Enid wailed.

"No! Elecka brought us here. She used dark magic to boost our Spell. That's how we got away from Killan. Gods, Enid, calm down."

"I can't. Don't you see? Landis has attacked a dark coven. They'll retaliate and Landis doesn't stand a chance. It's all my fault!" She spun and began to run through the grass.

"Enid! Wait!" Thomlin raced after her, catching up to her easily. He grabbed her arm, forcing her to stop.

"Let go!" she shrieked, tears pouring down her cheeks. "I have to get to Landis. He'll die. Because of me!"

"Enid, we'll ask Elecka to help. If she did it once, maybe she can do it again. Come on. Please."

Enid shook her head and backed away, her sobs coming hard and fast. "You don't know me. This was wrong, all of it. I'm not who you think I am. Go away!"

Thomlin stared at her, confusion and hurt raging through him.

"What in Tor's hell is going on?" Vantann cried as he and Elecka reached them.

"Enid says Landis has attacked the Session Chambers," Thomlin said. "She says he's looking for her. She wants to go to him. Elecka, can you Spell her?"

"But what about Ranen?" Vantann asked.

"Ranen!" Enid gasped. "Oh, saints! I forgot about him!" She turned wild eyes on Thomlin, her voice rising in panic. "What do I do, Thomlin? The dark coven will kill Ranen if they find him. Elecka, help me! Send me to Ranen at least. Or...or bring him here. I can't do this myself."

Elecka shot a quick glance at Thomlin but he only stared back in complete bewilderment. "All right, Enid," Elecka said calmly. "We'll work together to bring Ranen here. There's no way I can Spell all four of us to him. You reach him empathically, direct your magic, and I'll lend mine to pull him here. I'm warning you, though. This won't be pleasant for Ranen."

"It's better than dying," Enid replied.

Thomlin gaped at her, Elecka's words tumbling in confusion. Enid's magic? What magic? What was Elecka talking about?

He stumbled backward as Dirin magic permeated the air. Enid's gaze met his briefly, and suddenly he knew. A Nydiri! Enid was a Nydiri! Vantann took his arm firmly, twin-touching. ::Does it matter?:: he sent.

Thomlin's eyes went wide. ::You knew?::

::Elecka told me. She knew.::

::Why didn't you tell me?:: Thomlin demanded.

::Does it matter?:: Vantann asked again. ::You said you loved her, that you and she were SoulMates. Does it matter what she is?::

::Yes! No! Oh gods! I don't know.:: He looked at her, immersed in Dirin magic and dark magic and suddenly he had the urgent desire to get away. To turn and run. He felt his world crashing down around him. He was lost, his father who knew where, Elek and Kyel gone, Killan and his coven were busily waging war, and now...now he had given his heart to a Nydiri, the one race that drove fear deep into his very soul. Choking back a sob, he pulled away from Vantann and stumbled away. He had not gone more than ten steps before he was enveloped by Dirin magic and swept up into a TravelSpell.

Chapter Fifteen

Treyas winced as Glenna jabbed his arm with a long, slender, hollow needle. Blood oozed out and dripped into a small glass cup.

"Trey," Druce said, "you don't have to do this."

Treyas ignored him, concentrating what magic he could pull to stay the pain.

"You may as well save your breath," Darosenim put in. "He's not listening."

"I'm listening," Treyas said. "But it's nothing I haven't already heard." He looked up at Glenna, who was stirring something into his blood to keep if from clotting. "How much longer? There's not a lot of elfin magic left."

"I don't need much more blood," Glenna answered, as she massaged his arm with firm, downward strokes to encourage the flow of the red fluid.

Treyas regarded the myriad tiny puncture wounds that followed a vein on each forearm, then looked to Druce with an encouraging smile. He had a similar needle protruding from his arm, only his pointed downward and had been capped off with Glenna's magic. Each tiny cupful of blood taken from Treyas had gone drop by drop into Druce's veins, a procedure that had started after breakfast and continued most of the day.

It hadn't taken Glenna long to isolate whose blood had caused the reaction in Druce - Treyas'. She was convinced that she could cure the Yunyo by mixing elfin blood with Merian. There was a risk, she'd explained. A risk that Druce's body might fight against Treyas' blood, might make him sicker than he already was. It was a risk that Treyas had balked against, but one that Druce had accepted willingly. Until Glenna had started stabbing Treyas with the needles. By then, though, Treyas was committed and the blood sharing had gone on.

"There." Glenna set the cup aside, drew the needle from Treyas' arm and held a clean compress over the site. She looked up at Treyas. "How are you feeling?"

"Like I've done battle with a porcupine," he quipped.

"In a way, you have," the brownie replied. "These needles are porcupine quills. Well cleaned I might add." She gestured to Treyas to hold the compress, then picked up the cup and turned to Druce. "Your turn." She attached a tiny glass funnel to the needle in Druce's arm, released the magic cap and began to slowly drip Treyas' blood into it.

"Where did you learn all of this?" Darosenim asked in fascination.

"A little here, a little there," Glenna answered. "Some of my own smarts and some from healing animals. Treyas, drink your citrelle juice."

Treyas did as he was told, savoring the tangy, biting flavor. "When will Anwyl be back?" he asked.

"Soon. He's not as fast as he used to be, but if your boys are anywhere near, he'll bring them in."

Treyas sighed and started to rise but a warning grunt from Glenna changed his mind. She'd told him he might be dizzy and a little weak from the bloodletting. Rest and citrelle juice were the only cure. Darosenim guessed his mission and went to the window to peer out. He shook his head and Treyas sighed again. This was frustrating. He wanted to be out looking, yet didn't want to pass on a chance to help Druce. Especially if that chance involved a possible cure. "When will we know if this is working?" he asked.

"You've given him as much blood as I dare to use. We should know something by tomorrow," Glenna answered. "Either way."

Treyas met Druce's gaze, his heart catching. Druce gave a wry smile and Treyas reached out to grip his free hand. Neither of them wanted to think about the negative side of this radical procedure, yet it constantly asserted itself.

"Your SoulMateBond is going to help with this," Glenna told them. "As will the HealBond and the MindLink."

"Anwyl's back," Darosenim announced.

Treyas turned toward the door as the sorcerer burst in, his face flushed with excitement.

"You found them?" Treyas cried, sitting up.

"I did. They were too far away for me to Spell but strange luck intervened. Landis' coven, the Nydiri I told you about, attacked the Session Chambers. I think they were looking for Enid. Anyway, shortly after the attack, someone attempted a TravelSpell using a mixture of Dirin and dark magic. Then the whole Spell was diverted by Landis himself. I think your boys and the two girls are safe with Landis."

Treyas' mind quickly sorted out Anwyl's words. The dark magic had to be Elecka. But the Dirin? He regarded Anwyl in puzzlement. "Who helped them? Who lent the Dirin magic?"

"Enid," Anwyl replied with a proud grin. "Palls! I didn't think she'd ever use her magic."

"Enid's a Nydiri?" Darosenim breathed, shock evident in his voice.

"Yes. You didn't know?"

"Coals," Druce murmured. "I wonder how Thoms is handling this news."

Treyas grimaced. "How far away is Landis?"

"Not all that far," Anwyl answered. "In fact, I could Spell you there."

Treyas' gaze swung to Druce but Glenna shook her head. "Not Druce. Not yet."

"But I,"

"Trey," Druce interrupted. "You go. I'll be fine here. Just get the children and come back. By that time, I should be able to travel and we'll go after Kyel and Elek. Please, Trey."

"Druce, I...I can't leave you here," Treyas said quietly.

"It won't be for that long," Druce pointed out. "I'm sure the Nydiri can Spell you all back here."

"Can they, Anwyl?"

The sorcerer shrugged. "I don't see why not. They may need your help but even if they don't, the coven is only two days ride."

"Two days," Treyas murmured, his gaze again setting on Druce. Two days was a long time. Druce could die in that time. The HealBond didn't need much magic to stay intact, but Treyas didn't know what elfin magic was available out there beyond Glenna's Illusion.

"Treyas." Druce gripped the elf's hand. "Remember who it is behind all of this. You can't let Dukker get to Vans and Thoms. What happens to me is secondary. You have to go."

"I can stay with Druce if you want me to," Darosenim offered.

"No." Druce countered that at once. "Treyas may need your sorcery magic to get back. I'm well protected here. I've got Anwyl and Glenna, and the cottage is under Illusion. Please, Trey, go before it's too late. You don't know what Dukker has planned."

Treyas studied his face for a long moment, then nodded. "All right. Dar, get our packs and swords."

"Here now," Glenna said. She set the empty cup aside and pulled the quill-needle from Druce's arm. "Anwyl, bind this. Those packs are a might light on foodstuffs. Let me see what I can do."

It took her only a few moments to gather enough travelbread, cheese and dried fruit to fill both bags. It was more food than Treyas hoped they would need. He was praying that Anwyl had enough sorcery magic left to him to cast a clean TravelSpell. He had no desire to land in areas unknown. He rose dizzily from his bed, then bent and kissed Druce on the forehead. "Get well," he murmured, then joined Darosenim. "We're ready then, Anwyl." He looked one last time at Druce before Anwyl cast the Spell and the cottage faded away.

Thankfully, the Spell was clean and true. Treyas and Darosenim landed easily in the very center of a small, roughly put together camp. There were several small wooden structures and one larger one, all nestled comfortably amongst towering fir trees. A swift-flowing creek cut through one corner of the camp, and Treyas immediately drew Darosenim toward it, as four men, clothed in coarsecloth robes of yellow, stepped from the larger building.

"Welcome to Kell Coven," one of the men said. "How might I help you?"

"Anwyl sent us," Treyas said warily.

The man's face brightened. "Anwyl! Why that old goat! He can still cast an accurate Spell."

"I was told you might be harboring some elfin children," Treyas went on. "Is that correct?"

"Yes! Yes! Landis brought them in this morning. My name is Lutherum. These are my colleagues, Rohmer, Lunn and Parlin. You must be the boys' father. The resemblance is remarkable. Come. They're in the lodge." He gestured to them and turned back toward the larger building. "We couldn't have Spelled all of them if it hadn't been for the girl. She carries quite powerful dark magic." He chuckled. "More's the pity for poor Ranen. He's spent the entire afternoon relieving himself of prior meals. Here." He opened the heavy wooden door and stepped inside, Treyas and Darosenim following.

They were in a receiving hall of a type with several doors opening off it. Lutherum and the other Nydiri led them to a door on the far right.

"This is the dining hall," Lutherum said. "We were just about to sit for supper. Please, join us."

The dining hall was large with one long, narrow well-set table down its center and a huge fireplace occupying one wall, in which a roaring and welcoming fire had been kindled. But the best sight to Treyas' eyes were the twins and Elecka clustered in front of the hearth. He heaved a sigh of relief. "Vans! Thoms!" he called across the room.

The twins looked up in surprise, then fairly hurtled the table and benches in their haste to gain their father's side, their long robes hampering their movement. He wrapped one arm about each of them, hugging them close, then suddenly sagged with weakness.

Darosenim got him sitting at once, as the twins hunkered down beside him in worry.

"Papay, where did you come from?" Vantann cried. "Where's Uncle Druce?"

"It's a long story," Treyas replied. "Druce is safe. Are you all right?"

Vantann nodded. "Now. Landis let us bathe and gave us some clean clothes." He wrinkled his nose, looking down at the brown robe. "Not my taste though."

"I'm afraid that was all we had," Lutherum put in with a smile.

"It's more than adequate," Treyas told him. "I'd have taken them naked."

"Papay!" Vantann admonished, his gaze darting to Elecka who had remained near the fire.

Treyas looked past him to the brownling elf. He wished he had good news for her, wished he could produce Kyel. "I need to speak with Elecka."

"You still don't know where Grandpapay is, do you?" Vantann asked.

"No. That's our next task." Treyas glanced at Thomlin. "You're awfully quiet. Are you all right?"

Thomlin shrugged and Vantann spoke up. "Problems of the heart," he said.

"Be quiet!" Thomlin snapped.

Treyas gave him a gentle squeeze. "I heard about Enid's background, Thoms. If there is any way I can help,"

"No," Thomlin interrupted. "I'm fine. I'll deal with it."

"Where is this mystery girl?" Darosenim asked.

"I don't know," Thomlin muttered unhappily.

"Enid?" Lutherum asked. "She's with Ranen. I wasn't aware that there was a problem."

"There is no problem!" Thomlin cried, his voice rising a pitch. "I'm in love with a Nydiri is all! A Nydiri! Just like the ones who imprisoned me, who tormented me, who abused me, then tried to slice my neck open. How could that be a problem? She's a Nydiri! A damned Nydiri!"

"Thoms!" Treyas reached for him, then looked up as Enid stepped into the room. Treyas immediately saw the draw for Thomlin. Though Enid didn't resemble Cynthe in looks, she radiated the same maternal comfort. She regarded Thomlin through brown eyes filled with hurt and anger. Her posture was rigid, her hands clenched into fists at her sides. Her long, wild, brown curls were tamed with a simple ribbon of blue, bringing a spark of color to her brown robes. Treyas felt Thomlin's shoulders sag as Enid spoke, her voice cold and detached.

"M'Lords, Ranen is feeling better," she said, dropping a curtsy. "He's able to talk now and he has information regarding King Kyel and King Jansson."

Treyas' heart leapt with relief. "What information? Where is this Ranen?"

"This is the boys' father," Lutherum told Enid, then looked at Treyas in question.

"My name is Treyas, this is King Darosenim. May I speak with Ranen?"

"Certainly." Lutherum motioned them forward.

Treyas rose unsteadily, still dizzy from the bloodletting. Without a word, Thomlin and Vantann supported him, and the group followed Enid back into the receiving hall and through another door.

They entered what appeared to be a healer's ward. Twelve beds were set up and in one of them rested a young boy. His face was pale beneath a crop of short, black hair and dark circles ringed his green eyes. He looked at his visitors with a mixture of curiosity and fear. Enid stood near his bed and stroked his hair gently. "Ranen," she said, "these are friends of the people in the mountain. Tell them what you told me."

Ranen did so eagerly, as if he wanted both the words and the visitors to be gone. "An elf, a sorcerer and an empath are inside Iron Mountain. They're imprisoned. They can't get out."

"How do you know this?" Treyas asked.

"I'm an empath, too. The empath inside, Jansson, he...he talked into my head," Ranen stammered.

"An EmpathicLink," Darosenim murmured. "Baerns. No wonder you're sick."

"Iron Mountain?" Treyas repeated, then looked to Lutherum. "Does it live up to its name?"

"It does. It's extremely rich in iron ore."

"Which blocks Kyel's magic," Darosenim said with a frown. "And yours, Trey."

Treyas looked back to Ranen. "What did Jansson say?"

The boy scowled. "He scared me! I thought he was a demon. He told me to stay put or he would punish me. And...and he hurt me!" He sought out Enid's hand and gripped it tight.

"He didn't mean to," Treyas said soothingly. "EmpathicLinks are not normal for empaths and they're very hard to do. Tell me what he said."

"He told me who was with him. Kyel and Elek. He said I should find Treyas and tell him where they were. But then it started hurting really bad and he went away." His face brightened momentarily. "But he took all of the pain with him."

"Gods," Darosenim breathed. "It'll be a miracle if he didn't kill himself."

Treyas eyed him in alarm, then drew a deep breath and looked back at the boy. "When was this, Ranen? When did you talk to Jansson last?"

"Yesterday this time, maybe a little later." He gazed at Treyas. "Are you Treyas?"

"I am, and I thank you, Ranen. This is very valuable information."

"How are we going to get them out?" Elecka asked softly from the doorway.

Treyas turned to look at her, saw the fear in the blue eyes, and motioned her closer. She came, falling against him to softly cry.

"The Nydiri put them there," Darosenim said after a moment. "Maybe the Nydiri can get them out."

Lutherum shook his head. "I wish we could, but our magics are very different. And there are only twenty-two of us left here."

"Twenty-two?" Darosenim repeated. "But that's much more than at the Chambers."

"Indeed? You were unaware then that the entire official staff at the Chambers have been replaced?" Lutherum nodded at their amazed faces. Even Enid seemed surprised. "It's true," Lutherum went on. "We've been watching them for a year now. They have systematically replaced every official of Dalziel. We've tried to stop them on occasion and,"

"Lost half our population in so doing," another man interrupted. "Today, four more disappeared."

They turned to greet the tall, broad-shouldered man. He wore loose-fitting green robes, which set off his white hair and brown skin. Sky-blue eyes peered out from beneath bushy white eyebrows set in a strong, square-jawed face. The man approached them, gave Ranen and Enid a tender kiss on the forehead, then turned to Treyas. "I am Landis, the coven Leader. Enid has told me of your predicament."

"I'm afraid," Lutherum put in, "that Ranen has provided information to add to that predicament, Landis. It seems King Kyel, King Jansson and Elek are being held prisoner inside Iron Mountain."

Landis gave a small sigh. "At least we now know where Elek is," he mumbled.

Treyas fixed the Nydiri with a wary gaze. "You speak of Elek with some familiarity. Why?"

Landis smiled. "Elek is a dear friend. He has been for many years. There is no questioning who you are. Elek speaks of you often and fondly. One thing he rarely mentioned though, are your mis-matched eyes. But then, I suppose he no longer views them as unique." He looked to Thomlin and Vantann. "Your boys have provided me with a name. Dukker. I should have guessed this was his doing."

"Where is Dukker?" Treyas asked, anger picking at his gut.

"He has not yet crossed the Dimensional Border. He has sent his followers to pave the path. But, rest assured, he will come across and when he does, it will be with a vengeance."

"You seem to know a lot about him," Treyas said.

Landis fixed his blue eyes on Treyas. "I suppose I should. He's my brother."

Pepin brought Aleron down as close to the dragon mews as he could. He was stiff and sore from a full night and day of flight, and fairly fell to the ground. Ken must have been waiting his return, for he met Pepin almost immediately. "Where have you been?" he asked, his voice edged with both relief and concern. "I thought you were just taking a moonlight ride."

Pepin grimaced. "Aleron had other ideas. There are more eggs, Ken, more dragons on the way. They're in a cave west of the P'lays. Faolan is there. Teague spirited him and Rusulka there, too."

Ken stared at him in relief and astonishment. "Thank the gods. I was worried sick about him. I thought he'd left for Kelta without orders and without backup." He paused. "Eggs?"

Pepin nodded, and clucked at Aleron to head to the mews. He needn't have bothered. Aleron was more than willing to go rest and came close to trampling them both in his haste to get to his stall.

"This news may temper Queen El'leigh's anger," Ken said. "Though not by much."

"What's she mad about now?"

"Word's come up from Kelta. The fleet at Wydrell was attacked."

"Attacked at Wydrell! Coals! That's getting a little close. Was it the Nydiri?"

"No. Just a little skirmish with the Akuri. They were subdued easily enough but," he paused, "Andison is missing."

Pepin gasped. "His dragon?"

"Also gone."

Pepin's thoughts tumbled wildly. "If he's still with his dragon, he's probably all right. Where's Faolan's fleet?"

"They left for Kelta this morning on standing orders from Faolan."

"Good. He was concerned about the Nydiri down there. I'd better go speak with El'leigh. Get Jibben's fleet prepared to leave. I'll be flying down with them."

"On?"

"Jevra," Pepin returned. "I'll be taking the other dragonlings, too."

"But, Pepin, they don't have flame."

"Maybe not, but I'll wager the sight of ten dragons winging overhead will put a fear unlike any other into those Nydiri."

Ken grinned. "I like the way you think, Master Pepin. They'll be ready whenever you are."

Pepin nodded and headed for the palace. He found El'leigh in her solar, pacing furiously, her dark eyes red and swollen from crying. She turned on Pepin in rage. "Where have you been?" she demanded. "No one gave you permission to go anywhere!"

"I don't need permission to take my dragons up in flight," Pepin told her calmly.

"Your dragons?" El'leigh spat. "They're not your dragons, Pepin. They never have been! They belong to Mere Odain and me. You're not even qualified to be named DragonMaster! You're never here. You can't seem to break your ties with Glede and your precious elves."

Pepin drew a deep breath, aware that her anger was driven by her worry over Andison. "You are also an elf, El'leigh. Perhaps you have forgotten that."

El'leigh slammed her fist down on the back of a chair. "I am first and foremost Merian, King Be'an's daughter! The Queen of Mere Odain. I know where my loyalties lie. Do you?"

Pepin ignored the question. "Ken is preparing two fleets to go to south Kelta. I'll be leaving within the hour. I will also plan a flyover of Wydrell and the surrounding lands. Andison's dragon may answer to my call."

"Two fleets!" El'leigh cried. "And leave the palace unprotected? That's what the Nydiri are waiting for!"

"The palace will not be left unprotected. Ken's fleet will remain here. I am taking the dragonlings as a visual deterrent. I don't expect either the

Nydiri or the Akuri to choose to do battle with ten dragons, no matter their size."

El'leigh stared at him, the fight abruptly gone from her eyes. Tears gathered there and spilled across her cheeks. Pepin was empathically assailed by her raw emotions. Instinctively, he went to her and took her in his arms. She relaxed against him, crying. "I didn't want him to go," she whispered. "I really didn't. And now he's missing. I do love Andi, Pepin, I do."

"I know, El'leigh," Pepin said, smoothing her silky dark hair. He kissed the crown of her head, then laid his cheek against it, guilt and pleasure vying for attention. Why was it so impossible to separate himself from her? He loved her, he always had. But at the same time, he had no desire to be with her intimately, no matter how soft and inviting she felt in his arms. He released her gently and wiped the tears from her cheeks. "We'll find Andison. He probably just needed some time away. He loves you a great deal, yet you hurt him a great deal. He needs to find a way to handle that hurt. I have to go, but I promise when I return, it will be with Andison."

"Thank you, Pepi," El'leigh murmured, then kissed him lightly.

Pepin left the solar before his emotions could take over. He hurried outside and down the path toward the mews. Ken had rousted Jibben's fleet and the dragonlings. The latter seemed to be burning off excess excitement by roughly jostling each other. They were completely ignoring both the reproachful looks cast their way by the dragons and the repeated orders of Ken and Jibben to settle down. Pepin couldn't help but smile, though the moment he was close enough, he ended their playful romping with a quick series of clicks and whistles. Ken looked over at him gratefully. "They are a handful," he said. "Are you sure you want to take all of them?"

"Positive. They'll do fine."

"Pepin!" A frantic voice rang out and Pepin turned to see Avenal hurrying down the path from the palace. He reached them breathlessly.

"Galen says you're taking the dragonlings to Kelta. Do you need another rider?"

"Coals, Avenal! You've only ridden one day!"

"Two," Avenal corrected, brushing his brown hair from his face. "I worked with Miele today."

Pepin glanced at Ken, who nodded. "He did well, too."

"I still don't know about this, Avenal," Pepin said. "Kelta's a long ride."

"Pepin," Avenal said firmly, "if I'm to be a rider, I need to ride."

"He's got a point," Ken said with a smile.

"All right," Pepin agreed. "But don't come complaining to me with a sore backside."

Avenal tossed him a sour look and Ken chuckled. "So, which one will you take?"

"Miele," Avenal said without hesitation, casting a fond glance at the red and gold dragonling. Miele responded with a gentle hiss and nudged Avenal affectionately.

"Well," Pepin said, "it appears he agrees."

"I'll get the harnesses then," Ken said and walked away.

Pepin grinned as he watched Avenal scratch Miele, then started at a sudden flash of light. "Grandpapay! What are you," He stared in outright disbelief at the sorcerer who had materialized in front of him. Even Avenal dropped back several paces.

"Pepin!" Elek interrupted. "You have to come at once! Your father needs your help."

Pepin stared at him, aghast as the dragonlings hissed in alarm and danced away, nostrils flaring. Pepin shushed them and addressed Elek. "What's happened? I thought he was in Dalziel."

"He is. So are Dukker's coven. They're after the twins. You need to bring some dragons to stop them. It's your father's only hope."

"But I can't!" Pepin cried. "The dragons have to go to Kelta!"

"You must!" Elek retorted then cringed and flung one arm over his head as Jevra suddenly raised her head and shot a flame into the sky. The light sparkled on Elek's gold wristlet and something nudged at Pepin's memory but he was so startled at what Jevra had done, he ignored it.

"Coals!" Avenal cried. "Pepin, you didn't tell me they could do that!"

"I...I didn't know," Pepin stammered in shock, his mind whirling. "Avenal, you and Jibben take the dragons to Kelta as planned. I'll take Jevra, Shann and Tam with me. The other dragonlings can go with you."

"No!" Elek snapped, his gaze on Jevra. "Don't you understand? Your father and your brothers' lives are at stake. We must have the dragons!"

Jevra hissed again and shot another flame.

"We need flame," Pepin replied, confused. "That's all. Jevra seems quite adequate there."

Elek started to protest again but Jevra suddenly snapped at him, her sharp teeth barely missing his head. He leapt backward and Pepin quickly intervened. "Jevra, no!" he scolded. "I don't know what's wrong with her, Grandpapay. She's not usually like this. She must sense my emotions."

Elek glanced at her. "I suppose. You are an empath. You're most likely intensifying your fear and anger. The problem is, she thinks you're angry with me. She'll protect you well. However," Elek took another step backward, "it would be better for me to maintain some distance until either she, or you, calms."

"I agree. How do I get to Dalziel then?"

"I'll take you now."

"Pepin!" Ken's frantic cry split the air.

Pepin whirled toward the Foumen but before he could respond, Elek's TravelSpell swept him and the dragonlings away. They were deposited on a grassy slope overlooking a forest. Elek appeared a second later and Pepin turned on him at once. "Grandpapay! I don't have my pack or my sword. Why wouldn't you wait?"

"There's no time," Elek replied. "There. See that village? That's the Nydiri coven. And look there."

Pepin looked where he pointed. A column of men on horseback were crossing a wide field headed toward the village. "It looks like a hunting party," Pepin mused.

"It is and they have your father."

"What!" Pepin's gut tightened in alarm. "Then it's them I need to,"

"No!" Elek interrupted. "You risk killing Treyas, too. If you attack the village, it will draw the strength from the Nydiri WardSpell. I'll be able to rescue your father easily. Please, Pepin, do as I ask. Take your dragonlings and lay waste to that village. Let me rescue Treyas."

Pepin drew himself up, ignoring the little prick of doubt. "I will, Grandpapay." He spun. "Jevra, head down!" He mounted quickly. "Head up. Shann, Tam, up." He clung tightly as the three dragonlings shot into the air. He brought them into formation, then cast a hesitant glance at Shann and Tam. "Shann, flame," he ordered. "Tam, flame." He was surprised and thankful when they both complied. "All right," he murmured, "let's get some Nydiri."

Jansson trembled under the strain of holding magic and deftly directed just a bit to his pounding head wound and his wrist. It didn't do much to stay the pain and he brought his gaze up to meet Kyel's. He knew without asking that there was no more pain medicine left. He had consumed the last of it after lunch. Not that it did a lot anyway. He winced as he tried to move into a more comfortable position.

"Jansson," Kyel said softly. "Use the magic for your wounds."

"I have," Jansson admitted. "Some of it, but I still hold some."

Kyel sighed. "It is not enough. Please, make yourself comfortable. We'll try again later."

"No, Kyel, I," He was cut off by Elek's sudden re-appearance and the magic shot away, stinging him sharply. He yelped as the sorcerer, looking dazed, stumbled into Kyel's arms. The elf lowered him gently to the ground. "Welcome back," he said.

"Where were you?" Jansson asked. "What happened?"

"That Nydiri!" Elek mumbled, then seemed to regain some of his strength, at least verbally. "Tor's hell! That Nydiri used my image to coerce Pepin into,"

"Pepin!" Kyel interrupted. "Pepin is here?"

"He is now. That Nydiri impersonating me fetched him from Mere Odain. Him and some of his dragons."

"Why?" Jansson asked.

"To destroy a Nydiri coven." Elek gripped Kyel's arm. "It's Landis' coven, Kyel. They could help us if Pepin doesn't destroy them all first."

"He wouldn't do that," Jansson put in.

"He doesn't know the difference," Kyel replied grimly. "All he knows is that his grandfather wants it done. And I see precious little we can do to stop it." He rose, agitated, and went to brood near the fire.

Jansson watched him, his mind spinning. Pepin had to be stopped. If there were good Nydiri here, they were perhaps the only avenue of escape he and the others had. He leaned back against the wall of the cavern and pulled his blanket close. He and Pepin had shared an EmpathicLink before. Maybe they could again. But at what cost? Linking with Ranen had almost killed him and the boy had been just outside. There was no telling where Pepin was. Still, in the absence of anything else, he had to try. At least once.

Taking a deep breath, Jansson reached out, calling empathically for Pepin. He was rewarded with a strong, painful slap of magic. He gasped and his gaze swung to Kyel. But the elf was looking at him, confused. Confusion that quickly turned to understanding. And anger. "No, Jansson!" he snapped. "No EmpathicLinks! I will not risk it!"

Jansson cringed under the biting tone, but shrugged. "I can't do it anyway. I think the mountain's Warded."

Disbelief crossed Kyel's face. Disbelief and then rage. "It's not enough that I am surrounded by iron, now I must be Warded as well!" He swung out his arm, caught the stacked crates and sent them toppling.

Jansson came swiftly to his feet as the mountain shuddered, raining bits of rock and dirt upon their heads. Elek grabbed Kyel by one ankle and pulled hard, bringing the elf to the ground. Jansson yelped and danced away as a good-sized rock pelted him on the neck.

"Kyel! Stop it!" Elek commanded. "You'll kill us all!"

Kyel rolled and came to a crouch, his gaze darting to first Elek, then Jansson. Jansson's cry caught in his throat. Kyel's blue eyes had turned pale brown, the only true sign of dark magic use. But how? "Ky...Kyel?" he stammered, his heart pounding furiously.

Kyel shuddered, the ground stopped moving and he passed one hand wearily across his face. When he looked up again, his eyes were once more blue. "I'm sorry," he mumbled, then straightened and stepped away.

Jansson shot a quick glance to Elek, then went after Kyel. "How did you do that?"

"I lost my temper," Kyel replied without turning around. "That rarely happens. I apologize."

"But Kyel," Jansson persisted, "you used magic. How? I thought you couldn't. You said the iron here,"

"I am aware of my limitations!" Kyel snapped, then his shoulders sagged and he turned to face Jansson, his blue eyes distressed. "I'm sorry, Jans. It's not you I am angry with."

"I just don't understand," Jansson said. "If you can pull dark magic, why can't you get us out of here?"

"He didn't pull dark magic," Elek said. "He pulled at the Dirin magic surrounding the mountain."

"And most likely did nothing more than tighten the WardSpell," Kyel said. He drew a deep, calming breath. "Come, Jansson, let me brew some tea. We could all use it."

Jansson followed him to the fire, his mind whirling. "So you can pull against the Dirin magic? How tight can you pull it?"

Kyel gave him a cursory glance, then busied himself with the tea making. "It doesn't matter," he said.

"Tight enough to crush us," Elek supplied, then shrugged under Kyel's reproachful look.

"Don't worry over it, Jansson," Kyel told him. "I promise that won't happen."

"But we just might make use of it," Jansson said.

"Jans," Kyel said gently, "you don't understand the,"

"Maybe I don't understand dark magic that well," Jansson interrupted, "nor do I want to. But I do understand the power of a slingshot." He looked pointedly at Kyel. "Or have you forgotten all of the windows you've had to replace over the years at the palace?"

Kyel grimaced. "I have not forgotten, but I fail to see how your skill with a slingshot can help us now or what my magic capabilities have to do with it."

"Think about it," Jansson said. "I know this hasn't happened to you in a very long time, but do you remember the first time you tried to hold magic and it slipped away from you?"

Kyel looked at him blankly. "That has never happened."

Jansson frowned and went on. "Well, I remember. It hurts. A lot. And it tends to scatter one's thoughts for a few moments. What if we could do that to the Nydiri?"

Kyel shrugged helplessly, shook his head and looked at Elek for an apparent explanation. Elek's face brightened, his gray eyes aglow. "I think I see what you're getting at, Jansson. We might be able to distract those Nydiri with one good hit of pain."

"Exactly," Jansson agreed. "Maybe it wouldn't get us out of here, but just maybe it would stall Pepin's attack and wreak havoc with the Nydiri Illusions."

"Will someone kindly explain?" Kyel cried, then his eyes grew wide as understanding apparently took hold. "Oh! No! You can't be serious. If I pull that Dirin magic tight enough to create a rebound of the magnitude you're suggesting, there's no telling what might happen to us. No. It's far too dangerous. No."

"But, Kyel, what if I could provide us a sort of WardSpell?" Jansson asked.

Kyel looked at him, almost amused. "And you've mastered that in the last ten minutes?" He shook his head again. "No, what you're suggesting is,"

"Is the only thing we have left!" Jansson interrupted hotly. "What do you think those Nydiri will do to us once they have Treyas and the twins? They won't need us anymore, Kyel. With us gone, and a fake Treyas in a place of power in Glede, how long do you think war will wait?"

Kyel stared at him, aghast. "But, Jans, I may not be able to control it," he said softly. "This is Dirin magic. Not something I've accessed before. I could...I could bring the whole mountain down on top of us."

Jansson reached out and gripped Kyel's shoulder. "Then we'll die, but we'll die knowing we tried to help and we'll die together. I can't think of a better,"

"No, Jans," Kyel interrupted. "There are much better ways to die. Old age remains my personal favorite." He sighed, looking from Jansson to Elek and back. "All right. We'll try this. But if it doesn't work, be prepared to spend the rest of eternity in Veridia listening to I told you so."

Jansson was surprised at the unexpected bit of dark humor and, though his heart was thumping wildly, he replied in same. "As long as it's you saying it, I can handle it," he said.

Leagues away, Thomlin slouched woefully into a chair before the hearth, his thoughts on Enid and his rash words regarding the Nydiri. He had seen the look of hurt settle in her eyes at his comparison of her to Dukker and his coven. He knew the hurt was justified. These Nydiri in Landis' coven were nothing like the other. Herrick and Anyar had proved that. The spilling of elfin blood on the altar stone would have released their coven from dimensional imprisonment and yet they fought desperately to prevent the twins from being sacrificed. In the end, it was Dukker's own rage that had brought about his downfall. In stabbing Treyas, elfin blood had indeed been spilled and the Nydiri coven released. Thomlin could still hear Dukker's scream of disbelief as he and his followers had been whisked away. A scream of horror and rage that even now seemed to echo in the small room.

Thomlin's head snapped up. It was a scream! A real one, coming from outside! He leapt up and dashed to the window as the scream was joined by others. The sight that met his eyes was shocking.

Two buildings were aflame, as well as several large trees surrounding the camp. Thomlin watched in horror as two Nydiri, their clothes alight, ran from the burning buildings, shrieking in agony. Others ran to their aid, rolling them in the dirt, dousing the flames, then helping them up and towards the river. Men, women and children scattered in terror, their arms flung over their heads as if protecting themselves from some skyborne enemy. Thomlin's gaze swept the evening sky. At first, he saw nothing, then his heart leapt. Dragons!

He whirled and bolted from the room, meeting Vantann, Treyas and Elecka in the hallway. "It's dragons!" he screamed.

"Come! Quickly!" Lutherum appeared as if from nowhere. "We must get to the river."

He herded them outside to join the others in a mad, desperate dash for the safety of the water. Thomlin scanned the camp, his frantic gaze finally settling on Enid. She was stumbling toward the river, Ranen in her arms. A fierce shriek came from overhead and Thomlin froze. A large green dragon was bearing down on Enid, its yellow eyes locked on its target. Without another thought, Thomlin spun away from the river and raced across the compound toward Enid. He slammed against her, knocking her and Ranen to the ground, then covered them with his own body as flame shot from the dragon's mouth.

Though Thomlin felt the incredible heat sear into his exposed skin, he felt no fire and jerked his head up to stare at the dragon. Pepin stared back, his face contorted with disbelief and shock.

"Oh, gods!" Thomlin screamed, even as a sharp whistle pierced the air. "Pepin! Stop!"

The three dragonlings wheeled abruptly to the south and bore down on the river. Thomlin staggered to his feet, shrieking. "Pepin! No! Don't hurt them! They're friends!"

Pepin's brow furrowed in confusion, and he quickly emitted another series of sharp clicks and whistles. The dragonlings veered course, leaving the villagers cowering in the water. Thomlin stared at the devastation around him in disbelief, as Enid stood shakily, still hugging Ranen to her. "You...you know him?" she stammered.

"He's my brother," Thomlin breathed,

"Your brother?"

Thomlin turned to face her, saw hate and condemnation settle in her eyes. He reached out to take her arm but she moved away. "Your brother did this?" she seethed. "Why? Does hatred for the Nydiri run so deep in your family that you would kill innocent people? Children?"

"No!" Thomlin cried, truly aghast at her words. "No, it's not like that. We don't hate you, Enid. I don't hate you. There has to be a reason for this."

Enid stared at him a moment longer, then grabbed Ranen's hand and fled. Thomlin took a hesitant step after her but was stopped as the three dragonlings landed in front of him. Pepin leapt off and rushed to his side. "Thoms! What in Tor's hell are you doing here?"

Thomlin's rage, terror and heartache suddenly exploded. He drew back his arm, and slammed his fist against Pepin's jaw. Pepin staggered backward and stumbled against Jevra, who hissed menacingly at Thomlin. A quick motion from Pepin stayed any further retaliation by the dragonling

"How could you?" Thomlin screamed. "Why? Why did you do this?"

"Pepin! Thomlin!" Treyas reached them breathlessly, Vantann and Elecka close behind.

"Papay!" Pepin stared at him in bewilderment, holding his jaw. Blood trickled from the corner of his mouth and he blotted it away on his sleeve. His gaze flew from Treyas to Thomlin and back. "What the hell is going on?"

"What are you doing here? Why the attack?" Treyas asked, his voice firm, yet holding no reproach.

"Grandpapay, he...he said you needed my help," Pepin stammered. "He said you were a captive of the Nydiri. He told me to destroy the village so he could rescue you."

"Elek?" Treyas uttered an oath of frustration.

"These are good Nydiri, Pepin!" Thomlin snapped. "They were helping us! Why did you,"

Treyas stopped him with a firm grip to his arm, then looked back at Pepin. "Let's get these fires out." He started forward but Pepin held him back.

Another chorus of chirps and whistles, and the dragonlings again took to the air. They bore down on the river, scattering those villagers huddled there. But, instead of attacking, the dragonlings each drove forward, gathered a great scoop of water in a hollow at the base of their tails and proceeded to douse the fires in the village and the trees. Great smoky columns rose into the air, filling the air with the stench of burned wood, grass and flesh. Pepin's gaze flicked over the devastation, and he turned desperate eyes on Treyas. "Oh, gods! Papay, what have I done?"

Treyas hugged him. "It wasn't your fault, Pepin," he consoled, then turned as Lutherum and Landis joined them, their robes still dripping from the river. Both wore looks of confusion and outrage. Pepin backed away, seeking safety against Jevra, who simply hissed good-naturedly at the two Nydiri.

"Landis," Treyas said, "let me explain."

"There is little to explain," Landis said hotly. "It is clearly evident that Dukker has crossed the border."

"Dukker?"

"Yes. This attack was no doubt his doing. Dragons and dragonlings would not willingly attack us. They seem to have an innate ability to read the truth in a Nydiri soul, whether they be good or evil." His gaze settled on Pepin. "That they would follow your command to do something so against their nature, suggests your position. You can be no other than the DragonMaster."

Pepin turned a startled gaze on Treyas.

"I don't care who you are!" Thomlin shouted. "Why did you do this? Look what you've done, Pepin! Look!"

"Thoms!" Treyas admonished. "Pepin is quite aware of what he's done. Perhaps you need to be aware of what you have done."

Thomlin looked at his brother's swollen, bloody lip and tears filled his eyes. He felt completely out of control, as if everything that had once made sense no longer existed. He had struck his own brother, had felt a searing hatred for the man before him. He was violently defending the very race of people he'd sworn to hate. And not only that, but he was deeply and unquestioningly in love with one of them. One who now thoroughly despised and hated him. It was too much to bear and Thomlin broke into sobs. He felt arms go around him, thought it to be his father, was surprised to find it was Pepin.

"Gods, Thoms," Pepin murmured, "I don't know what's going on, but I'm sorry. I'm so very sorry."

"Come," Landis said quietly. "Let us talk further inside. I, for one, would like dry clothes. Lutherum, would you tend to the wounded?"

"I'm sorry," Pepin mumbled. "I never...I didn't...I'm sorry."

Treyas put an arm about his shoulders. "You thought you were helping. Put it behind you and let's come up with a plan to stop Dukker before it's too late." He paused. "Maybe your dragons could go graze or something. I don't think the Nydiri here would appreciate them staying around."

"Nonsense," Landis retorted. "The dragonlings were doing what they were told to do. My people hold no animosity toward them." He looked at Pepin. "You on the other hand, may not be so easily forgiven. But, rest assured, they will understand. Dukker and his malicious ways are well known to this coven." He turned and strode inside the lodge, one of the few buildings left standing. The others followed slowly.

Once inside they sat quietly around the table, their gazes on Pepin. He shifted uncomfortably, then told them what had happened, how Elek had appeared and demanded his assistance in rescuing Treyas.

"I should have known something was wrong," he said quietly. "Jevra was upset with Grandpapay. And the dragonlings...they didn't really want to attack the village at all. I...I forced them to. I thought they were just frightened. Gods! I should have paid more attention to what she was trying to tell me." He cast a helpless gaze at the others. "But how could they make Grandpapay act like that?"

"Because it was highly doubtful that you talked to your grandfather at all," Landis replied. "It was most likely a Nydiri under Illusion."

"Papay," Thomlin said quietly. "I need to find Enid. I need to explain what happened."

Treyas nodded. "Go on, then, but keep in mind what she witnessed. Try to view it from her perspective."

"I will. Pepin, I'm sorry about your mouth."

Pepin gave him a lop-sided grin. "Apology accepted. Maybe you can teach me that right cross sometime."

"Maybe," Thomlin agreed half-heartedly, then slipped away. He hadn't wanted to go so much to search for Enid as to get away from anymore talk of Dukker. Just the name sent chills coursing through him. Gods! What was he doing here? With her? He shook his head, forcing back his tears of despair and followed the hallway.

It ended in a small room at the far end of the lodge. Incense hung heavy in the air, and Thomlin took a deep breath of its warm, spicy fragrance, before moving into the room. He caught his breath. Enid had just set a small metal cup on what appeared to be an altar. Light gray tendrils of smoke spiraled from the cup, and Enid dropped to her knees before the altar, her head bowed. She was mumbling softly but her words were in another language. A language Thomlin did not understand but knew to be Dirin. He guessed she was praying for the wounded and sank down on the nearest bench, unsure what else to do. Her voice startled him.

"What do you want?" she asked without turning or rising.

"N...nothing. I..."

"What do you want?" she asked again, her voice tight and angry.

Thomlin sagged. "I want to talk to you. I want to explain both my words and my brother's actions. I was wrong, Enid. I know I can't condemn a whole race because of a few. Your coven is nothing like Dukker's. I feel warm, safe and cared for here. I never felt anything even remotely resembling that in Dukker's coven." He rose, saw her stiffen and stopped. "My brother, Pepin, was sent here by someone, probably..." He couldn't bring himself to say the name, "by someone impersonating my grandfather. Pepin would do anything to help us. He couldn't know who you really were. He...he thought he was saving us from...from..." New tears appeared and Thomlin's thoughts unexpectedly spun back to Winze. He shuddered violently, closing his eyes, once more reliving the terror. He could still see the strange orange moon rising over the altar, still see the knife blades glistening, still hear the chilling, mysterious chanting of Dukker and the others. It was the same language Enid had been using only moments before.

His legs went wobbly and he sank down on the bench, using the bench in front as a support. "Dukker was going to kill us," he whispered. He leaned forward, resting his head on his hands. "Me and Vans. He was going to sacrifice us to release his coven. He...he had us on the altar stone...and the knives..." He felt dizzy, flushed, nauseous.

"Thoms." Enid's voice was close and Thomlin gasped, his eyes snapping open. He realized he was trembling, and tears fell. He didn't have the strength to wipe them aside. "I'm sorry," he sobbed. "I'm sorry I said those things. I'm sorry I condemned you with Dukker's kind. I know you're not the same. I know that."

She was quiet a moment, then sat beside him and placed her arm about his shoulders. Thomlin caught at his breath, arching away from her as pain tore across his back. Enid gasped, her gaze flying to his neck.

"You're burned!"

Thomlin frowned, then remembered how he had thrown himself over Enid and Ranen to protect them from the dragon's flame. He still wondered how Pepin could have called off the attack of flame so quickly, and his awe over his brother's talents increased tenfold.

"You offered your life for mine," Enid said softly, her voice holding true surprise.

Thomlin looked over at her. "I love you. I would die for you."

She appraised him thoughtfully, then reached up and gently brushed his tears aside. "I love you as well, Thoms."

Thomlin's heart leapt. It was the first time she had called him by his nickname. "Will you marry me, Enid? Will you?"

She gave a small, teasing smile. "Ask me in three years," she said again. "When you're eighteen and considered a man."

Thomlin smiled back. "And every month until," he whispered and their lips met in a gentle, yet passionate kiss.

Chapter Seventeen

Treyas frowned and exhaled sharply, his unease clearly evident. "You only have three, Pepin," he said again. "Dragonlings, not even dragons. This is too dangerous."

"But what other choice do we have?" Landis put in.

The group had gathered before the hearth in the dining hall. Landis, the twins, Elecka, Enid, Darosenim and Pepin all looked to Treyas for a possible answer to the question. Treyas had none.

"Papay, listen," Pepin said. "Dukker doesn't know I'm onto him. If I can show him that I followed his orders and destroyed this village, it'll,"

"Get you killed!" Treyas interrupted. "No, Pepin. You can't trust Dukker. Just because you did his bidding, doesn't mean he won't turn right around and kill you. He has no great love for you or your dragons. You said yourself that Jevra almost bit him in half. Why would he want you around?"

"Besides," Landis said. "By now Dukker is aware that you failed to destroy our coven. He would have felt it had we all died."

There was a moment of resigned silence before Treyas spoke again. "Was the Nydiri wearing Elek's wristlet?"

Pepin nodded. "He was. I remember, because Jevra's flame shone off it." He frowned, then suddenly gasped. "Oh coals! That's what was wrong! He was wearing it on the wrong wrist. I knew something was different. I should have paid more attention."

"Pepin," Treyas said softly, "you would never have guessed what was going on. Don't condemn yourself for that."

Pepin looked at him grimly. "No, I suppose I have enough else to condemn myself for. Coals, Papay, the dragonlings didn't want to attack. I made them. I took their reluctance for fear and uncertainty. I should have listened to them. I'm not a DragonMaster. I'm an elf, just an elf and I want to go home."

The words rang sweet in Treyas' ears, though the look of grief on Pepin's face tugged at his heart. He squeezed Pepin's hand tenderly. "Glede is always your home, Pepin. You know that. But I need you to be the DragonMaster for just a while longer. We need to get Elek's wristlet to him. I think the dragonlings may be our answer."

"How so?" Landis asked.

"If anything can defeat Dukker, it'll be the dragonlings," Treyas replied. "If we can get the wristlet from whoever holds it, the dragonlings can take it to Iron Mountain. If Kyel, Elek and Jansson are indeed being held inside as Ranen said, there has to be some sort of air vent to keep them alive."

"An air vent that can be spotted from above," Darosenim mused.

"And into which a small gold wristlet can be dropped," Landis finished with a grin. "At last, a plan that bears merit."

"Landis!" Lutherum burst into the room, his thin face flushed. "You need to see this! I was scrying the area as you instructed and...well, come look."

The group rose as one and followed Lutherum and Landis to a large study. A crystal sphere floated several inches above a polished burlwood table at the room's center. The candlelamps in the room were reflected against the crystal, but an image could quite clearly be seen in the orb. Iron Mountain, rising in its black glory out of a grassy field. Treyas could see nothing untoward but Landis scowled unhappily.

"Dukker's Warded the mountain," he stated.

Treyas sighed as his plan shattered, but Lutherum clutched at Landis' arm. "Watch, Landis," he instructed.

Landis looked at the crystal globe, then his eyes went wide and a small gasp escaped him.

"What is it?" Treyas asked.

"The WardSpell...it seems to be shrinking."

"Shrinking?"

"Yes. It's as if someone were pulling it inward." Landis exchanged a puzzled glance with Lutherum, who shrugged, obviously just as confused.

Darosenim frowned, peering closely at the crystal.

"What would be the purpose of pulling it in?" Treyas asked.

"I don't know," Landis replied grimly. "But if it doesn't stop, it'll crush the whole mountain. That is, if it doesn't rebound first and rip the top off the mountain."

Treyas gasped. "We have to get them out of there!"

"But who's pulling it in?" Vantann asked.

Landis shrugged. "I don't know. If Elek is without his conduit, and Kyel is without his elfin magic, that leaves only King Jansson with his bardic. And that would not be sufficient to tighten a WardSpell."

"But dark magic would," Elecka said softly.

"Kyel?" Treyas asked.

Darosenim's gaze flew to Treyas. "A slingshot!" he cried.

"What?"

"A slingshot," Darosenim repeated. "Pull it nice and tight, then let it go. Jansson once told me that was what it was like to have MagicStrands slip away. Like a slingshot. This is Jansson's idea, I'll bet."

"But do you realize what a rebound like that will do to Dukker and his," Landis broke off with a big smile. "Palls! That'll scatter their Illusion magic far and wide. Pepin! That's when you need to attack. As soon as that WardSpell is released, it'll knock Dukker senseless. He and his followers will be vulnerable."

"But I don't even know where he is!" Pepin cried.

"Don't worry about Dukker. Find the one holding the wristlet. Your dragonlings can guide you."

Pepin looked to Treyas, who frowned. "I don't like the idea of,"

"Please, Papay," Pepin interrupted. "I need to do this. Please."

Treyas studied his son for a moment, seeing the anguish that lay in the dark eyes. He knew Pepin was punishing himself, would be for many months, over what he had forced his dragonlings to do. Maybe helping the Nydiri would help him as well. Treyas nodded. "It may just work, Pepin. Landis, can you tell how much time we have?"

Landis looked again at the crystal. "I'd wager that's King Kyel working that magic. His control is legendary. Still, this is Dirin magic. I wouldn't think he's used it much. I don't know how tight he'll be able to pull it. Too tight and he risks himself and the others. Not tight enough and the rebound won't be sufficient. I'd say maybe another hour."

"An hour," Treyas repeated. "Pepin, you need to get your dragonlings in position. One to go after Dukker, the other two to attack the Nydiri at the Session Chambers."

"Then they'll need riders," Pepin pointed out. "Someone who I can tell them to obey."

"Let me," Thomlin said quickly. "I have a score to settle with Dukker."

"Revenge, Thomlin?" Treyas asked softly.

"Why not?" Thomlin retorted, then his gaze went to Enid. "No," he amended, "no." He took her hand and kissed it gently. "Not revenge. I just want to help."

"I do need someone light and small enough to ride the dragonlings," Pepin admitted.

"Elecka and I can do it, then," Vantann said.

"I can do it!" Thomlin asserted.

"Papay?" Pepin looked to him for a decision.

Treyas' gaze settled on Vantann and Elecka. Both lithe and light. Both strong willed and determined. And both heirs to the throne. But what other choice did he have? Thomlin and Enid? The former, who no matter his words, burned with the need for revenge. The latter a Nydiri herself who would be killing her own kin. No. Neither was a good choice. "I'll go," he said, his voice firm, holding no invitation for argument. "Me and Dar."

Darosenim started, his blue eyes alarmed. "I hardly consider myself light or small," he protested.

Pepin gave a half-smile. "Tam can carry you. Easily. That is, if you're not too scared."

"Scared!" Darosenim flushed, his gaze darting amongst those around him. "I am not scared." He threw back his shoulders. "And I'm not small. I'm just a little bit shorter than most men. And a little lighter. But, I'm not small."

Treyas kept his smile to himself. "All right, Pepin, you have your riders. Let's go. There's no telling how long Kyel will be able to hold that magic, despite his renowned control."

They all trooped outside to where the three dragonlings waited. They'd attracted quite an audience, something they were reveling in. Shann, a striking purple and green dragonling, had her head lowered and was puffing smoke in bliss as Ranen scratched one hornfan. Pepin chuckled softly, and motioned Darosenim toward Tam, a sturdy looking blue-on-blue dragonling. The mage approached him warily, light blue eyes meeting dark blue. Tam hissed a greeting and Darosenim leapt backward, his face alarmed. "Pepin?"

"Tam says hello," Pepin told him, then addressed the dragonlings as if speaking to humans. "Tam, this is King Darosenim. He'll be your rider for a while. I want you to listen to his orders. Shann, this is my father, Crown Prince Treyas Merripen. He'll be your rider. You will take your orders from him." He whistled shrilly and all three dragonlings lowered their heads. Pepin gestured to Darosenim and Treyas. "You can mount now. If you sit just there, at the base of their wings, you'll be able to stay on no matter what maneuver they do."

Darosenim looked at him, startled. "They'll just fly, won't they? I mean, we aren't going to do anything fancy right?"

Pepin gave him an amused smile. "Just blow flame, that's all. Now mount up."

Darosenim grimaced but climbed up on Tam and settled himself into the spot Pepin had indicated. Treyas turned to the twins and Elecka, not sure of what to say. In the end, he said nothing but gave them each a heartfelt hug and kiss before turning and climbing up on Shann.

Pepin leapt up on Jevra. "Heads up!" he ordered the dragonlings and all complied.

"Remember, Pepin," Landis called. "Trust the dragonlings. Trust yourself."

Pepin nodded, met Treyas' gaze briefly, then gave the command that sent all three dragonlings shooting into the sky. They circled once, gathered their bearings, then winged silently east.

In the cavern, Jansson had his gaze locked on Kyel. The black elf's eyes were a muddy brown, his mouth set in a tight frown. Jansson could almost feel his concentration on pulling the Dirin magic. He glanced at Elek, who gave him a reassuring, though wan, smile. "Now, Elek?" he whispered.

"I will say when!" Kyel snapped. "My control hasn't suffered so far."

"I didn't say it had," Jansson replied calmly, soothingly.

"I'll thank you to deliver bardic help only when I ask for it," Kyel said tightly.

"Firesass," Jansson mumbled through clenched teeth.

"And change your language!" Kyel snapped.

"Gods!" Jansson surged to his feet and strode to the food crates, where he began to repack the food Kyel had earlier toppled.

"Sit down!" Kyel's voice was commanding. "How do you expect me to concentrate when you're flitting about like a butterfly?"

Jansson's own anger and worry surfaced and he spun on Kyel, but before he could say anything, Elek snagged him by the arm. "This is dark magic, Jansson. You know how that affects you both."

"I certainly know how it affects him!" Jansson seethed.

"Do you?" Kyel retorted. "Do you really? Perhaps you would like to feel just a bit of this struggle. It was, after all, your brilliant idea."

Jansson gasped as sharp pain swept through him. Pain that was gone as quickly as it had come as Kyel regained control. But it was enough of a shock to jolt Jansson out of the dark magic's grip. "Kyel," he murmured, "I'm sorry. I didn't know it would cause you pain. Let it go. It's not worth it."

"If it will free us from this prison," Kyel said, "then it's worth it." He shuddered and closed his eyes briefly. When he opened them again, they were black.

The mountain trembled violently and dirt fell from the ceiling. Jansson ducked, covering his head with his arm.

"Now, Kyel!" Elek cried. "Let it go now!"

Kyel's gaze shifted to him, his stare blank and uncomprehending.

"Kyel!" Jansson yelled as the ground shook beneath his feet. A low rumble filled the air, bouncing from wall to wall, creating a deafening roar. Dust billowed up as chunks of rock fell from the ceiling and walls.

"Let it go!" Elek shouted, then collapsed with a cry of pain as a large piece of rock hit him on one shoulder.

Kyel trembled, his brow furrowed and, for a moment, the ground calmed. But, as quickly as it had settled, it began again with a new vengeance, knocking Jansson off his feet. He came to his knees, gasping. Kyel stared his way, without seeing him. Jansson stared back in horror.

"No," he mumbled aloud. "I will not let the dark have you, Kyel!" He doubled his hand, swung out with all of his strength and slammed his fist against Kyel's jaw. The elf staggered and his gaze flew to Jansson, the black eyes registering disbelief and then rage. Jansson recoiled only briefly, then struck him again. This time Kyel went down.

The mountain roared with the release of Dirin magic, and Jansson flung himself on top of Kyel as the ceiling began to collapse. The food crates toppled, landing on his back and head. For a split second, time seemed to stand still, then blackness engulfed him.

Outside the mountain, Pepin drove Jevra down hard and fast. A lone Nydiri stood on the grassy field outside the Session Chambers, his gaze intent on Iron Mountain. He wore a look of disbelief and astonishment as the magic shuddered over the land. He whirled as Jevra's form cast a shadow over the meadow, but he was not fast enough to stop her attack. She loosed her flame, catching him in its fiery embrace, wrapping him in a solid wall of flame. He shrieked as his robes ignited, and batted at them, his magic too scattered to use. Jevra once again spit fire and Pepin recoiled in revulsion as the Nydiri dropped to his knees, his skin already melting from his bones.

Out of the corner of his eye, Pepin saw the golden wristlet fall to one side. He whistled to Jevra, who immediately stopped her attack, swept down and deftly plucked the wristlet from the grass with one long claw. Pepin leaned hard into her side, driving her away from the Session Chambers, toward Iron Mountain. Behind him, Shann and Tam were turning the Chambers into a raging inferno. Nydiri, subdued by their temporary loss of magic, ran screaming from the building, robes and hair flaming.

Pepin reached Iron Mountain in a matter of moments and circled it anxiously. He could see no vent, no opening of any kind. In fact, it looked as if the mountain were collapsing on itself. Jevra pulled hard to the right and Pepin corrected her, circling the mountain again. And again, Jevra pulled at him. With a start, Pepin remembered Landis' words. 'Trust the dragonlings, trust yourself.'

"All right, Jevra," he said, "this is yours. Drop the wristlet where you must."

Jevra threw back her head, blew a stream of fire, and dove. Pepin gasped as the dragonling came perilously close to the jagged black rock, then released the wristlet, before soaring upward, leaving Pepin's stomach behind. He swallowed hard to keep from retching and waited anxiously to see what would happen.

Just a few moments later, the entire side of the mountain blew outward, showering the grassy fields with rock and dirt. The percussion hit Jevra hard, sending her rolling through the air. Pepin hung on through sheer terror alone, until the dragonling managed to regain her stability. Pepin clung to the reins, gasping, sweat trickling down his neck and back. Nausea tore through him and won. He retched, narrowly missing Jevra and himself. Magic spun through the air - sorcery and dark mixed together and Pepin let out a sigh of relief. Kyel and Elek were free! He whistled to Jevra and they turned toward the Session Chambers, where great columns of smoke pierced the sky. Only then did his success hit him. Along with euphoria. "We did it, Jevra!" he yelled. "A dragonling and a halfling. We did it!" He leaned forward and planted a kiss on her scales. "I'm no DragonMaster and you're no dragon," he murmured. "Just the same, I think we make a pretty good team. Come on, Jevra, let's go home."

By the time Pepin had regrouped his dragonlings, the Session Chambers were no more than a black, smoking pile of ashes. Darosenim and Treyas had dismounted, shaky but unhurt. A small group of servants huddled nearby, stunned and silent.

Treyas turned at once to Pepin. "Are you all right?"

"Fine," Pepin replied, grinning. "In fact, I feel great."

Treyas winced at the note of pride in Pepin's voice. Now, Pepin felt great, euphoric from the kill, the success of his actions. Later would come the remorse, the guilt. And for Pepin, an empath, it would be a hard road. Treyas gave him a small smile, and squeezed his shoulder.

"Baerns," Darosenim groaned. "I didn't plan to destroy the place." He gasped in surprise as a group of dazed-looking officials abruptly materialized on the field behind him. Elek was with them. He immediately grabbed Treyas in a firm hug, then Pepin.

"I take it these are the real Dalziel officials," Treyas said.

"They are. Dukker had them all imprisoned at his camp several leagues from here. Neslin, this is my son, Crown Prince Treyas Merripen, and his son, Prince Pepin Merripen. This is King Darosenim Quartermane of Karsaba."

But Neslin was looking past them all to the smoking remains of his home and offices. "The Chambers," he mumbled.

"We'll help you rebuild," Darosenim said quickly, then leapt back as Kyel appeared, Jansson, the twins, Elecka, Enid and Landis in tow. "Baerns! I need to sit down!" He dropped to the grass, his face pale.

"I know the feeling," Jansson said and sagged down beside him.

"Papay!" Vantann and Thomlin hugged him with relief.

"Neslin," Landis said, placing a hand on the official's shoulder. "Consider our home as yours until the Session Chambers are rebuilt."

Treyas stepped forward. "Please accept our sincerest apologies for the devastation caused here. And allow me to remedy this situation. Glede has an abundance of hardwoods, and many skilled craftsmen. I would be glad to offer their services."

Neslin looked at him numbly. Slowly a hesitant smile crossed his face. "Thank you, Your Highness. And perhaps we can repay your kindness with citrelles." He glanced at Elek. "Strange how an alliance of a sort has been formed and I wasn't even here."

"Believe me, Neslin," Elek said, "that isn't the strangest of it."

Landis gave a weary smile and motioned some of his people forward. "Take Neslin and the others to the lodge. Get them something to eat, then find them a place to rest."

The Nydiri nodded, and led the subdued officials away. Treyas turned to Landis. "My sympathies, Landis. Dukker,"

"Is not dead," Landis interrupted.

Treyas caught his breath, his gaze darting to Thomlin. The boy had paled noticeably, but said nothing. Treyas gripped his arm in reassurance. "Elek, if things are in control here, I have an urgent need to get back to Druce. And I would like the twins returned to Lidgerwood."

"Where is Druce?" Jansson asked.

"He's with a brownie and a sorcerer."

Jansson rose. "Mind if I tag along then?"

"I'd like that," Treyas told him, not wanting to dwell on the reasons for the offer. "The problem is, I have no idea where Anwyl's cottage is."

"Anwyl?" Elek grunted. "That old goat? He's the one who started this whole mess!"

"Yes," Landis said gently. "And there but for the grace of the gods,"

"I know, I know." Elek waved him away.

"Grandpapay," Pepin put in. "I need to get back to Mere Odain. There are still the Nydiri there to deal with and I have to find Andison."

"Andison is missing?" Treyas cried.

Pepin sighed. "It's a long story, Papay. I'll fill you in later. But I need to go."

Treyas nodded, ignoring the sense of duty Pepin was showing for Mere Odain. "Elek, this won't be too much for you will it?"

"Too much?" Elek boomed, then drew a deep breath and flexed his arms, his wristlet glistening in the sunshine. "Hellfires! It feels good to have my magic back!"

"What about us, Papay?" Vantann asked.

"I just want to go home," Elecka murmured, clinging to Kyel's arm.

"I second that," Darosenim put in.

Treyas looked to Thomlin. "Thoms? Are you ready?"

Thomlin drew a deep breath and gripped Enid's hand. "Papay," he said firmly, "I've asked Enid to marry me."

Enid, Vantann and Elecka gasped together.

"Thomlin," Treyas said gently, "you're only fifteen."

"I know. That's what Enid said. But in three years I'll be eighteen. That's when she'll give me her answer. In the meantime, I'd like her close. If you don't think it's appropriate for her to stay at the palace, maybe she can stay with Uncle Jansson, Uncle Dar or Uncle Quinlin."

Treyas hesitated, eyeing Enid. "What do you have to say to all of this?"

Enid flushed, looking to Landis. He smiled and tipped his head, as if in agreement. Enid looked back at Treyas. "I...I would appreciate any form of lodging you could provide, Your Highness. I have been fully trained as a kitchen servant. Perhaps I could serve one of the palaces."

"She makes wonderful bread ties," Jansson put in. "Mayfaire has extra rooms."

Treyas shot him an amused look. "So does Lidgerwood. We'll discuss proper living arrangements later. For now, Enid, consider Lidgerwood your home, not your place of employment. Oh and, Enid, if I'm to be your future father, you needn't address me as Highness." He leaned forward and kissed her lightly on the cheek, furthering her blush. "Elek, send the children home, then send Pepin and his dragonlings back to Mere Odain, and me and Jansson to Druce." He looked at Kyel thoughtfully. "You seem a bit quiet. Is there something wrong?"

Kyel shook his head. "No," he mumbled. "My jaw seems rather sore. Talking is painful."

"What happened?"

Jansson clutched his arm. "Don't ask," he whispered, then gave Kyel a hug. "See you at home, Papay."

Kyel managed a small smile and gestured to Elek, who sent him, Darosenim and the children swiftly on their way. Pepin and the dragonlings went next. Jansson heaved a sigh of relief. "Gods, if Kyel remembers what happened, I'm doomed."

"What did you do?" Treyas asked, puzzled.

"I hit him, Trey." Jansson shuddered. "Twice. It was either that or be crushed by the mountain."

"And he doesn't remember that?" Treyas asked doubtfully and Jansson frowned in worry.

Elek grinned and prepared the Spell to send them to Druce. Just before he cast it, he caught Jansson's eye. "Kyel knows perfectly well what happened. He said he'd deal with you later."

Jansson's eyes went wide but before he could retort, the three of them were whisked to Anwyl's cottage.

"Trey!" Druce greeted them before they were fully down.

"Druce!" Treyas stared at him in shock. Not only was he up from bed, he looked healthier than Treyas had seen him in a long time. Treyas looked to Glenna and Anwyl.

"It worked," Glenna said simply.

"I'm cured, Trey," Druce put in. "The Yunyo is completely gone."

"Gone?"

"Gone. That's pretty powerful blood you have there," Druce said, his voice soft. "Now, we're more than SoulMates, Trey. We're brothers."

"Druce, we're..." Treyas' voice cracked with emotion and tears flooded his eyes.

Druce gave an awkward grin and hugged him. "I guess we're even now. Three years ago in Winze, it was me who didn't know whether you lived or died. I guess it worked out well in both instances."

"You guess?" Jansson cried. "Firesass! You guess?"

Treyas smiled and went to Glenna. "How can I ever thank you? There are no words."

"It is I who should be thanking you," Glenna replied. "My life has been a long one, Treyas Merripen. Who knows how much time Anwyl and I have left. But I can die happy and satisfied now, knowing that I have done this."

Treyas hugged her gently, then clasped Anwyl's hand between his. The sorcerer glanced over at Elek. "I know I brought a lot of this on," he said, his voice holding remorse and apology. "I guess I should realize that I'm not as young as I used to be. My reflexes aren't quite as sharp. I think from here on out, I'll leave the dimensional hopping to those more qualified."

Elek grunted. "That'll be the day, Anwyl," he grumbled, though Treyas noted it was said with no animosity. "Come on, then, Treyas, Jansson, Druce. I'm tired. I just want to relax in front of a warm fire with a good glass of wine."

"We have that here," Glenna said quietly.

"Hmpf, so you do." Elek glanced about. "You go on ahead, Treyas. I think I'll visit with Anwyl for a time."

Treyas smiled. "I'll see you at home, then."

Jansson moaned. "I'm sick of these TravelSpells. Give me a good horse. Please?"

"Right," Druce teased. "Then you'd be complaining of a sore,"

"Enough!" Elek interrupted. He cast the Spell and sent them home.

Pepin arrived from Mere Odain two days later and went straight to Treyas in the study. The latter looked up in surprise from his paperwork on Dalziel. "Pepin? Where did you come from?"

Pepin glanced toward the TravelPortal, then back at Treyas. "Um...Papay, I have a request," he stammered, then motioned Treyas to the window.

Treyas dropped his quill and rose to join his son. The afternoon sun was shining down on the palace grounds and had encouraged all of the resident children outside. Even the twins, Enid, and Elecka were there. And all were clustered in squealing excitement around five very colorful, very large dragonlings, while Faolan and Rusulka appeared to be fielding questions. Treyas caught at his breath.

"Papay," Pepin said quickly. "I know they seem big, but they're not really. And they're quite harmless. Really!"

"Harmless!" Treyas cried, remembering all too well the ruins of the Dalziel Session Chambers.

"Papay, they won't throw flame unless I tell them to. And they don't eat meat. Fao and Rusulka found out that they're vegans."

"All right," Treyas said slowly. "But what are they doing here?"

"Finding a new home?" Pepin asked warily.

"What?" Hope surged through Treyas at the words. So far, neither he nor Pepin had discussed his move to Mere Odain. And, although Treyas knew Pepin had been in conference with Kyel, he did not know what had occurred. He knew only that Pepin had spent the last few days away from Lidgerwood. He had supposed it was to set up a place in Mere Odain for him and his family. Now, though, if Treyas was hearing him correctly, those plans might have changed. He waited patiently for Pepin to continue.

Pepin ran a hand through his dark curls. "I know this is a bit of a surprise, Papay, but it's the only thing I could think of. I've turned over the title of DragonMaster to Andison."

"Andison? I thought Faolan was the,"

"Hear me out," Pepin interrupted quietly. "Andison wasn't missing. He'd gone to see Veya and Jak. It took some convincing but I got him to go back home to El'leigh, and to his position as King. Despite her actions, she was overwhelmingly glad to see him safe and sound. Anyway, I came to the conclusion that it was extremely important to El'leigh that she be united with the DragonMaster. Andison's love and loyalty for Mere Odain goes far deeper than anything I could ever experience. He is Merian, Papay, he is the armsmaster and he is the King. It seemed fitting that he should also be the DragonMaster. And there is nothing more to the name than the title itself. A title that now belongs to Andison."

Treyas paused, eyeing his son. He heard much more behind the words than were being spoken. Pepin was trying to convince not only Treyas, but himself, that his connection with the dragons of Mere Odain was merely in title. He doubted that was true, not after the way Pepin had controlled the dragons in Dalziel. Still, there was such quiet determination behind the dark eyes Treyas did not question it. What he did question was where Pepin called home. He just couldn't bring himself to ask. Not yet.

"What do the dragons think of this?" he said instead. "And Faolan?"

"The dragons are fine with it. They respect and love Andison. It was an easy fit, really. As far as Fao - he's always been the DragonMaster in more than title. He'll continue to be so. He's quite happy with the arrangement. He'll keep doing what it is he does best, working with Ken in handling the dragons. And," Pepin paused for a moment to look down at the dragonlings, "he'll have help from his new wife - Rusulka."

Treyas started. "Does Thoms know about this?"

"I expect he does now," Pepin said, pointing.

Rusulka and Thomlin had separated from the others and looked to be in deep conversation. Treyas watched as they embraced, then Thomlin motioned for Enid to join them. Faolan did as well and, after a moment, he and Thomlin clasped forearms in friendship. Treyas smiled. His family was growing up. His gaze went back to the dragonlings, who were happily suffering the younger children clambering across their backs and tails. "The dragonlings, Pepin," he prompted. "You still haven't explained them."

"Well," Pepin said hesitantly. "El'leigh doesn't want them. Not in view of the fact that fifteen more dragons just hatched out. Aleron showed Fao and me a nest on the west side of the P'lays. That's where Fao and Rusulka have been this past week, hatching out dragons. They're all back at the palace now but it was a bit crowded with the dragonlings there, too. Since El'leigh prefers the dragons over the dragonlings and since there was no place else to take them..." His voice trailed off as Treyas looked his way.

"And since there's still a part of you that is a DragonMaster," Treyas put in, "this seemed logical?"

Pepin nodded weakly, then grasped Treyas' arm. "Please, Papay, can I keep them here with me? I'll build the mews for them. I'll take them to Kartonn to feed. They really don't eat much despite their size. And you can see how good they are with the children. I'll take full responsibility for them. I promise. Please?"

Treyas eyed him for a moment. "And what of you personally? Will you be here or in Mere Odain?"

"Here. That is if you,"

Treyas silenced him with an upraised hand. "Your place here has never been in question." He paused, then added, "Your allegiance has."

"No longer," Pepin told him firmly. "I've made my choice. Kyel and I discussed it at length. Believe me," he added under his breath, then again turned a beseeching gaze on Treyas. "So, can I keep them?"

Treyas chuckled. "Do you know how often I've heard this from you? It started with those two kittens when you were seven and now it seems it ends with five dragonlings."

"It would have been six, but Miele didn't want to leave Avenal, so it's just the five," Pepin pointed out, as if that made a huge difference. "Please?"

Treyas looked deep into his son's eyes, then broke into laughter and draped an arm about Pepin's shoulders. "Welcome home, DragonMaster. Welcome home."

JennaKay Francis has been writing since she was 12 years old. She has written in many different genres - science fiction, childrens, mainstream, poetry - but truly found her voice and love in fantasy. She writes fantasy adventure, fantasy romance, dark fantasy and children's picture books.

Her first official publication was a children's poem that was the Grand Prize winner in a contest sponsored by Half-Price Books. Her prize was a $500.00 gift certificate at Half Price Books: something she took great delight in spending. She has been published in several local newsletters, several print magazines, as well as numerous online magazines in both fiction and non-fiction.

Jenna lives in the beautiful Pacific Northwest with her husband, their three delightful children, two wild cats, a chihuahua that thinks he's really a dog, one rat, one anole and a several tanks of tropical fish, frogs and newts. Oh, yeah, and a forest full of elves, fairies and magic.

JennaKay was also Writers Exchange's Senior editor for many years.

You can keep track of all her books on her author page:

http://www.writers-exchange.com/Jennakay-Francis/

If you want to read more about other books by this author, they are listed on the following pages...

Blood Bred Series

{Fantasy: Vampire}

Book 1: Gift of Blood

Jaeger needs blood. Half Vector, half human, newly coming of age, Jaeger is now drawn to human blood for the first time in his already long life.

Rhiannon, a witch, has too much iron in her blood to safely live. She wants to propose a partnership with the Vectors, but, before she can approach them, she's attacked and left for dead beneath a pier. Jaeger finds her unconscious and bleeding. Fighting against the lure of her blood, he takes her to a place of safety instead. His actions set them both on a course of pain, hunger, terror and love. Can he save her from himself?

Publisher: http://www.writers-exchange.com/Gift-Of-Blood/

Book 2: From the Heart

Baris has everything: A wife he worships, a child he adores, a life of comfort and security. But his idyllic existence changes suddenly and dramatically, with no explanation. Anika, his wife, shuns him and orders him to leave her side. His child claims his mother is not really his mama. And Dierdre, a devastatingly beautiful young woman slides into Baris' life with seduction on her mind.

When Baris attempts to help his wife, she flees, leaving him alone with their son and Dierdre. To add to his agony, the child is bitten by a poisonous snake and Baris has no choice but to take him to the Lair to save his life. Once reunited with Dierdre, the pair set off in search of Anika. But, as the days turn to weeks with no sign of his wife, Baris must accept the possibility that she has no wish to be found.

As his life grows increasingly entangled with Dierdre's, he makes the mistake of feeding on a young man addicted to a powerful drug called Hack.

Baris is soon addicted as well and must struggle to reclaim everything that he once held dear...or die.

Publisher: http://www.writers-exchange.com/From-the-Heart/

Book 3: New Beginnings

A powerful Vector roams the dark alleys and streets searching for his next victim. But he he's not interested in those with normal blood--only those whose veins runs blood thick with the highly-addictive drug Hack. If Adan can't find someone who's just ingested the potent drug, he has no compunction about using his powers to coerce them to do so before he feeds.

For Vector Sovereign Darius, Adan has become a problem he needs to fix...

Publisher: http://www.writers-exchange.com/New-Beginnings/

Guardians of Glede Universe:
Beginnings Series

{Fantasy: Young Adult}

When the balance of power is threatened in the land of Glede, the powerful Triskelion calls for its master.

Book 1: The Triskelion

The Triskelion, a powerful magical amulet, once torn into two parts to protect the world of Glede, now must be found and re-united to save Glede. Two boys are summoned by the magic of the Triskelion to perform this dangerous task -Treyas Beckering, a 14 year old elf from Bailiwycke in the west; and 13 year old Jannson van Tannen, the newly orphaned King of Odora Dava to the east. Both will endure more than they ever thought possible, and both will become men in the process.
Publisher: http://www.writers-exchange.com/The-Triskelion/

Book 2: Dark Prince

Prince Rugan Merripen, once thought to be the rightful master of the Triskelion's magic, was cast aside by the medallion itself when it chose his half-brother Treyas Beckering as master. Now Rugan is on a quest to regain the magic and power he thinks is rightfully his. Befriended and manipulated by Vaalde, an evil sorcerer who has only his own goals in mind, Rugan attempts to drain Glede of elfin magic. Once gone, only sorcery magic will remain and Vaalde can then rule the world. It is up to King Jansson and Treyas to stop him and restore the balance of magic once again. Each boy will face what seem to be insurmountable odds, and both will discover that friends are there to depend on in times of travail. And Treyas will move towards a destiny that he never envisioned.

Publisher: http://www.writers-exchange.com/Dark-Prince/

Book 3: Sorcerer's Pool

Firmly embedded into Prince Rugan's mind, the sorcerer Vaalde once more manipulates Prince Rugan into wresting the Triskelion magic from Treyas Beckering Merripen, now the Crown Prince of Lidgerwood. This time Vaalde spirits King Jansson van Tannen and Treyas to Karsaba, a land void of magic and the ability to drain memory. Three days outside of magic and their memories will be wiped clean. Unfortunately for Vaalde, King Kyel Sylvain has hitched a ride. The black elf, reknowned for his magical prowess will prove to be a formidable adversary. But will Jansson and Treyas survive the strange power of Karsaba or will they lose everything that makes them who they are?

Publisher: http://www.writers-exchange.com/Sorcerers-Pool/

Book 4: Dragons of Mere Odain

Far away in the land of Mere Odain, a dragon calls out for help to her master--Pepin Merripen, now living as the son of Crown Prince Treyas Merripen and his wife, Cynthe. Pepin must answer, or die. Shocked and terrified, Treyas gathers his closest friends, and goes to Mere Odain. But the country is in turmoil. An ethnic cleansing is going on--any black or brown skinned person must die. Treyas is determined to save his young son's life even if it means taking on the whole of the Keltin Empire and ending a war 40 years in the making.

Publisher: http://www.writers-exchange.com/Dragons-of-Mere-Odain/

Book 5: Dragon Master

Pepin Merripen learns that the two countries that had promised to protect the dragons, his dragons, have withdrawn their forces. Furious at this betrayal, he goes to Karsaba to take council with Mere Odain's young Queen.

Although his father is willing to let Pepin resolve this situation, he soon finds out that Pepin has disappeared. Treyas follows his son's trail, but it ends where magic begins.

Increasingly worried, Treyas attempts to follow the magical trail and ends up in Northern Karsaba. It soon becomes apparent that he has more to deal with than a disgruntled runaway youth. A powerful magiker claiming to be Pepin's birth mother has summoned him, and she will stop at nothing to see his control over the dragons become her own. With Pepin at her command, and thereby his dragons, she intends to rule not only Karsaba, but any land she chooses. It is up to Treyas and his friends to make sure that doesn't happen. But will Treyas lose his son to the powerful pull of the dragons?

Publisher: http://www.writers-exchange.com/Dragonmaster/

Book 6: For the Love of Dragons

Pepin Merripen, now a young man of fourteen, has forged a strong bond with the elves. So when Queen El'leigh of Mere Odain informs him that the dragons have disappeared, he is torn between his allegiance and his love for the dragons. Still, he is steadfast in his loyalty to his father, Treyas Merripen, and refuses El'leigh's request to join her in the search.

Furious, El'leigh sends Pepin's love, Nila, to the wilds of South Kelta, the last known place of the dragons. As she suspected, Pepin quickly follows before any harm befalls Nila. No sooner have the two young lovers arrived in Kelta, than they are captured by Keltin warriors, who quickly ascertain that they have the DragonMaster in their grasp. And if they can force Pepin to make the dragons do their bidding, they'll regain their lost advantage in Mere Odain. All they have to do is use Nila as incentive.

Publisher: http://www.writers-exchange.com/For-The-Love-Of-Dragons/

Guardians of Glede Universe Continued:
Next Generation Series

{Fantasy: Young Adult}

Return to the land of Glede for new adventures with the next generation!

Book 1: Caves of Challenge

Their heads filled with stories of adventures spun by their father and uncles, Princes Vantann and Thomlin Merripen decide to have an adventure of their own. Through an old book, they learn of the Caves of Challenge. If they can survive the challenges within the caves, they will emerge as men.

Blackmailed by their young friend, Shuri, the boys agree to take her along. Before they trio has a chance to adequately prepare, however, they are sent to the Caves by haphazard magic. Once there, Shuri and Vantann are captured by War Gnomes, while Thomlin is lost in a dark swamp. His only consolation is that, somehow, he has snagged King Jansson van Tannen on the magic strand.

Jansson is reassuring, telling Thomlin that there will be a rescue party sent out and all they need do is wait. But the rescue party is having trouble of their own, and they find much more than they bargained for in the Caves. The question now becomes, who will be forced to stay in the Caves of Challenge forever.

Publisher: http://www.writers-exchange.com/Caves-of-Challenge/

Book 2: Blood Sacrifice

Tormented with guilt over the happenings in the Caves of Challenge, Prince Vantann Merripen watches over his siblings with a critical, judgmental and sometimes violent scrutiny. Prince Thomlin finally rebels and accidentally sets the course for an even more dangerous adventure than the one he and his brother endured in the Caves. Swept into a land that demonizes the second-born of twins, forbids magic, and is currently being terrorized by a coven of Nydiri, the twins very survival is threatened.

Any use of magic carries the penalty of death. Contact with the coven means the same, for the Nydiri are actively seeking twins to complete a powerful spell they intend to weave at the height of a mysterious orange moon. And elvin twins are especially prized.

Publisher: http://www.writers-exchange.com/Blood-Sacrifice/

Book 3: The Coven

Pepin reclaims his title as DragonMaster, not fully understanding the ramifications of such a move. Is his allegiance with the elves, or with Mere Odain? The announcement of his decision couldn't have come at a worse time – the Crown Prince is to leave the next day on a diplomatic visit to Dalziel.

Once in Dalziel, things rapidly begin to fall apart. Politically, Kyel and Jansson are at each other's throats, Vantann and Thomlin make friends in the wrong places, and Treyas finds out that his SoulMate and squire, Druce Sinclair, suffers from a horribly painful and incurable disease.

To top it off, Treyas discovers that Dalziel has been overrun with Nydiri with the power of Illusion in their grasp.

When Vantann, Thomlin and others disappear, Treyas must find a way to free the captives and destroy the Nydiri threat once and for all...

Publisher: http://www.writers-exchange.com/The-Coven/

Book 4: Fire Stone

Stranded after a river float trip goes horribly wrong, Brann van Tannen and his friends Tavin, Elek and Janna are caught by slave traders. To make matters worse, on board the barge are three trolls, descendants of the tribe that destroyed Mayfaire and killed Brann's grandfather. Brann will need to rely on all of the strength, wisdom and courage his father instilled in him while their lives are changed beyond wildest imagination.

Publisher: http://www.writers-exchange.com/Fire-Stone/

Book 5: The Fane Queen

Attempting to escape the past can have devastating consequences...

Ask Tavin Sylvain, who is trying to forget all about the abuse he suffered at the hands of the trolls six months earlier.

Ask Kitiara, who would like to escape her sordid past in Kartonn, where she was known as the Princess of Pleasure.

Or ask King Jansson van Tannen, who would like nothing better than to keep his family intact and not have to face the possibility of losing one of his own beloved children to fate.

When the past rears its ugly head, all three are thrown into turmoil. Tavin, Brann and Kitiara are lost in Karsaba, without magic, without direction, without hope. And in the middle of a troll invasion. In a race against time, King Jansson and King Kyel gather their closest friends and allies to find the children before the trolls find them first.

Publisher: http://www.writers-exchange.com/The-Fane-Queen/

Book 6: Battle for Argathia

A desperate plea for help, written on a scroll and sent with magic, falls into the wrong hands, and with a few misplace words, Treyas' young daughter activates the spell, sending her and her friends to a world controlled by the Albino.

The Albino, not content with being dictator of only one world, now has a hostage--and one of royal pedigree--with which to extend his empire. It is up to Treyas and his companions to stop the Albino and free the world he has claimed as his own.

Publisher: http://www.writers-exchange.com/Battle-for-Argathia/

Guardians of Glede Universe Continued: Reckonings Series

{Fantasy: Young Adult}

Return to the land of Glede during a time when the Nydiri intend to destroy not only Treyas but the whole of the elven empire.

Book 1: Dukker's Revenge

Elek is missing and Dukker has returned. The Nydiri will not stop until not only Treyas is destroyed but the whole of the elven empire. When the palace is infiltrated, chaos ensues. Floy, the son of a visiting dignitary, becomes an unwitting pawn in Dukker's plans. Through him, Dukker captures three of the royal youth.

Treyas and his companions set out to rescue the young people, but their TravelSpell is severely compromised, sending them in different directions. They will all need to rely on new friends, and a powerful, mysterious dagger, to set things right and defeat the Nydiri.

Publisher: http://www.writers-exchange.com/Rukkers-Revenge/

The Faery Sickness

{Fantasy Romance}

Vala Kalei was saved from death by the fae but condemned by her own neighbors. When she goes to the faery realm and retrieves the babies that have been dying, she opens up another world filled with mystery, pain, heartache...and love.

Publisher: http://www.writers-exchange.com/The-Faery-Sickness/

Free Spirit

{Fantasy Romance}

Diesa de Tyronmen escapes from a brutal master only to be sold to an elf. Though mesmerized by his beauty, Diesa struggles for her freedom...and against her own growing love for her new master. Was she purchased only to win a wager? And, as her mother had claimed, will an elf claim her heart with his words, her very soul with his touch?

Publisher: http://www.writers-exchange.com/Free-Spirit/

Nitesh

{Fantasy Romance}

Thalassa, a sea-witch, is captured when the warlord Rhaeven sends his troops to her small village. After the hard life she's already lived, she's resigned to her fate. Married at a young age to an abusive man she doesn't love, she's secretly glad to see her husband die. Now, pregnant, enslaved and stricken with a deadly disease, she only waits for her own death to release her from the torment that is life.

Elfin Crown Prince of Diraenia, Terran, must choose a mate and produce an heir before his thirtieth birthday or risk forfeiting the crown to his youngest brother Unwin. Time is running out. Terran is twenty-nine, his fiancee is dead, and he believes Unwin responsible despite the lack of proof. To make matters worse, Terran's other brother Sinclair has disappeared, and Terran fears the worst.

Bothered by a strange, haunting beat of drums no one can hear but Terran, the Crown Prince thoughts continually turn to a brief encounter he shared with a young woman from Zal. For three days, he'd walked her back to her village, delivering her to her pre-ordained life there. For three days, he fell in love with the wife of a woman who could never be his. When he returned to his own palace, he'd seen the emptiness and despair of his own life.

The drums call to Terran until he can longer deny his own need to revisit the village where he'd fallen in love. If he sees Thalassa one last time, can he make himself let go?

Publisher: http://www.writers-exchange.com/Nitesh/

You can find ALL our books on our website at:

http://www.writers-exchange.com

all our fantasy novels:

http://www.writers-exchange.com/category/genres/fantasy/